**Secret L

What Society doesn't know...

Meet Julian Carlisle, the Duke of Lyonsdale,
Gabriel Pearce, the Duke of Winterbourne,
and Phineas Attwood, the Earl of Hartwick.

In the eyes of the *ton*, these three gentlemen
are handsome, upstanding men who (mostly!)
play by the rules. But what Society doesn't know
is that, behind closed doors, these men are
living scandalous lives and conducting
sinfully scandalous affairs!

Read Julian's story first in
An Unsuitable Duchess
Available now

And look for Gabriel's and Hart's stories,
coming soon!

Author Note

I've been interested in history since I was young, and that interest was fueled by many visits to many museums. The idea for this story came to me while I was visiting Washington Irving's home in Tarrytown, New York. I confess I have a bit of a historical crush on Irving, who was one of America's first internationally acclaimed authors. For a time, he lived in London during the Regency era and also served as a diplomat there in the last few years of the reign of George IV. While hearing about Irving's time in London, I began to imagine what life could have been like for the daughter of such a man. I'd also often wondered about the courtship of the first American woman to breach the walls of the English aristocracy. With these two thoughts in my head, this story was born.

While writing this book, I used some creative license and changed the name of the United States Minister to Britain who served in 1818 from Richard Rush to the fictitious Mr. Forrester.

If you're interested in learning more about some of the historical details in this book, please visit my website at lauriebenson.net and click on the link to my blog. You can search *An Unsuitable Duchess* for relevant articles. And while you're there, please subscribe to my newsletter for information about my upcoming books.

I hope you enjoy *An Unsuitable Duchess*, which is the first book in my Secret Lives of the Ton series.

Laurie Benson

An Unsuitable Duchess

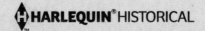 HARLEQUIN® HISTORICAL

If you purchased this book without a cover you should be aware that this book is stolen property. It was reported as "unsold and destroyed" to the publisher, and neither the author nor the publisher has received any payment for this "stripped book."

Recycling programs
for this product may
not exist in your area.

ISBN-13: 978-0-373-30740-1

An Unsuitable Duchess

Copyright © 2016 by Laurie Benson

All rights reserved. Except for use in any review, the reproduction or utilization of this work in whole or in part in any form by any electronic, mechanical or other means, now known or hereinafter invented, including xerography, photocopying and recording, or in any information storage or retrieval system, is forbidden without the written permission of the publisher, Harlequin Enterprises Limited, 225 Duncan Mill Road, Don Mills, Ontario M3B 3K9, Canada.

This is a work of fiction. Names, characters, places and incidents are either the product of the author's imagination or are used fictitiously, and any resemblance to actual persons, living or dead, business establishments, events or locales is entirely coincidental.

This edition published by arrangement with Harlequin Books S.A.

For questions and comments about the quality of this book, please contact us at CustomerService@Harlequin.com.

® and TM are trademarks of Harlequin Enterprises Limited or its corporate affiliates. Trademarks indicated with ® are registered in the United States Patent and Trademark Office, the Canadian Intellectual Property Office and in other countries.

Printed in U.S.A.

Laurie Benson is an award-winning historical romance author and Golden Heart® finalist. She began her writing career as an advertising copywriter, where she learned more than you could ever want to know about hot dogs and credit score reports. When she isn't at her laptop avoiding laundry, Laurie can be found browsing museums or taking ridiculously long hikes with her husband and two sons. You can visit her at lauriebenson.net.

An Unsuitable Duchess
**is Laurie Benson's fantastic debut
for Harlequin Historical**

Visit the Author Profile page at Harlequin.com.

Acknowledgments

I'll always be grateful to my wonderful editor, Kathryn Cheshire, for giving me this opportunity and for helping me bring Julian and Katrina into the world. Thanks for your guidance and support. You're the best! And thank you to everyone at Harlequin Historical, especially Linda Fildew, Nic Caws and Krista Oliver for all that you've done for me.

Thanks, Courtney Miller-Callihan, for having my back and for just being you.

To the history bloggers and the people who answered my historical questions, thanks for making research fun.

Lori V. and Lisa D., this book might not have been written if it weren't for the two of you. Thanks for encouraging me to put this story to paper and for not running the other way when I asked you to read it—a number of times. I love you both!

To Jen, Mia, Marnee and Teri, thanks for riding this roller coaster with me and for being such great friends.

Thanks, Mom, for teaching me that I could do anything if I put my mind to it. To my boys, you mean the world to me. Thanks for never complaining when deadlines have me ordering takeout for dinner. And thank you to my husband for always believing in me and for proving that love at first sight really is possible.

Finally, thank you, kind reader, for picking up this book. I hope this story makes you smile, and you enjoy this brief armchair vacation in Regency-era London.

Chapter One

Mayfair, London, 1818.

Katrina Vandenberg had come to the conclusion that the ballrooms of London were rather dangerous places.

As she stood under a glittering chandelier in the Russian Ambassador's ornate drawing room she rotated her sore foot beneath her gown. It didn't help. Anticipating its tenderness, she held her breath and gingerly lowered her slipper to the red and gold rug.

'Why does Lord Boreham continue to ask me to dance?' she groaned as her foot began to throb. 'Each time we do he stumbles through the steps and blames it on me being American and not knowing the movements. This time he stepped on my foot so many times I stopped counting.'

'Perhaps he is enamoured with you,' replied Sarah Forrester, the daughter of the American Minister to the Court of St. James.

'Perhaps he's waiting for me to issue a war cry in the middle of the dance floor and wishes to have an excellent view.'

The friends laughed and a number of the finely dressed gentlemen and ladies looked their way. One of them was their hostess, the Russian Ambassador's wife, Madame de Lieven.

'I suppose you could wear boots under your gown to protect your feet from clumsy partners,' Sarah whispered, hiding her amusement behind her fan. 'Although it would not be very fashionable.'

'I do not believe even that would help. But perhaps I could pretend the orchestra is too loud and I cannot hear them speak. Then maybe I could avoid listening to them boast about how important they are or prattle on about some ancient relative's great accomplishment.' Katrina nodded towards a group of gentlemen. 'One day I wager one of them will show me his teeth in an attempt to impress me. London would be lovely if it weren't for the men.'

When they laughed again Madame de Lieven narrowed her eyes and gave them a chastising shake of her head.

Katrina took a deep breath and shifted her gaze. 'I do believe our hostess is attempting to inform us that ladies in London do not laugh out loud during entertainments such as this.'

How she wished there was somewhere she could go to avoid the constant scrutiny. And that smell! Had someone forgot to bathe?

She rubbed her forehead and a drop of wax hit the embroidered forget-me-nots on her white silk glove.

Evenings like this were always so tedious.

This evening could not become any more tedious.

Julian Carlisle, the Duke of Lyonsdale, didn't know how Lady Morley and her daughter Lady Mary had cornered him. And that bloody chandelier! He was certain his valet would have an apoplexy when he saw how much wax was falling onto his new black tailcoat.

Tonight's crush was so great it had become difficult to

raise his glass of the Russian Ambassador's fine champagne to his lips. If he tried he might inadvertently brush his hand over the front of Lady Mary's dress. It would be interesting to see her mother's reaction to *that*. Most likely Julian would find himself embroiled in the scandal of the evening, with a wife he did not want.

He would stay thirsty.

'And so I told her,' continued Lady Morley, 'that if Madame Devy moved back to Paris we simply would not know what to do. She is the best in London. She makes all of Mary's dresses. Not that she needs any help to show as well as she does. Has the bearing of a duchess, I always hear.'

Thirty-three. Thirty-four. The peacock feather in Lady Morley's turban bobbed with every nod of her head. Julian continued counting. The unique sound of soft feminine laughter floated from behind him and he wished he were part of that conversation instead of this one. He made a conscious effort not to sigh.

Before he could school his features into his usual bored expression he wrinkled his nose. What was that smell? It reminded him of his gardeners in the heat of summer. A man's sweat should not be mixed with an abundance of flowers and sold in a bottle.

Julian managed to down the remainder of his champagne in one gulp. The bubbles tickling his throat were a welcome distraction. 'I understand cards are being played across the hall. Is that where your husband is this evening?' he asked, with no real interest.

Lady Morley blinked at his sudden interruption. 'Oh—oh, yes, I believe it is.'

'I'll be off, then.'

Both ladies curtsied to Julian, and he began to attempt a shallow bow. He bumped into something soft. As he turned to excuse himself high, soft breasts met his hard male chest.

A startled woman with pleasant features and a pair of deep blue eyes looked up at him. Then her gaze travelled slowly down to his waistcoat and back up to his face. When her white teeth tugged at her lower lip, he had a strong urge to lick and soothe that lip. Mentally shaking himself, he tried to gain control of this unexpected yearning.

Her eyes widened, and a faint blush swept across her cheeks. 'Please forgive me, my lord,' she murmured.

Nine years had passed since anyone had addressed him simply as 'my lord'. Everyone knew he was the Duke of Lyonsdale and should be addressed as 'Your Grace'—even if he didn't care to know *them*. 'I assure you no apology is necessary. I believe the fault is mine.'

She bobbed a shallow curtsey and turned away from him. As he watched her make her way through the crowd something inside him shifted. Suddenly he was striding across the room, not even aware of the parting of finely dressed people before him.

Stepping onto the terrace, Katrina closed her eyes and filled her lungs with fresh night air. For a brief time, at least, she would not have to be conscious of her every action.

The amber glow of candlelight, shining through the tall windows and doors of the large brick house, streaked this outdoor haven. In the far corner was an unoccupied area that called to her. It would be an ideal place to escape inquisitive stares and pointed whispers.

The stone of the marble balustrade felt cool against her gloved hands and was a welcome contrast to the warm crush inside. Peering out into the dimly lit garden, she gradually began to relax, enjoying her first bit of solitude all evening. It was wonderful to finally be alone.

'We are fortunate the evening air is so pleasant and there's no rain,' rumbled a deep voice to her right.

Resisting the urge to push the intruder over the railing, Katrina held back a sigh. 'Yes, we are quite fortunate,' she said, in what she was certain was a bored tone. She kept her eyes fixed on the landscape below, hoping it would discourage further conversation.

'The quality of the Ambassador's garden is well noted. Have you walked through it yet?'

'No, I have not. Fortunately for us there are lanterns placed along the pathways so we can enjoy the beauty from up here.' He would soon learn she was not a woman who dallied in the shrubbery. Perhaps he would move on.

When Katrina glanced over at him, she was surprised to discover the handsome gentleman she had clumsily bumped into a few minutes before. He was standing tall, facing the garden, in formal black evening clothes, with the moonlight shining on the waves of his neatly trimmed dark hair. She studied his profile with its chiselled features and square jaw. He must have noticed, because he turned his head towards her and their eyes met.

It happened again. The ground seemed to shift, and this time their bodies hadn't even touched. Deciding it was best to focus on the flowering shrubs and manicured lawn, she diverted her attention away from the man at her side.

Julian closed his eyes and clenched his jaw. Was he actually reduced to discussing the weather and gardening with this woman? When had he become this dull? And he was certain she had just dismissed him. No one *ever* dismissed him.

For the first time in his life Julian felt the need to capture a woman's attention. 'Are you new to town?'

In whose world was this captivating conversation?

'I suppose. I have only been in London for a few weeks.'

'Your accent escapes me.'

She crossed her arms under that pair of lovely small breasts and turned towards him. 'I'm American.' When he remained silent, she tilted her head and studied him. 'Pardon me, but have we been introduced?'

He shook his head, amused at her candour. 'Not that I recall—and I am fairly certain you are not someone I would forget.'

'Then speaking with you would not be proper.' She glanced at the French doors, as if she expected to see someone. 'Did you follow me out here?'

Julian never followed women, and he never acted improperly. He had needed to get away from Lady Morley, and that smell had been unbearable. There had been no reason to consider it further.

'We must have had the notion to step outside at the same time.'

'And you just happened to find yourself standing next to me?'

He shifted under her sceptical expression. 'It appeared to be a pleasant spot.'

She narrowed her eyes momentarily before she turned her attention back towards the garden and began to drum her fingers on the stone.

Below them, a figure walked in and out of the shadows, along one of the garden's gravel paths, as the flames inside the lanterns flickered. Julian traced the figure's movements. 'You wouldn't happen to be hiding from someone, now, would you?'

She looked at him with a curious glint in her eyes. 'Why would you think that?'

'When a woman as striking as you is alone at a ball teeming with men, one must conclude that her solitude is by choice. Are you attempting to avoid a foolish suitor?'

Her lips twitched. 'What makes you believe I have foolish suitors?'

'Ah, I said suitor. Apparently there is more than one.'

'Perhaps I was simply seeking a breath of fresh air.'

'Then I would say any man who wasn't wise enough to accompany you out here to take the evening air was foolish.'

The silk of her ice-blue gown shimmered in the moonlight as she turned her body to face him. 'And why is that?'

He had the strongest urge to step closer. She smelled like lemons. 'Because in this secluded spot he has left you free to be charmed by another man.'

'Are you attempting to charm me?'

'Do you find me charming?'

'Not in the least,' she replied, even though her expression said the opposite.

'Then I suppose your suitor is safe in his position of favour.'

A soft laugh escaped her lips before she quickly pursed them together.

'Or perhaps not,' he amended, revelling in the odd satisfaction that she found him amusing.

'My purpose in coming out here was simply to enjoy a bit of solitude.'

'And I have intruded on your privacy—not well done of me at all. Perhaps we might enjoy the solitude together?'

'Then it would not be considered solitude.'

'Semantics,' he replied with a slight shrug. 'So, why are you seeking solitude?'

She looked down at her slippers and appeared to give her answer great consideration. 'I grew weary of people telling me how important they are.'

He wondered if he was like that. He didn't think he was. Nevertheless, it was probably best not to let her know how important he really was. 'A bold admission.'

'An honest one. And what brings *you* out here? If you were planning on having a clandestine meeting, I fear you are keeping some lady waiting,' she said with a teasing smile.

'I'm not. Perhaps I too grew weary of spending time with people I have no interest in.'

'Than we are of a like mind.'

'It appears we are.'

Her lips rose into a full smile and for the first time in his life Julian forgot to breathe. 'You are lovely,' he admitted, before he could stop himself.

'Thank you, but I have been told I am much too expressive.'

'Not to me.'

'You're trying to charm me again.'

'Am I? I thought I was simply being honest. I appreciate a true smile. I find the false ones maddening.'

What in the world had got into him? Perhaps her candid speech was infectious. Her unguarded manner and their frank discussion should not appeal to him, yet he found her entertaining.

She shifted her stance, and her skirt rustled as if she was shaking out her foot. 'Well, it appears that you, my lord, are not a typical member of the *ton*.'

If she only knew.

It was as if he was being pulled to her by some magnetic force. His heartbeat quickened as he stepped even closer. Her lips looked so soft. As his gaze travelled down to the small swell of her breasts his fingers instinctively curled. He needed a distraction.

Turning back towards the balustrade, he focused his attention on the stars. He had never attempted to count them before. For a moment longer he could feel her watching him. Then she turned and tipped her face up to the inky night sky.

* * *

Katrina wondered at the sudden change in her companion's demeanour. There must be some unspoken rule of English Society she had unwittingly broken. During their brief encounter he had managed to make her forget she was a stranger, navigating uncharted waters. But his silence spoke volumes. She would have to peruse *The Mirror of Graces* again tonight before she fell asleep, to find some clue as to her *faux pas*.

Their engaging conversation had improved her mood, and she was determined to hold on to that feeling for as long as she could. 'It appears as if every star in the heavens is out,' she mused, testing the waters for his response. 'Do you enjoy stargazing?'

She glanced at him and smiled at his friendly, inquisitive expression. 'I have been known to occasionally look upon the stars, if that is what you mean.'

'But can you identify the constellations? Do you know their names?'

She shook her head.

He leaned closer and his sleeve brushed her arm. 'See that grouping of stars over those trees? That's the constellation Cassiopeia.'

It took her a moment to attend to what he'd said, with his body so close to her. 'That's the name of an ancient Ethiopian Queen.'

He nodded. 'And that is her constellation. What do you know of her?'

'Only that her excessive pride in her daughter Andromeda angered Poseidon so much that he commanded the Queen to sacrifice Andromeda to him.'

'Very good. In fact Andromeda is over there.'

She took note of the stars he pointed to.

'It is said Poseidon was enraged because Cassiopeia's sacrifice was not completed,' he continued. 'As punishment, he placed the Queen on her throne in the night sky. Do you remember what happened to Andromeda?'

Katrina could feel him watching her and she shifted her gaze back to him. 'She was rescued by Perseus, whom she married.'

'She was. Now, Perseus is over there.' He leaned across her and pointed to another grouping of stars. He smelled wonderful—like champagne and mint.

Their faces were mere inches apart. His lips looked so firm and smooth. For a moment their breaths mingled. Suddenly he jerked his head back, and unwelcome cool night air blew across her face.

She needed to shift her attention away from his lips and recall what they were discussing. 'Is that truly Perseus, or are you attempting to appeal to my sense of the romantic?'

'That truly is the constellation Perseus. It is said that Athena placed Andromeda next to Perseus in the night sky when Andromeda died.'

'Oh, that *is* romantic.'

He wrinkled his brow as he stared at the stars. 'I suppose some might consider it that way.'

'But you do not?'

'I never gave it much thought until now,' he replied with a slight shrug.

Their eyes met, and it was as if every part of Katrina's body was straining to get even closer to him. She needed to get away before she did something embarrassing, such as caress the arm that was now pressing against her own.

Taking a deep breath, she clasped her hands together. They were safer that way. 'Well, I should return. My party will wonder where I have disappeared to and hopefully the air inside will have cleared.' She smiled at him and moved away from the balustrade. 'Thank you for showing me the stars. I can truly say I was not bored in the least.'

He bowed, and when he raised his head she caught the

laughter in his eyes. 'I am glad. I was not bored either. I hope you will find some pleasure in what is left of your evening.'

She curtsied in return and walked to the doors leading back to the drawing room. As she reached the threshold she couldn't help glancing at him over her shoulder. When their eyes met she lowered her head, and attempted to hide her satisfied smile.

From the moment she'd left his side it had been impossible for Julian to look away from her. If he had looked away he might have missed that one last glance she'd given him before she entered the house. It didn't matter that she had caught him staring like an untried boy. That last look had told him everything. She wanted him just as much as he wanted her.

Pulling his shoulders back and crossing his arms, he tried unsuccessfully to suppress a grin. The novelty of knowing that this woman desired him without knowing his prominent position in Society was exhilarating. Her lemon scent lingered in the air, and Julian took in a deep breath while leaning his lower back on the balustrade.

This night was turning out to be far from tedious after all.

'Now, that's quite odd. It almost appears as if you are smiling. But I know that can't be, because while *I'm* returning from a pleasurable time spent in the garden *you*, my friend, are all alone.'

Lord Phineas Attwood, the Earl of Hartwick, sauntered up the terrace steps. He was dressed all in black except for his crisp white shirt. The knot of his cravat appeared askew, and a lock of black hair was draped over his right eye. He ran his fingers through his hair, attempting to comb the lock back into place. It was no use.

Stopping next to Julian, he also crossed his arms over

his chest and followed Julian's gaze to the French doors. 'Does she have a name?'

'Who?'

'Whoever she is that has caught your interest.'

Julian closed his eyes and with an exasperated sigh turned his attention from the doors to his friend. 'What makes you think it's a woman?'

Hart raised both brows. 'Come, now, I always tell you what has put a smile on *my* face. We can compare notes. I'll tell you about my lady, and you tell me about your lady.'

'There is nothing to tell.'

'Very well—I'll start. Margaret has the most amazing mouth. She can—'

'You were in the garden with Lady Shepford?' Julian closed his eyes. 'You are mad. Not two hours ago you took over two hundred pounds from Shepford at cards, and now you take his wife.'

'Exciting, isn't it?' Hart replied, adjusting his cuff. 'I can't help if she finds me irresistible, and he is positively unlucky tonight. It was impossible not to win his money.'

'One day some husband is going to challenge you, and I have no desire to be your second.'

'I am aware that you believe widows are preferable, but I'm not you. Married ladies are infinitely preferable to un-married ones. At least they aren't fishing for a title. Hon-estly, you worry for nothing. My coach is always at the ready, and I'm very competent with pistols and swords.' He pushed himself off the balustrade. 'I'm bored—let's go to White's. Stop scowling. You look like my old tutor.'

Julian shook his head. There was no reason to stay. He would have enjoyed spending more time with the Ameri-can woman. Had she been a member of the *ton* he would have re-entered the Ambassador's townhouse and imme-diately sought an introduction. Unfortunately, with the responsibility of his title, a relationship with an American was not possible.

When he married again it would be to an English-woman of prominent lineage—just as his ancestors before him and just as he had done before. Respectable English noblemen did *not* marry American women.

Why was he even thinking of marriage? Hart was right. It was time to leave.

Chapter Two

Reading the *Morning Chronicle* should not be so difficult. Katrina had done it every morning since she and her father had arrived in London a few weeks ago. However, today she was finding it impossible to read even one article—and it was all because of that English gentleman she had talked with out on the terrace the previous evening.

The dining room in the house her father had leased in Mayfair was quiet except for the occasional tinkling of a Wedgwood cup hitting a saucer and the crinkling of paper as her father turned a page of the document the American Minister had sent over.

Feeling frustrated by her lack of concentration, Katrina pushed the newspaper aside and reached for a piece of toast from the silver rack in front of her. As she began spreading honey on the bread she couldn't help but smile recalling their conversation for the hundredth time since last night.

Why couldn't she stop thinking about him? She was not attracted to Englishmen—at least she hadn't been until last night. Most of those she had met since arriving in London had been proud, patronising and too self-possessed for her taste. But this gentleman had appeared to be none of those things. He hadn't even made any foolish comments about her being American. On a night that had begun so poorly he had managed to make her laugh and forget about the pain in her foot. And she couldn't deny that being close to him had made her heart race.

Honey began to drip through her fingers, and Katrina shook her head as she licked away the sticky sweetness. How long would it be until she saw him again? Once he obtained a proper introduction they'd be able to speak openly, and she would finally know his name. He might even ask her to waltz.

While she had no desire to tie herself to an English gentleman, spending time in that man's company during the various social engagements she was obligated to attend while she was in London would be an excellent diversion.

Smiling to herself, Katrina returned her attention to the newspaper and tried to concentrate on reading it one last time.

In another part of Mayfair, in a much larger house, Julian walked out of his suite of rooms and rubbed his pounding forehead. He needed more sleep. Several times during the night he had awoken from vivid dreams about the American woman. Now this lack of sleep left him very irritable—and very frustrated. What he needed was a quiet, peaceful morning.

From the sounds drifting out through the doorway of his breakfast room, there was little hope of that happening.

Crossing the threshold, he noted his mother and grand-mother were deep in conversation at the elegantly set table. Grasping at his last few moments of peace, Julian passed the livery-clad footmen on his way to the mahogany Sheraton sideboard and filled his plate. The smell of ham made his stomach growl, making him realise how hungry he was. The moment he sat down coffee was poured into a porcelain cup.

Just as he was about to bring the aromatic liquid to his lips, the chatter around him stopped. His mother's sharp eyes were focused on him, and Julian cursed himself for not taking breakfast in his study.

'Good morning, Lyonsdale,' she said, while refolding a note that had been lying open next to her plate. 'How was the Ambassador's ball?'

'It was a crush, as usual, but surprisingly tolerable.'

'And Lady Wentworth? Did she enjoy the evening?'

Julian had been trying to keep his association with the widow discreet. Obviously he needed to try harder. He blew into his cup and decided to be evasive.

'She was not there.'

'Then who held your attention for so long on the terrace?'

Julian's fingers clenched the handle of his cup before he carefully placed it down on the saucer. He was one and thirty. Was it too much to ask for some privacy? He needed to speak to his secretary about seeing what could be done to hasten the renovations of his mother's townhouse.

'Pray tell, how is it possible that you possess such information?'

His grandmother Eleanor, the Dowager Duchess of Lyonsdale, paused in spreading butter on her toast. 'Your mother has already received a note this morning from Lady Morley. Isn't that correct, Beatrice?'

'Your friend has written to you about what I did last night?' Julian asked indignantly.

'She has only commented on your actions because she says you left rather abruptly and she had thought you were about to speak with her husband regarding their daughter.'

'Why would she assume I intended to approach Morley about her?'

His mother trailed her slender finger around the gold

rim of her cup and raised her pointed chin. 'She, and every other member of the *ton*, is aware that you are in need of an heir. It is obvious that Lady Mary is a suitable choice. Her father is an earl, and she is the niece of a duke. And you have spoken with her. Your conversation confers distinction upon any gel you single out.'

'I have not spoken with her.'

'You must have. You've danced with her. Surely you had *some* manner of discussion on that occasion.'

Had he? Julian tried to recall any remnant of conversation, but he could not. Nothing about Lady Mary set her apart. All the chits who had recently entered Society resembled one another, twittering behind their fans and taking measure of him when they thought he wasn't looking. They were all so young. He must have spoken to her, but he honestly could not recall doing so.

'I may have also mentioned to Lady Morley that you might consider their daughter.'

Julian had stopped listening to his mother moments before, but that declaration caught his attention. The pounding in his head increased. He would not let her dictate which woman he would marry—*not* this time.

'It was not your place to speak for me,' he bit out.

'I made no promises, but surely you see you cannot keep wasting your time with Lady Wentworth. That woman is an unacceptable choice. Her family is of no true consequence. It is time you secured this line. If Edward hadn't been foolish enough to race his horse that day we would at least have had him as your immediate heir. But with his death the line falls to your grandfather's incompetent nephew, should you perish, and he will destroy our good name.'

A familiar hollow feeling opened in Julian's chest—which was why he never wanted to think about Edward. The way his mother had so callously mentioned his dear brother's death fuelled the anger welling up inside him. Was there ever a time that she thought of either of them as more than a necessary part of fulfilling her own duty to bear an heir and a spare?

'You have avoided marriage long enough,' she continued. 'It's high time you fulfil your duty to marry again and finally bear an heir. Lady Mary will make us a perfect duchess. You should be thanking me for saving you from the trying task of finding you a suitable wife.'

'Thanking you?' he sputtered. 'You chose a wife for me once. It did not end well. You will not dictate my choice to me again.'

His mother appeared hesitant to say more, and the tension eased somewhat in his shoulders. Maybe he would be lucky enough to have her abandon the conversation entirely.

'At least *consider* Lady Mary.'

Or maybe she would continue to pester him till he lost his appetite completely!

He swallowed a mouthful of tepid coffee and pushed the cup away in disgust.

Before he could reply, his mother rushed ahead. 'She is from a prominent family, has been trained from birth to assume such a title, is accomplished, and appears strong for breeding. You could not possibly require anything else.'

But he did. He felt it. Only he wasn't certain what it could be. He simply knew he could not continue this conversation while he was still suffering from lack of sleep. This decision was too important—and his coffee was cold.

'You never did say who you were with last night on the Ambassador's terrace.'

'No, I did not.'

His mother held out her cup for more tea. A footman immediately appeared at her side. She wasn't leaving the table any time soon. Julian rose from his chair and dropped his napkin onto the table.

His grandmother glanced at his untouched plate and looked at him with soft, sympathetic eyes. 'You have not eaten a thing. Surely you must be hungry? Would you like Reynolds to fetch you something else?'

Her genuine concern softened some of his anger. 'No, thank you.'

'I could have a tray sent to your study. Surely we can find something to tempt you?'

'There is no need. I believe I have lost my appetite.'

Hart's breakfast room was blissfully quiet. No one was pestering him to make a decision that would affect the rest of his life. Julian knew he needed to marry soon. He couldn't keep delaying the inevitable. The longer he waited, the younger the girls would be. However, each time he considered marrying again his stomach would do an uncomfortable flip. This time was no different.

Why couldn't he find a woman among the *ton* like the American woman who had captivated him last night? Staring sightlessly at his plate, Julian gave a slight start when Hart's butler cleared his throat.

'Is there anything else you require, Your Grace?'

'Actually, Billings, would you see if His Lordship has any lemon curd?'

The butler exited the room as a sleepy Hart wandered in, wearing a black brocade dressing gown. A lock of hair covered his heavy-lidded blue eyes. Hart's gaze followed his butler as Billings re-entered the room and placed a Wedgwood bowl before Julian.

'So this is what my breakfast room looks like,' Hart said through a yawn. 'I was told you were here, however, I didn't believe it.' He dropped into his chair and stared in horror at his friend's toast. 'What has happened to the butter?'

'It's lemon curd.' Julian took a bite of toast and closed his eyes, savouring the flavour.

'I've never seen you eat lemon curd before. I did not even know I *had* lemon curd—and why the bloody hell are you putting it on your toast?'

'I have no idea.' Julian took another bite and wiped his lips with his napkin. 'I woke with the oddest desire for lemons.'

Hart accepted a cup of coffee from Billings and reclined in his chair. 'So what has brought you to my door at this ungodly hour of the morning?'

'It's past ten—hardly ungodly.'

Hart stilled, his cup halfway to his lips. 'In all the years you have known me, and with all you know about me, do you *really* think I rise anywhere near this hour?'

'Point taken. Your coffee is quite good. I do not believe I've tasted it before.'

'That's because you knew enough not to come here for breakfast. Now, enjoy this pot. I do not expect you to bother me for breakfast again any time soon.'

Julian continued to eat his toast. *Lemon curd on toast was exceptional.* He licked his lips, wondering why he hadn't thought of eating it before.

'What does bring you here?'

Perhaps if he talked about it with his friend he might release some of his frustration. Leaning back in his chair, Julian took a final sip from his cup. Billings was at his side in an instant, refilling it. Hart eyed his butler and the man retired from the room, closing the door quietly behind him.

'She wants an heir.'

'Who?'

'My mother.'

'That's no secret. She has made it quite clear that you have been remiss in fulfilling your duty. Is that why you are here at this hour? You have run away from your mother?'

Julian flung a piece of toast at Hart.

'I say, that was quite undignified of you.' His friend picked the toast from his chest and bit into it. 'This is quite good.' He licked his fingers. 'Has she selected another simpering chit for you?'

'Yes, but this time she has spoken to the family, indicating that I have an interest. She has gone too far.'

'And who is this paragon of the *ton* she has so carefully chosen to bear the next Duke?'

'Lady Mary Morley.'

As if he was trying to recall her name, Hart momentarily shifted his gaze. 'Could be worse. She has the most delicious-looking breasts I've seen. They're so full and tempting. Here—pass the lemon curd over.' He picked up the bowl from Julian's hand, dipped his spoon in and licked it clean. 'See…now you've done it. I will not be able to look at Lady Mary's delectable breasts without recalling this taste.'

'Would you please focus?'

'I am!' Hart took another scoop of lemon curd.

'On my problem, dolt!'

'I would if I saw one! You've told me you need to marry again. She is a better choice than any of the other chits your mother has favoured. She's a prime article, appears biddable, and those breasts—'

'Can we please not focus on Lady Mary's breasts?' Julian bit out through clenched teeth.

'Maybe *you* can stop focusing on Lady Mary's breasts. I, on the other hand…'

The pounding in Julian's forehead was back. The fact that he could not recall any conversation with Lady Mary was not promising, and the thought of educating a girl as young as seventeen about marital relations made his stomach roll.

'I did not come here to listen to you tell me what an excellent choice Lady Mary would be. Believe me, I am well versed in her virtues.' He ripped off pieces from a slice of dry toast, trying to hold on to his composure. 'I've danced with her before, but I cannot recall any of our conversations. And I do not believe I've ever seen her smile. I mean a genuine smile, not a false one. Have you ever seen her smile?'

'Can't recall…probably not. Most of them don't.' Hart took a sip of coffee and studied him. 'I was not aware that smiling was a requirement of yours.'

'I am simply stating that a woman should be able to smile if she wishes.'

'I suppose…' Hart said hesitantly. 'I don't understand why you're so angry. Do whatever you wish. You could run through Almack's naked, drink brandy for breakfast, wear puce—it would not matter. No one ever questions you. Actually, the brandy sounds like a splendid idea. Do you think I have any in this room? I honestly don't know the last time I was in here.'

Hart scanned the room for a decanter of amber liquid and turned back to Julian. 'If the chit is not to your liking, do not pursue her. But I am curious. Why do you continue to say you need to fulfil your duty and find a bride when it appears you do everything in your power to discount all the choices? You do realise the sooner you choose someone, the sooner your mother will stop casting you in a dudgeon.'

He scooped some lemon curd onto a slice of apple and popped it into his mouth.

Why did Hart have to be so insightful? Julian knew he needed to marry soon. As it was, he was thirteen years older than most of these girls—fourteen, in Lady Mary's case. In a few more years he might be bedding someone young enough to be his daughter.

Julian rubbed his chest. He wished he had more time.

Lady Mary was as good a choice as any for his duchess. Lineage was important, and the Morley family could trace their blood back to the Tudor courts. So why did Julian feel sick each time he thought of marrying her?

Suddenly clever blue eyes and a warm smile filled his thoughts. If only Lady Mary was like the American he wouldn't think twice about marrying her.

Shaking his head, he resumed slathering his toast with lemon curd.

Chapter Three

Later that evening Drury Lane buzzed with a multitude of voices as a large crowd awaited the evening's performance. Katrina found the theatre impressive in size, with three rows of boxes above orchestra level and two additional rows of open seating above. Chandeliers were suspended from each box, illuminating the theatre and making it easy to see its occupants.

Scanning the colourful attendants, Katrina found her gaze was drawn to a box close to the stage in the row above her own. She adjusted her opera glasses to get a better view.

'I thought English gentlemen were more discreet in their intrigues. Lord Phelps appears rather bold,' she whispered to Sarah as they sat together in the Forresters' box.

They both watched as a tall blonde woman turned adoringly to the portly older gentleman as he slid her mantle from her shoulders. Katrina's eyebrows rose as the cut of the woman's dress was revealed. The last time she'd seen a dress cut that low, she'd been in Paris.

'Perhaps that woman is his daughter,' Sarah said, clearly not believing her own suggestion.

'What do you think possesses a man to seek a mistress?'

'Lack of contentment, I suppose,' replied Sarah with a slight lift of her shoulder. 'It appears much more common here than it does back home. Most of these *ton* marriages seem to be for convenience and not love. That may explain why there are so many indiscretions.'

Katrina's gaze drifted back to Lord Phelps, who appeared to be introducing another older gentleman to his mistress. 'I am grateful joining the ranks of the *ton* is not to be my fate. I would never want my future tied to a man who would likely have liaisons.' She turned to Sarah and her spirits lifted. 'Hopefully when I return home I will find an honourable man who will think me so captivating he will have no choice but to offer for my hand.'

'Hopefully he will be handsome, as well as honourable,' Sarah said with a grin.

Before Katrina was able to respond her father sat down in the vacant seat on her other side. 'And how are the two of you enjoying the evening thus far?'

'We have been admiring the sights,' Katrina said as she smiled affectionately at him. 'It appears a number of boxes are garnering quite a bit of attention, and it's lovely not having stares and whispers pointed in *our* direction for once.'

But in a box across from where Katrina sat in comfortable conversation a man *was* staring—a very surprised man.

Julian narrowed his eyes and studied the woman in pale pink satin. He lifted his spyglass for a better view. She had rich golden hair, delicately curved shoulders, and her face moved with animation as she talked with the woman to her right. There was no mistaking it: this was the American he had spoken with on the de Lievens' terrace the night before—the same one who had plagued his thoughts throughout the day.

The older gentleman sitting next to her smiled indulgently, and Julian had an unnatural urge to drag her away from her companions. What the hell was wrong with him?

'I believe you have not heard a single word I've said for the last five minutes,' Hart complained with annoyance as he flipped a guinea in the air and caught it.

'Of course I have. You were discussing one of your latest liaisons.'

Hart let out a deep-throated laugh and leaned back in his chair, tipping it precariously. 'Not unless her name was Royal Rebel. Which, come to think of it, would be an exceptional name for a princess I am intimately acquainted with… I was speaking of the race I attended this afternoon and the amount of blunt Royal Rebel brought to my pockets. Came from behind and all. It was quite exciting.'

Julian was unable to keep his gaze from returning to the American, even though he tried to focus on his friend.

'What's her name?' Hart asked, flipping the guinea again.

'Whose name?'

'Whomever the lady is who has your attention—attention, I might add, that should be focused on *me*. It was sporting of you to invite me out this evening, but you really are an abominable host.'

Julian glanced at this friend. 'What makes you think it is a lady who has my attention?'

'Foolish of me. I suppose you are studying the folds of some gentleman's intricately tied cravat?' When Julian gave no reply, Hart shook his head. 'You realise it will not take me long to determine who has captured your attention?'

Placing the coin in his pocket, Hart took his spyglass and openly scanned the boxes across the way. 'There is the Montrose box—nothing new in there. Rothschild has some guests, but unless you are interested in *much* older women I think we can safely say your attention was not focused there. Then there is the box with the American delegation... Hmm...potential there. Next we have—'

'You know that box?' Julian closed his eyes, praying his friend hadn't heard the inane question.

Hart laughed softly and arched a cocky brow. 'So your thoughts were of a political nature?'

He didn't have to look so smug.

'Oh, very well, Julian. The gentleman and lady seated to our far left are Mr and Mrs Forrester, the American Minister and his wife. The other gentleman in the front row is Mr Peter Vandenberg, an American author who has recently arrived in London and will be one of the American representatives at the Anglo-American Conference. Surely you have heard of him? My understanding is that he has been welcomed all over the courts and drawing rooms of Europe and has lived for the past eight months in Paris. It's interesting that President Monroe has entrusted him to successfully negotiate the treaty between our countries.'

A mischievous sparkle flashed in Hart's blue eyes. 'Sorry to say I am not acquainted with anyone else in the box. Are you disappointed?'

'Dolt.'

'I can make some enquiries if you like.' Hart smirked and eyed Julian with open curiosity.

'No need. I am simply enjoying the view.'

Julian wondered if Peter Vandenberg was the American woman's husband. They were obviously well acquainted, considering the way she occasionally touched his arm when she spoke. He was too old for her, but Julian knew of many marriages arranged between young women and much older men. If he did not give proper attention to spending time with Lady Mary, his marriage might eventually resemble that one.

It hadn't occurred to him when they spoke that she might be married. Crossing his arms tightly over his chest, Julian forced his jaw to unclench. Why should he care if she was married?

The orchestra struck up its opening chords and the red velvet curtains of the stage parted. The narrator stepped out, and Julian was grateful for the distraction. However, when the interval was announced it annoyed him that he noticed the exact moment when the American woman left her box.

Once the performance had ended Julian couldn't help searching for her as he prepared to enter Hart's carriage. He turned towards the people still exiting the theatre and scanned the crowd for a pale pink gown. Not far away, to his left, he saw her standing next to Vandenberg while the man spoke to a coachman.

As if some strange force of nature had tapped her on the shoulder, she turned his way. Their eyes met. Recognition mixed with pleasure lit her features and the commotion around them faded away.

She pulled her mantle closed, appearing to hold off a chill. There were a number of interesting ways *he'd* like keep her warm. Her head tilted slightly, as if she was trying to read his thoughts, and then her lips rose into that alluring warm smile.

There was movement by her side, and Julian's gaze darted to the older gentleman next to her. When Vandenberg's hand moved to her elbow Julian's grip tightened around the gold handle of his walking stick. Meeting her eyes once more, Julian tipped his hat to her before climbing into Hart's coach.

'Where shall we go next?' Hart enquired as he settled himself on the green velvet bench and adjusted the cuffs of his black coat. 'Shall we try White's for cards?'

'Have your driver take me to Helena's. I promised I would make an appearance at her card party this evening.'

'I still do not understand this attraction you have to Helena. She, my friend, is the devil. Tell me she is nothing more than a passing fancy.'

'I do not understand why you are so against my association with her.'

Hart leaned forward across the carriage. 'She wants to improve her rank.'

'As do most women of the *ton*.'

'Tell me you are not thinking of marrying her.'

'It hasn't crossed my mind. You are mistaken about Helena. She has informed me that she has no wish to marry again.'

'And you believe her?'

'She has not given me a reason to doubt her.'

He and Helena shared a mutual physical attraction. She was the widow of the Earl of Wentworth and missed her marriage bed. She told him she enjoyed her independence. It was the perfect arrangement. Julian would never pay for sex. He wanted shared desire.

Hart opened his mouth to say something, but then turned and looked out of the window. 'Mark my words: Helena is trouble. You'd best remember that.'

However, at that moment Julian was having a difficult time remembering anything about Helena at all. His thoughts kept returning to a warm smile and a pair of lovely eyes.

Chapter Four

For days Julian couldn't seem to rid himself of the pull the American woman had on him. Suddenly she seemed to be everywhere. Each time he saw her their eyes met briefly, but he refused to pursue an introduction. Any enquiries he made about her would lead to speculation. He did not need members of the *ton* thinking he was panting after some American, even if that was exactly what he was doing. She was too tempting—and all wrong for a man who needed to live up to the Lyonsdale title.

The crackling and popping of the fire broke the silence in the library, where Julian and his grandmother faced each other over a chessboard. Absently twirling a glass of his favourite brandy on the Pembroke table, Julian wondered if the American would be attending the Langley ball later that evening.

'Your mother went to a musicale at the Morleys' tonight. I assume you were invited as well? You had no desire to attend?'

'I had already accepted another invitation,' Julian said as he slid one of his black pawns along the board.

'You do not like the girl?'

He gave a careless shrug. 'I have not spent enough time with her to form any opinion of her character.'

'You have danced with her recently.'

'She is a rather quiet partner. Do not fret. I am aware of her family's history and I know she is an appropriate choice.'

'It matters not to me if she is the one you will choose. I will not be marrying her. She does show quite well, though. I wouldn't think it a hardship to produce an heir with her.'

Julian jerked his head up. 'This is hardly a topic you and I should be discussing.'

'Why not? You're a grown man. We have both been married. I doubt there is anything you could say that would shock me.' She arched a challenging brow.

His stomach gave a queasy flip. 'You are my grandmother.'

She took a sip of her sherry and waved her glass in the air. 'Is that the best you can do?'

'It was not meant to shock. Discussing my marriage bed with you is unsettling, to say the least.'

'I am mentioning it because I know how important finding a suitable partner in bed can be for a happy marriage. Your grandfather and I had a happy marriage. Did you?'

Every muscle in his body turned to stone. She knew he hated discussing Emma. It was too painful.

He shifted his attention back to the board, trying to blink away the wretched image of his wife's lifeless form lying on the bloody sheets of her bed. He'd been holding her hand when she had slipped away. Offering her comfort at the end had been the least he could do, since it had been his fault she would never see her twentieth year.

'I had a satisfactory marriage,' he bit out, moving a random chess piece.

His grandmother's attention was back to analysing her next move. 'You were never cruel to Emma, however, I always had a sense that you were indifferent to her presence.'

He forced his jaw to unclench. 'And you think I was wrong in that?'

'I suppose it depends on what you want in a marriage.'

He rarely lost his patience with his grandmother, but she knew as well as he that what he wanted in life for himself did not matter. His parents had chosen his bride for him when he'd been away at Cambridge. When he had returned home one Christmas he had been informed that he would be married to a girl he'd never met. It had made him ill, but he'd understood that his needs and desires did not come before his duty. What mattered above all else was the legacy he left to the Lyonsdale name. He had known that to be true then, just as he knew it to be true now.

'I accepted my responsibility,' he said, looking his grandmother in the eye and raising his chin.

'Yes, you did—quite well, I might add. To my knowledge you never questioned your father's decision.'

'You know I could not cry off, even if I had wanted to. A man does not break an engagement. It is not done.'

She leaned in. 'But would you have done so if you could?'

If he had, Emma would still be alive today.

He took a large swig of brandy. 'I knew how important it was to have an exemplary woman share the Lyonsdale name. Father made an appropriate choice in Emma. There was no reason to protest.'

'And yet even though you accepted their choice the spark in your eyes you had as a child went out when you made your vows, and it has not returned since. You need to find that spark again.'

She made it sound simple, but Julian knew that honouring the responsibility of his title meant he would be bound, yet again, to a marriage of convenience. The only sparks that mattered were the ones he could fire off in his speeches at Westminster.

'Why am I certain you are about to tell me how I can regain what I have lost?'

His grandmother gave a slight shrug. 'I was fortunate. I married your grandfather and we fell in love. Your father was not as fortunate. We were certain your mother would be a rose in his pocket, but she had thorns. Being married to her killed something precious inside him, and he became consumed with politics and Westminster.' She leaned across the table and levelled him with a pointed stare. 'There is more to life than that. It did him no good.'

His father had been the very model of what an English duke should be. Nine years had passed since he'd collapsed and died while delivering a speech to the House of Lords, and to this day people continued to tell Julian how much they had admired him. If only Julian could be half the man he had been.

'I disagree. He helped this country achieve great things.'

'And it cost him his life. No one will convince me that his heart did not give way because of the strain of his political career.' She drained her glass of sherry. 'We were wrong in preventing him from choosing his own bride, and he was wrong when he did the same to you. Life is too brief, Julian. Trust someone as old as I. Do not waste your life tied to someone you do not want.'

If only it were that easy. Out of an entire ballroom of girls the only one he had been drawn to wasn't an appropriate choice—to say nothing of the fact that she was probably married to a man old enough to be her father. The point of taking a wife was to produce an heir. His father had told him many times that it wasn't necessary to like the person you married. You just needed to tolerate them.

Thankfully his grandmother's attention was back on the chessboard. 'Oh, and Julian…? I seem to have misplaced my edition of *A Traveler's Tale* by that American author—Vandenberg. Would you mind purchasing another one for me the next time you are near Hatchards?'

The Vandenberg name should *not* follow any conversation about marriage. He needed to concentrate on finishing this game of chess. Soon Hart would arrive, and they would be off to the Langley ball. However, tonight, he vowed, he would not search for the American at all.

Only the flutter of shuffling cards and the soft murmur of voices could be heard in the card room at Langley House. Footmen stood along walls that were hung with yellow silk damask, ready to refill crystal glasses at the mere lift of a hand. Purposely removed from the hubbub of the ballroom and the front public rooms, this drawing room was located near the end of a long hallway. Serious gambling was always done at the Langley ball, and serious gambling required concentration. It was the ideal place for a man who needed to keep his mind occupied. It didn't even matter to Julian that he was losing miserably.

'Perhaps a new table is in order?' Hart suggested as he collected his winnings.

A new table would not change his luck, but Julian surveyed the other seven tables for open seats anyway. As his gaze skimmed past the doorway he caught sight of Helena, in a jonquil satin gown, its bodice cut to accentuate her womanly curves. With an air of confidence she scanned the room until her grey eyes landed on him.

The beginnings of a smile tipped the corners of her full mouth as she made her way to his side. 'Do not tell me luck is against you tonight,' she said in a silky voice.

'It definitely is now,' mumbled Hart, low enough for Julian to hear.

He shot Hart a look of reproach and turned to her. 'I've had better luck,' he replied congenially.

'Have you been to the ballroom yet? The orchestra is exceptional.'

The American woman was probably in the ballroom— dancing with some braggart. 'The ballroom does not interest me tonight. Perhaps I'll try another table.'

She cocked her head to the side, exposing the pale skin of her neck. 'Perhaps we could play together,' she whispered.

'Perhaps we could.' He should have found the smooth skin of her neck enticing. He had before. However, looking at it now, he found his body surprisingly unaffected.

They were about to search for an open game when a footman approached him with a request for his presence at the Duke of Winterbourne's table. He felt an unprecedented sense of relief in having to leave Helena's side to join his friend.

Excusing himself, Julian followed the footman across the room.

Helena watched Lyonsdale walk towards the table full of his friends who were playing whist. As he leaned over to whisper into Winterbourne's ear Lyonsdale's black tail coat stretched across his broad shoulders. It was a pity the tails covered the outline of his muscular legs and his firm backside...

She could feel Lord Hartwick's eyes on her. For the last five years he had never once attempted to hide his hatred of her. It was perfectly reasonable, considering what she had done to him. However, watching the drama unfold around her at the time had been so entertaining she refused to feel any remorse. Her only regret was that she had believed his father's lies. He had told her that he would marry her if she helped him with his plan—a plan that she was certain had devastated the man's son.

Why hadn't Hartwick walked away when Lyonsdale left?

He tossed a lock of hair out of his eyes and pulled back his shoulders. 'He will never make you his duchess. I will see to that.'

Although he was splendid to look at, his confidence grated. 'Do not imagine you will be able to dissuade him.'

'But I find I rather like the idea, and I don't believe it will take much effort on my part. I suggest you search elsewhere for that elevated title you so desperately seek.'

The foolish man thought he could best her. 'I do not follow suggestions—least of all from you.' She shook out her fan and pasted on a sly smile, glancing pointedly across the room at the woman she knew to be Hartwick's current conquest. 'You should tell your friend she should not wear emerald. The colour does nothing for her complexion.'

Hartwick turned his head and followed her gaze. His lips pressed together as he took a glass of champagne from the tray of a passing footman. 'Maybe in this instance you should follow my suggestion. I hear Ponsby is on his last breath. You might want to try him. You'd have better luck.' He did nothing to hide the sarcasm from his voice.

Why would she want a decrepit duke when she could have a handsome, virile one? 'It appears you are worried for your friend. Do you believe I will damage him?'

'Your excitement is stirred by breaking people. You won't be able to do that with him.'

'You mean like your Lady Caroline? It's a pity she is no longer with us. Your father enjoyed her immensely.' She arched her brow and anticipated his reaction.

He brought his glass to his lips and his nostrils flared. 'I see you have no remorse for your part in bringing an innocent woman to his bed.'

Why should she? The foolish girl hadn't been forced to accept every glass of champagne Helena offered her. She hadn't poured them down the girl's throat.

Recalling that entertaining night brought a smile to her lips, and she leaned close to Hartwick, purposely pressing a full breast into his arm. 'You might not want to discuss this here, where someone may overhear us,' she whispered into his ear. 'You don't want them to guess the truth about her death, now, do you? Tell me…did she choose poison, or was it something more dramatic?'

His jaw clenched, and his athletic body stiffened against her breast. If they had not been in a drawing room, with a good number of the *ton* around them, she might just have provoked him enough to strike her.

She couldn't help but smile. 'I do believe I have found a weakness of yours, Lord Hartwick. Everyone has at least one, and it is so delicious whenever it is discovered.'

'I warn you—if you cause any problems for Lyonsdale you will regret it.' He moved from her side, downed the remainder of his champagne, and strode across the room to join his friends.

It was amusing that he thought he could stop her. She deserved that title, and all the wealth and power that went with it. She should have had such an advantageous marriage the first time. Instead, due to one minor indiscretion, she had found herself married to a gambler and a drunkard.

Hartwick's father had promised to make her his marchioness and laughed at her when she'd reminded him. No one made a fool of her. It would be her turn to laugh when she became Duchess of Lyonsdale.

Near a corner of the Langleys' ballroom, in front of a large potted palm, Katrina was learning that she was not the only one who regretted dancing with Lord Boreham.

'I do so wish I did not have to agree to dance with everyone that asks me.' Lady Mary Morley pouted as she stood beside Katrina. 'On that last turn Lord Boreham managed to elbow me quite hard in the stomach.'

'How was that even possible?' Sarah asked, staring at the area in question, which was covered in elaborately embroidered white muslin.

'I can assure you it's possible,' Lady Hammond commented dryly while fanning herself. 'He once knocked heads with me during a quadrille.'

They began to laugh, and Lady Mary immediately covered her mouth to stop herself. The diamond bracelet on her wrist sparkled in the candlelight.

'Surely there must be a way to avoid him,' Sarah said.

Lady Mary shook her head. 'Mother says one should have a full dance card if one is to be considered an incomparable, and if you decline even one offer to dance you must decline all the others.'

Katrina found that rule of social conduct one of the hardest to accept. She suspected she was not the only woman in the ballroom who felt that way. 'That hardly seems fair.'

'That might be. However, it is the way of things. Mother says if one is to catch a duke or a marquess one needs to rise above all the other girls vying for such a title and become an incomparable.'

'And how does one become an incomparable?' Sarah asked with amusement.

Lady Mary was not as naïve as she appeared. She tilted her head coyly. 'I suppose if everyone knew the answer to that, no one girl would stand out.'

'Well done, Lady Mary,' Sarah said with a smile, glancing around the crowded ballroom. 'And are there many dukes and marquesses for you to choose from?'

'I'm afraid there are very few, and I don't think I'd like

to settle for an earl.' She turned to her friend and offered Lady Hammond a genuine apologetic smile. 'Sorry, my dear. I didn't mean anything against your Hammond.'

Lady Hammond waved her fan carelessly in the air. 'I'd much prefer a young earl to an old duke.'

Both Lady Hammond and Lady Mary appeared to be a number of years younger than Katrina, and she wondered just how old the girl's husband was.

'Isn't your father an earl?' Katrina couldn't help pointing that out to Lady Mary.

Lady Mary adjusted her bracelets. 'He is. However, my uncle is the Duke of Ralsteed. I was born to be a duchess. I do not have to settle for an earl.'

Lady Hammond let out a delicate sniff. 'You'd change your mind if Lord Hartwick made an offer for you. With his looks and those blue eyes, you'd forgive him his title.'

A blush spread across Lady Mary's cheeks, making her appear even younger. 'That might be true. However, my sights are focused on one specific duke—even if he does make me nervous.'

'Being nervous around a man can be a good thing,' Sarah offered helpfully. 'It might mean you find him very attractive.'

'Oh, I do,' Lady Mary agreed, nodding vigorously before she caught herself. 'I do think he is very handsome... except he is a bit old.'

'He is the same age as Lord Hartwick,' Lady Hammond said with exasperation.

Lady Mary looked as if she was fighting the urge to stamp her foot. 'Well, he appears older.' Stepping closer to Katrina and Sarah, she shook out her fan to cover her lips. 'He comes from one of the most respected houses and has great influence in Parliament. His manner is very formal, and each time I am in his presence I find him austere and imposing. He seldom speaks. I don't believe he needs to. He can fluster people with just the lift of his brow.'

He sounded like a bore to Katrina. 'And this is the man you would like to marry?'

Lady Mary nodded again, with excitement in her eyes. 'Just imagine the respect his duchess will be granted. And he's rich. He is a man who does not need to marry an heiress. Should we marry, we might very well be the wealthiest family in Britain.'

'Which would be wonderful,' Sarah remarked, 'as long as you can stay awake long enough to enjoy it.'

'Sarah!' Katrina chided her friend with what she hoped was a stern expression.

These two girls had been nothing but kind since being introduced to them by Madame de Lieven. They were eager to hear about America and about Katrina's time in France. She didn't want Sarah's unchecked honesty to ruin a pleasant discussion.

'I am simply stating that should a man be that…flinty, it might be difficult to stay awake in his presence,' Sarah explained.

Lady Hammond let out a small laugh before she pressed her lips together. 'I can't imagine anyone falling asleep in His Grace's presence.'

He was sounding more and more like everything Katrina didn't want in a husband. She turned to Lady Mary. 'But if you were married to him, eventually you would fall asleep beside him.'

The rosy colour drained out of the girl's face and she glanced about the room, as if this fine specimen of an English nobleman might overhear them and curse them with an arched brow. 'I could never do that. I am certain he would never approve.'

Yes, this duke was definitely someone Katrina was grateful would not be part of *her* future. 'Could it be possible that you might forgo this favourable duke and marry someone for love?'

Lady Mary and Lady Hammond looked at one another with confusion. There was no way to know for certain, but from her perplexed expression Katrina would guess that Lady Hammond's marriage had been an arranged one. There still might be hope for Lady Mary.

However, she now addressed Katrina as if she were a small child. 'I imagine that is an American way of thinking. Why would I marry for love when I could marry a duke?'

She would never understand the English. But there was no sense in filling the girl's head with romantic notions. Katrina had spent some time this evening in the presence of the girl's mother. It hadn't taken her long to see how determined she was to promote her daughter for an advantageous match. Good luck to the man who married into *that* family!

While Katrina had been contemplating what it would be like to be married to a man such as Lady Mary's duke, the discussion had turned back to life in America. It was making her feel nostalgic for her friends back home. As Sarah was regaling them with tales of life in Washington, Katrina excused herself, to slip away for a few minutes to the ladies' retiring room.

She was about ten feet from the end of the long hall when she almost walked directly into the last person she had any desire to see. It was that self-important Englishman from the Russian Ambassador's terrace, who appeared to be too proud to associate openly with an American.

She hadn't been aware that he was in attendance, and he seemed just as surprised to see her. His green eyes widened momentarily with recognition, but as usual he said nothing—no greeting at all. Not one to be intimidated,

Katrina looked directly at him and waited. Even without seeking an introduction it would be a great insult if he completely ignored her this time. Now she would see how high in the instep he really was.

This was the closest she'd been to him since the night they'd talked under the stars. He'd nodded acknowledgement to her one night at the theatre, but each time she'd seen him after that he had avoided making eye contact. A number of times she'd caught him staring at her, but he had always diverted his gaze so quickly, she'd been certain he must be giving himself a headache with each sudden shift of his eyes.

And now he was standing less than five feet in front of her, impeccably dressed in formal black evening attire, with candlelight shining on the chestnut waves of his hair.

Perhaps it was because they were so close, or maybe he had had too much to drink, but this time his gaze roamed over her body. The hallway was growing very warm, and she shook out her fan to cool her heated skin.

He gave her a polite nod. 'Pardon me.'

That was it? That was all he would say?

It was quite obvious from his demeanour that he had no intention of saying more.

He must be great friends with Lady Mary's duke.

They wouldn't be able to continue down the hall unless one of them moved to the side. Katrina was tempted to take both her hands and push him over, but instead she inclined her head and swished around him, doing her best to ignore the fluttery feeling she'd got from hearing the rumble of his deep voice.

Chapter Five

The next morning Julian could barely finish his paperwork. His attention kept drifting to the American. He'd been astonished at the sense of longing he'd felt when she had walked past him last night. While she hadn't exactly given him the cut, her brief response to his apology for almost knocking into her for a second time had been anything but friendly. They hadn't spoken since the night of the de Lievens' ball. What could he possibly have done to warrant the daggers she had thrown at him with her eyes?

He was angry with this woman he didn't even know for turning his life upside down. Thoughts of her popped into his mind at all hours of the day, and each time he saw her his body immediately snapped to attention. He hadn't bedded Helena in weeks, and as of late his blood was only stirred by thoughts of the American. How could he get any work done?

He needed sex. His lack of release was playing havoc with his mind—that must be why he was so fixated on a woman he'd barely spoken to. He needed to see Helena.

Walking into the entrance hall of her townhouse, Julian handed her butler his hat and walking stick. The sound of footfalls on the wooden staircase caught his attention, and he watched Helena make her descent, her curves straining against a blood-red dressing gown. He should have felt like dragging her somewhere and bedding her for hours. He didn't.

Perhaps it was because they were in a very public area of the house, with her butler not far away. Julian shifted his eyes to her drawing room door, giving her a wordless command. As they entered the sparsely furnished room Helena closed the door and locked it. She always had been good with discretion.

Before she could utter a word Julian pushed her up against the door and kissed her. He needed her to help him forget the American right now. But the kiss felt all wrong—awkward and unpleasant. He closed his eyes, willing his body to react. Her lavender scent filled his nose.

Why did it suddenly seem so overpowering and unappealing?

He pulled his head back and looked down at her inviting expression. She was one of the most beautiful women in England. *Wasn't she?* He'd used to think so. His brow wrinkled as he studied her delicate features. The outline of her breasts was not even enticing him to undress her.

Helena slid her hand up his chest and combed her fingers through the hair by his temple. 'We could retire to my bed.'

That would be the ideal place. However, he could barely kiss her, let alone bed her. He turned away from her eager expression and glanced towards the settee. 'This room will suit our purposes.' He placed distance between them and took a seat.

'Would you care for some brandy?' she asked.

His body was tied in knots of uncomfortable tension. If only he could relax… He nodded, and when she sat down he felt her right thigh push up against his left. He took a long draw from the glass. The warm liquid eased some of the tightness in his shoulders and he shifted his thigh so it was no longer pressing against her leg.

She sketched circles on his knee with her finger and avoided his eyes. 'You are quieter than usual. Have I done something to displease you?'

'No. I find I have much on my mind today.' He forced himself to smile reassuringly. It was not her fault his body wasn't co-operating. He took another drink.

'What has brought you here? You've never called on me during the day.'

Unable to voice the real reason, he shrugged. 'I needed to see you.'

That seemed to satisfy her, and she attempted to hold back a smile. 'I see.'

She was giving him time to elaborate, but how could he? He had no idea why his body wasn't responding to her. He kissed her again, more demandingly this time. In his mind he saw magnetic blue eyes and a warm smile— so he squeezed his eyelids tighter. He told himself that Helena could do amazing things with her mouth. It was no use. He wasn't even remotely hard.

Julian released her and drained the contents of his glass. The burn washed away the taste of their kiss. This visit had been intended to cure him of the affliction brought on by the American. Instead it had made him want her more. He was out of ideas on what to do. He needed advice.

Helena watched Lyonsdale swallow the remaining contents of his glass. When he was finished, the glass landed on the table with an audible thud.

He stood rather abruptly. 'Pardon me, but I have matters I need to attend to today.'

Without giving her a chance to reply, he walked out of the room.

Picking up his discarded glass, she ran her tongue over the rim where his lips had been. He never called on her during the day. Surely this was the sign she had been looking for. She had finally caught him. This time all her plotting and planning would land her the title she so richly deserved. He might even have left to make arrangements about asking for her hand.

How she wished she could be there when her brother heard she would be the next Duchess of Lyonsdale! Her new title would trump his title of earl. Finally she would be above him. He and that puritanical wife of his would regret the day they had said they wanted nothing more to do with her when she had become obligated to marry Wentworth. They could beg all they wanted—they would never dine in Lyonsdale House!

She poured herself a small splash of brandy. No longer would she have to sell items from her home to purchase this fine vintage. It was exhausting, hiding her financial situation. Soon that would all be a memory. Soon she would dine at Carlton House with the Prince Regent and his set while she wore the Carlisle diamonds.

Not far away, Katrina was preparing herself for an onslaught of advice as she was escorted down the hallway of Almack's towards the assembly room where Madame de Lieven was waiting. When she'd received her note, requesting a meeting regarding a matter of the utmost importance, Katrina had been curious as to what the summons could possibly mean. Could she be about to enter into a lengthy discussion about the consequences of not following the strict rules of English etiquette? Or was Madame de Lieven about to inform Katrina in person that she was revoking the vouchers she had granted? Katrina wished she had someone besides her maid,

Meg, to accompany her. Madame de Lieven was known to be quite commanding. There would have been safety in numbers.

Stopping before a set of double doors, Katrina raised her chin and took a deep breath, reminding herself to remain polite no matter what the woman had to say.

Light poured into the cavernous room from the large windows, brightening the white walls and gold trim. In the very centre of the room sat Madame de Lieven, at a white linen-covered table set for tea. Closing the book she had been reading, she motioned Katrina forward.

'I am pleased you accepted my invitation, Miss Vandenberg. I realise it is a bit early in the day for making calls, and the venue is unusual, but I do have my reasons.' She turned her head to the doorkeeper. 'Please see that Miss Vandenberg's maid is taken care of downstairs, Mr Willis, while we settle things here.'

That didn't sound very promising. As Katrina watched Meg trail Mr Willis out of the large ballroom she wished she could follow them. Shifting her gaze, she accepted the chair that was offered.

Madame de Lieven was a woman of strong self-importance, who moved with ease among the leading political figures of London. She had a way of influencing the people around her. Katrina was certain she wanted to keep her eye on 'the Americans', and that was why she'd offered to sponsor Katrina and the Forresters at Almack's.

She handed Katrina a cup of tea with milk and sugar. 'You intrigue me, Miss Vandenberg. I have noticed that you are a woman very much like me—a fish in a different pond.'

Katrina steadied herself under Madame de Lieven's intense gaze. 'Forgive me, I don't understand.'

'Since I am also a foreigner here, I am aware that it is not always easy to adjust to English customs. You have shown yourself to be a woman of intelligence and diplomacy. Two qualities I admire.'

'I see no reason to hide the knowledge I possess, but I try not to appear too forward in my opinions.'

'You should be aware that you have impressed me enough that I believe together you and I could accomplish great things here.'

Katrina's brow furrowed. 'I do not understand,' she said again.

Madame de Lieven placed her cup on the table. 'Let us be American and speak plainly.'

Katrina bristled at the insinuation. Anticipating what Madame de Lieven might say or do had kept Katrina amused since she had arrived in London. This time she sensed the next thing she said would cause her orderly life to be changed in ways that wouldn't be pleasant.

'I have noticed that you can be a bit too honest with your emotions at times. However, you possess a keen mind. Your presence is a refreshing change for me, and I have decided I will find you a husband here in London, so you can remain even after your father's negotiations are settled. It is the reason I extended the vouchers for Almack's to you. Our assemblies will prove helpful in finding you a husband.'

'A husband?' Katrina placed her cup down on the table and clasped her hands together on her lap. What had she ever done to give Madame de Lieven the impression she was looking for a husband? Whatever it was, Katrina knew she needed to stop doing it. 'I do not want a husband.'

'Of course you do. Every woman wants a husband. A husband provides a woman with…security.'

'What I mean to say is I do not want a husband here… in England.'

Madame de Lieven appeared sceptical.

Katrina continued. 'I will return to New York when my father's work here is finished. I plan to marry an American.'

'Nonsense,' Madame de Lieven said, appearing appalled. 'I can help you secure an excellent match. There are a number of rich, untitled Englishmen who would be pleased to marry an attractive woman with knowledge in the art of diplomacy, regardless of your background. You could live in wealth and splendour. Besides, you do not have many more good years left. You are almost on the shelf.'

Katrina was not about to tell her that all the luxury in the world couldn't compensate for a wandering, haughty husband. 'I appreciate your thoughtfulness,' she managed to say evenly, 'but we also have wealthy gentlemen back home. And, more to the point, money will not figure prominently in my choice of husband.'

Madame de Lieven gave her a dubious look.

'Of course it is desirable to live comfortably,' Katrina amended. 'But you should be aware that, while I appreciate your offer to assist me in finding a husband, I intend to follow my heart.'

'You are referring to love?'

'Yes.'

'You are so very American. Love has no place in marriage. No one of consequence marries the person they love. They marry the person who is in a position to provide the best life possible.'

'And by "the best life" you mean one with wealth and privilege?'

'What else is there?'

'Companionship, humour, trust—'

'That is what your friends are for.'

Katrina rubbed her lips together, trying not to show her

frustration. 'Although I appreciate your interest in finding me a husband, it is not necessary.'

Madame de Lieven smiled regally, then let out a low sound that was almost a laugh. 'I believe finding you well settled here will be highly entertaining. I expect I will see you at tomorrow night's assembly. We can begin our search then.'

Katrina opened her mouth to protest again, but before she could get the words out Madame de Lieven motioned someone forward with her hand.

Mr Willis approached the table and bowed. 'The musicians are ready,' he informed her.

Clapping her hands together, Madame de Lieven motioned to the balcony and soft strains of music began to drift through the room. 'I've asked you to meet me here today because Mr Willis believes he has found us a new orchestra and I am to determine if they will suit. I will be interested in your opinion of their abilities.'

Katrina was grateful for the change in subject. She had no desire to marry an Englishman, and she hoped she would be able to convince the persistent Madame de Lieven to let the matter rest.

Julian should have been reading the latest reports from his steward in Hertfordshire. Instead he had sought out Hart at Tattersalls. Luckily, his friend was predictable. Hart was inspecting the horses that were to be auctioned off tomorrow. He did little to hide the surprise in his greeting, but after a few minutes they fell into companionable silence while they watched three horses parade around the paddock.

'That black thoroughbred looks very fine. Perhaps I will bid on him tomorrow.' When Julian didn't reply Hart watched him from the corner of his eye. 'Although I am considering purchasing a mule instead. Do you think that would do?'

'Yes…' Julian murmured, while he considered once again his time at Helena's. When had he stopped feeling the desire to bed her? They had agreed to a relationship based on satisfying each other's physical needs. If he no longer desired her was there any reason to continue visiting her?

'Splendid. I will send the bill to your house.'

'Of course.'

Hart yanked him to a stop. 'Julian, you have just agreed to buy me a mule. What the devil is wrong with you? All week your mind has been elsewhere.'

It took Julian a few blinks before Hart came into focus. Turning away from his friend's inquisitive gaze, he looked out towards the horses. 'Apologies, I've been woolgathering.'

Hart placed his booted foot on the lower rung of the fence enclosing the horses and leaned his arms on the upper railing. 'You don't say? Will you tell me what has you so distracted?'

Julian stepped closer to his friend and crossed his arms over his chest. He hoped he would not come to regret this. 'You know women…'

Hart grinned. 'I like to believe I do.'

Taking a deep breath, Julian watched the horses as they ambled around the pen. If anyone overheard them it would stir up gossip. He moved closer to Hart and lowered his voice. 'I went to see Helena this morning.'

'A daytime visit—that's a bit unusual,' Hart said slowly.

'I'm baffled. She's a beautiful woman, but the entire time I was in her company my thoughts were elsewhere.'

'On another woman?'

'Yes.'

Hart rubbed away a small smile with his gloved hand. 'Who?'

'I don't know her name,' Julian said, in a low, forceful voice that did nothing to hide his frustration.

'I don't understand.'

'She is new to London and we haven't been introduced.'

'So seek an introduction.'

'It would only lead to more speculation on my affairs. It would not do for people to think I have an interest in her.'

'Why not? It's just an introduction—unless you're planning on seducing her on the dance floor?'

That thought had crossed Julian's mind—more times than he would care to admit even to himself. 'It is not amusing. I have not been able to get her out of my head. I search for a glimpse of her whenever I am out. I think I hear her voice in crowded rooms. *This* is not normal.'

'Maybe not for you, but at least it explains your odd behaviour.'

'What do I do? How do I remove her from my thoughts?'

Hart shrugged his shoulders with careless ease. 'Why would you want to? It's evident that you want her, so end this association you have with Helena and pursue this woman.'

If only he could. 'That is not an option,' Julian replied, squeezing the bridge of his nose.

Hart faced him and crossed his arms. 'What hold does Helena have on you?'

Julian let out a snort of disbelief. No woman directed his actions, and he would find a way to forget this American. He just needed to determine how to do that. 'Helena has no hold over me.'

'Prove it. End your association with her. If your interest lies elsewhere, follow it. You are making this more complicated than it needs to be.'

'With this woman everything is complicated.' Julian's

gaze drifted to the horses. 'Besides, nothing could possibly come from an association between us. She's an American.'

An indecipherable look flashed in Hart's eyes. 'So? Do you believe all Americans are cannibals, perform war dances, and run around with hatchets when they get angry? Make certain you do not call out another lady's name while bedding her. She might scalp you.'

'Very amusing.'

'Don't let her nationality prevent you from pursuing her. I imagine American women are quite uninhibited in bed.'

'Well, I'm not going to find out.' And it was driving him to distraction.

'You need to stop being so bloody proper. I cannot see one benefit to not doing what I want, when I want. End what you have with Helena. It's obvious your attention has shifted elsewhere.'

'It is not that easy.'

'Of course it is. You say, *Helena, I am finished with you.*'

'Truly? Have you ever ended a relationship with a woman?'

'That's beside the point. We are discussing you. I know you too well. You, my friend, are boringly monogamous.'

'Let it alone, Hart.'

'Very well. Then continue to tup Helena while you imagine a certain miss who shall remain nameless.'

The statement left him unsettled and guilty. There was only one thing to do.

Chapter Six

Julian was not looking forward to seeing Helena before leaving for Westminster the next day. He might have sent her a note. It would have been far easier and much less painful on his part. But he could not be so callous. It wasn't her fault that he'd met someone he couldn't stop thinking about.

This time when he knocked on her door her butler didn't appear surprised to see him. He was left to wait for her in the drawing room. The idea of sitting was not appealing, so he walked around the room to relieve his restlessness. A few minutes later Helena walked in, wearing her blood-red dressing gown.

'Forgive me,' he said. 'I did not realise you would be preparing for the evening.'

'I was resting, and didn't see the point of dressing when I heard you were here. This is a pleasant surprise. Would you care for a brandy?'

He would have liked the entire bottle, but that would just muddle his brain so he politely declined.

She trailed her fingers down his chest. 'Do you wish to retire upstairs? I could see to your comfort.'

No matter what room they were in, Julian knew he would not be comfortable. 'I believe I'd prefer to remain here.'

A questioning look flashed in her grey eyes as she gestured towards the settee.

Julian chose an armchair instead.

Prowling behind him, Helena skimmed her fingers along his shoulders before lowering herself into the slightly worn silk armchair closest to him.

'What brings you here today?' she asked, reclining back. 'You left rather abruptly the other day.' She tipped her chin towards the box on his lap. 'Is that your way of apologising?'

He handed her the blue velvet box. 'It is…for a number of things…'

A look of confusion crossed her face before she slid her hand up his thigh. 'I hope you will stay longer today, so I may thank you properly.'

The boldness of her gesture forced him to shift in his chair. He nodded towards the package in her hand, relieved to know that she was easily distracted by expensive objects. 'Open it.'

Her eyes sparkled with eager anticipation as she lifted the lid. Slowly she pulled out the long strand of pearls and arranged them between her breasts, which were suddenly exposed through her open dressing gown.

He wished he could tell her she was wasting her efforts on him. 'They suit you,' he said. It was as much of a compliment as he could muster.

'They are beautiful,' she said, more interested in the pearls than in Julian. 'They will go well with the new gown I have ordered from Madame Devy. Perhaps we could attend Drury Lane or Vauxhall, and I will wear them for you.' She finally looked up at him. 'I know how you dislike attracting attention, but I think we will turn some heads.'

Julian's jaw clenched as he studied his brown leather gloves. 'Helena, there is something I need to ask you.' He turned his attention to her expectant expression. 'You are aware that I have a deep regard for you?'

She smiled up at him. 'I am.'

'Well... I was wondering if you are content with the state of our friendship?'

'What are you trying to say?'

'When we began this liaison both of us knew it could not continue indefinitely the way it is.'

'That is true,' she said through a seductive smile. The scent of lavender filled the air as she leaned in closer.

'And we both entered into this with a mutual understanding that eventually we would part ways.'

Her mouth fell open. 'You are *ending* this?'

'While I have enjoyed our time together, surely you knew that it would not last?'

'I cannot believe you are doing this,' she whispered. The sound of her heavy breathing mingled with the ticking of the clock. She jumped from her chair and poked him in the chest—hard. 'Lord Hartwick is behind this.'

He pulled his brows together in puzzlement. 'He has nothing to do with this.'

'Then there is another woman.' She eyed him up and down in disgust. 'Have you offered for Morley's chit? Your mother acts as if an announcement will be made any day.'

'I have not offered for her. There is no other woman.' She didn't need to know the truth.

'Why are you doing this?' she demanded, clenching her fists at her sides.

'I did not think you would be upset. You told me you had no intention of marrying again,' he stated firmly.

'And you *believed* me?' she screamed. She stormed across the room with her head high, and then spun around. 'And you give me *pearls*? We have been together all this time and you give me *pearls*!'

'What is wrong with pearls? They are quite expensive.'

Her body visibly shook with rage. 'You are the Duke of Lyonsdale! You should be giving me diamonds!'

His sympathy for her was quickly diminishing upon seeing her greedy nature. 'I did not have to give you anything!' he bellowed.

'You selfish boor!' She picked up a silver candlestick from the table closest to her and flung it at his head.

He ducked just in time.

'I am worth diamonds—not pearls!'

Before his control slipped further he needed to leave. Striding across the room, he unlocked the door and didn't look back.

When he stepped outside the soft breeze cooled his heated skin. His body hummed with anger at her selfishness. Sitting in his carriage would do him no good. He needed physical exertion. He would walk home—but first he needed to make one more stop.

Chapter Seven

Descending the staircase in the centre of Hatchards, Katrina scanned the room below her. This bookshop was one of her favourite places in London. The soft whispers and the occasional sound of the turning of pages were welcome after spending the entire morning on social calls with Mrs Forrester and Sarah.

As she continued to search for her maid Katrina let her gaze skim over the few patrons who were selecting books from the dark wooden bookshelves that lined the walls. An older woman in an elaborately decorated black hat was comparing books with a younger woman dressed demurely in lavender. Near them a dandy dressed in a navy jacket and puce trousers stood in a studied pose, reading the book he held through his quizzing glass.

Scanning the room further, Katrina felt her heart skip a beat. Standing near her maid, at a table piled with books, stood a broad-shouldered, dark-haired gentleman in a finely cut bottle-green coat, buckskin breeches and top boots. Was her time in London destined to be cursed with the presence of the rude Englishman from the Russian Ambassador's ball?

Katrina hesitated on the staircase, wondering if she should turn around and go back upstairs before he spotted her. Suddenly he lifted his head, as if sensing her gaze, and their eyes met. She could not turn back now. Taking a breath, she gripped the wooden banister and proceeded to slowly walk down the stairs towards Meg.

Katrina picked up the first volume of *Frankenstein* and thumbed through the pages. 'Have you found anything of interest?' she asked Meg.

Her maid smiled and showed Katrina the book in her hand.

'I do not believe *Clarissa* is an appropriate choice for you,' Katrina said.

'I've heard it's scandalous, and I'm hoping they have it at the lending library. The heroine is told to marry an unappealing gentleman and then is tricked into running away by a rake. I bet there is a dungeon in the story. I love a story that takes place in a dungeon.' Meg sighed and then glanced inquisitively at the book in Katrina's hand.

Taking into account her maid's vivid imagination, Katrina quickly placed *Frankenstein* back on the table. 'I'm well aware of the plot. You do know you can borrow any of my books?'

'Do they have dungeons, kidnappings, evil earls or ghosts?'

'No.'

'Then why do you think I would want to read them?' Meg asked, wrinkling her brow.

There was a deep laugh from across the table. Keeping her head averted under the rim of her bonnet, Katrina blocked her view of the gentleman across the table. Searching for a more appropriate novel, Katrina spotted a copy of her father's book. As she reached for it her hand brushed against a strong hand encased in a brown leather glove. Startled, she looked up.

'We meet again,' the annoying Englishman said.

No, we don't, because you are too rude to seek an introduction!

Katrina took a breath to compose herself before she spoke. 'So it would seem.'

'Forgive me. I believe that is the book I have been searching for.'

'This book?' Katrina asked, holding it up to show him the title on the spine.

'Yes, that is it.' He reached for another copy and began to turn the pages. There was a hesitation before he looked up at her. 'I've heard it's a very good book. You would not happen to know anything about it, would you?'

'I can highly recommend it. The book presents the observations of a traveller and contains much happy humour.'

Katrina glanced around the shop to see if anyone was watching them. Meg had moved to a nearby bookcase, engrossed in *Clarissa*. What was the point of having your maid accompany you around the town if she walked away when the man you wanted to avoid began speaking with you?

He walked around the table and stood next to her, smelling of leather and fresh air. 'The account is humorous?'

'Yes, Lord Byron has said he knows it by heart, and Scott has said it is positively beautiful. I understand the book is selling rather quickly. You might wish to purchase one before they are all sold.' She looked closely at him, challenging him to actually buy it.

'You appear intimately acquainted with the book,' he commented, his eyes narrowing.

'I suppose I am. My father is the author.'

'You are Mr Vandenberg's daughter?' he asked in a rush of breath.

'Yes, my lord, I am.' She crossed her arms over her

chest. If he said one disparaging thing about the fact that her father was a writer she was leaving immediately. He would deserve the cut.

He tipped his head to her. 'Then I shall be certain to take your recommendation. My grandmother speaks highly of it as well.'

'Your grandmother?'

'Yes. My grandmother seems to have misplaced her copy. I came here today to purchase a new one for her.'

He was intending to purchase her father's book because his grandmother had lost her copy? That seemed rather...sweet.

Katrina caught herself before she smiled. *He wasn't sweet. He was rude!* Still, she couldn't help asking him if he was a doting grandson.

'I suppose I am.'

He smiled at her and he appeared even more attractive.

'She seemed truly distressed to discover it missing.'

He stepped a bit closer and inhaled. Was that some odd English custom?

Katrina eyed him and placed her father's book down. 'Did you just *sniff* me?' she whispered.

A small smile raised one corner of his lips. 'Now, why would I do that?'

'Why, indeed?' Katrina replied, narrowing her eyes at him.

She edged a little further down the table. The heat from his body somehow made its way over to her. This man had ignored her for days. Why couldn't her body do the same to him? She could practically feel his every breath. That slightly unsettling feeling was back.

'If you will excuse me?' she said, turning to leave.

He blocked her way with his body. 'You do not need to leave yet, do you?'

'I cannot stay. You must realise our speaking without

an introduction is highly improper.' It was easier not to look at him, and she picked unseen strings from her pale blue and white spencer.

He glanced around and edged closer to her. 'That didn't bother you before.'

'A momentary lapse in judgement.'

'No one here knows we have not been formally introduced,' he said quietly.

'*We* know we have not,' she chided. 'And you have done it again! You sniffed me.' She stepped away from him, feeling more than a little unsettled. 'I can assure you Americans do bathe.'

His lips twitched. 'Why do you smell like lemons, Miss Vandenberg?'

Katrina's brows drew together in confusion. 'That is irrelevant—and I refuse to carry on this conversation when I do not even know your name.'

'We could remedy that easily. I could simply tell you what it is.'

'Do you always flout the English rules of conduct?'

He appeared to ponder her question for a moment. Then he shook his head. 'Actually, I never do. However, I see no harm in it this time. But if you insist we will do this in the proper manner. I shall need to borrow your maid.'

'You'd like to borrow my maid?'

'I would.'

He walked to Meg, who was watching the interaction between her mistress and this perplexing Englishman. They bent their heads together, and a short while later both walked towards Katrina.

'Miss Vandenberg,' Meg said, trying unsuccessfully to hide her smile, 'may I present His Grace the Duke of Lyonsdale? Your Grace, this is my mistress—Miss Katrina Vandenberg.' She curtsied and watched them both closely.

The scoundrel! Katrina's eyes widened. 'You're a *duke*?'

A slow smile made his lips turn up invitingly. 'I am.'

'You are the Duke of Lyonsdale?'

'Yes, I believe we have established that.'

Meg, as if sensing her mistress's temper, smartly moved back to her place by the bookcase.

'Why didn't you tell me?' Katrina demanded.

'My name? I was going to, but you seemed to need a proper introduction so I had your maid do it.'

'That's not what I meant,' Katrina said as she shook her head. 'You led me to believe you were simply a lord.'

'How did I do that?'

'You did not correct me when I addressed you. You must have found my ignorance vastly entertaining,' she replied waspishly.

It had been bad enough when she'd thought he might be a titled gentleman, such as a baron, but he was a *duke*! In England, his station in life was so far above hers he probably would never have spoken to her again if it had not been for this accidental encounter.

She would not show him that it hurt.

'Miss Vandenberg—'

'I'll not be played for a fool. I'm sure you have enjoyed telling your friends how ignorant Americans can be. Well, let me tell you—'

'Miss Vandenberg,' he interrupted more forcefully. 'I didn't correct you because we had not been introduced. I had no opportunity to tell you my name or indicate my station.'

'You could have corrected the way I had addressed you.'

'And sound like a pompous fool? I think not.'

He certainly would have sounded like a pompous fool, but Katrina was not convinced he didn't have another motive for not telling her the truth. He must have had a great laugh at her expense.

'In any event, what you did was rude.'

Both his brows rose and he jerked his head back. 'I assure you, causing you any distress was most unintentional.'

Then his lips twitched, and she wanted to throw a book at him. The man was insufferable.

'You are laughing at me,' she said through her teeth. 'I believe I have spent too much time here today. I bid you good day—Your Grace.'

As she stormed out of the bookshop she wished she could restrict her engagements to those he would never consider attending.

Julian's encounter with Miss Vandenberg left him perplexed. No one had ever schooled him in proper behaviour before. No one would ever have dared. And yet this American had thought it necessary to inform him that he was rude.

He should have been insulted by the way she'd spoken to him, but she had been so certain in her conviction, so passionate about the way she deserved to be treated, he had not been able to fault her.

He was a man of strong convictions as well. When he had entered the shop it hadn't occurred to him that he would leave finding Miss Vandenberg even more desirable than he already had.

By the next day he was still reliving their discussion and anticipating when he would speak to her again.

Deciding to visit the woman who was indirectly responsible for their encounter, Julian sought out his grandmother when he returned home from his committee meeting. Upon entering her private sitting room, he found her resting in a bergère chair, with a book in her hand.

'Come in Julian,' she said, waving him closer. 'You truly have spoiled me.'

He walked across the gold and white Aubusson rug and sat down next to her. 'I see you are enjoying your book.'

'You were slippery, presenting me with that volume yesterday. The arrival of this copy was quite unexpected.'

'This copy?' he replied, perplexed.

'Yes—the one you had Mr Vandenberg inscribe.'

Julian gestured to the copy of *A Traveler's Tale* that she held in her hands. 'May I…?'

His grandmother placed a black ribbon between the pages and handed the book to him. 'It is a lovely inscription.'

He eyed his grandmother through his lashes and turned to the title page. He was speechless. Obviously Miss Vandenberg must have arranged this—but why?

When she had stormed out on him yesterday Julian had not known if he should go after her. No one had ever walked out on him before. What had possessed her to have her father inscribe a book for his grandmother?

'I did not do this,' he admitted, handing back the book.

'Of course you did. I have told no one else I misplaced my copy.'

'I believe Mr Vandenberg's daughter arranged this.'

'His daughter? How would she know?'

'I mentioned it to her yesterday, when we spoke at Hatchards.'

'How very delightful of her. You have never said that you are acquainted with the family.'

'I am only acquainted with the daughter.'

His grandmother arched her brow. That was not a good sign. 'Just the daughter? How unusual for you. How did you make her acquaintance?'

'A mutual friend,' replied Julian, picking a speck of lint off the sleeve of his navy tailcoat.

'I see. And is the lady in question married?'

'She is not.'

'And how long have the two of you been acquainted?'

'Not long.'

Her eyes narrowed, causing Julian to shift restlessly in his seat.

'Tell me about this girl.'

'She is not a girl.'

'How old is she?'

'I do not know. I thought it wasn't polite to enquire.'

His grandmother chuckled. 'When the lady in question is my age, it absolutely is not. But for a younger one I do not think it at all beyond the pale.'

'And a lady of your age would be how old, exactly?'

'You impertinent man—we are discussing your friend, not me.'

'And why exactly are we discussing Miss Vandenberg?'

'She had her father send me this lovely book. I am curious as to what kind of girl would do such a thoughtful thing. You say she did this completely without your influence?'

'I doubt the lady could be influenced into doing anything at my bidding,' he muttered.

'Nonsense—you are Lyonsdale.'

'At the moment that fact does not seem to be to my advantage with her.'

'Why not?'

'Miss Vandenberg is a little cross with me at the moment, due to my title.' He knew it was absurd, and saying it out loud made it appear more so.

'I do not understand. Does she not realise the significance of your station?'

'She does. However, I do not believe she cares.'

'Because she is an American?'

'Because she is Miss Vandenberg. In truth, I find at

times that she baffles me with her logic.' And his reaction to her mere presence baffled him more.

His grandmother tilted her head and he realised he'd said too much. Miss Vandenberg wasn't a woman he was courting, or even a woman he should be thinking of courting. And yet he'd told his grandmother more about her than he had about any other woman.

Knowing that she was annoyingly perceptive, he knew he needed to place distance between them before she started asking a litany of questions. He pushed himself off the chair and walked to the window overlooking Grosvenor Square.

'Would you take me to Almack's tonight?' she called to him.

Dear God, he should have just left the room. The last place he ever wanted to go was Almack's. He might as well place a notice in the *Morning Chronicle*, stating that he was shopping for a wife.

'Why in the world would you want me to do that?' he asked, trying to think of an excuse as to why he could not take her. 'You've been going there for years without me.'

'Yes, and it is about time you used those vouchers of yours. Each year you pay for them, and each year you never use them.'

He wasn't giving in. Her reasoning wasn't good enough.

She rubbed her knees and sighed. 'If I don't move these bones they may stiffen permanently.'

Crossing his arms, he arched a sceptical brow. If the woman hadn't been born into the aristocracy, she might have made a fine living on the stage.

'I do not have many years left,' she continued. 'Is it so wrong for me to wish to spend time with my grandson? I rarely see you any more, with all the time you are spending with Lord Kenyon's committee and other Parliamentary affairs.'

She blinked a few times, and Julian wasn't certain if he saw tears in her eyes.

Should he remind her that they saw each other most mornings over the breakfast table? He searched the frescoed ceiling for an answer, but the cherubs just laughed down at him. He allowed her to live with him in London during the Season because he cared about her, and knew they probably didn't have many more years left together. Perhaps it was time he hired her a companion and rented her a townhouse.

Letting out a deep breath, Julian knew he was going to regret agreeing to go with her. And yet he was unable to say no.

Chapter Eight

As Julian stepped into the cavernous assembly room at Almack's the large mirrors magnified the many women and men who turned to look. Heads poked around the gilt columns to his right, and some people even had the impudence to raise their quizzers at him. This was why he avoided mixing with the likes of the marriage mart. Their unabashed interest in him was tiresome.

He walked further into the room, with his grandmother on his arm and his mother at his other side. They left a buzz of voices in their wake.

'This is a testament to how much I care for you,' he whispered down to his grandmother. 'Do not expect me to escort you here again.'

She blinked up at him innocently and readjusted her hand on his arm. 'Evenings such as these have a way of turning unexpectedly. You may change your mind.'

'There is nothing in Christendom that would make me enjoy myself tonight,' Julian replied through a polite smile, knowing the people around them were trying to listen to their conversation.

His mother nodded regally at the Duchess of Skeffington and Lady Harlow. Julian knew his mother was not fond of the gossipy pair. He wasn't either, and had no qualms about pretending he did not see them.

'You are shocking people tonight with your presence, Lyonsdale,' his mother said from behind her fan. 'They see a man in search of a wife. Perhaps you might consider announcing your intentions and quelling their interest?'

'Madam, tonight I have no intention of announcing anything.'

His mother pursed her lips together and looked away. Julian was surprised she hadn't broached the subject of Lady Mary sooner. He assumed she was here somewhere. Lady Morley would not be remiss in displaying her daughter to the eligible men of the *ton*. There was no sense in delaying the inevitable. Tonight he would speak with Lady Mary and discover if he would be able to endure sitting across the breakfast table from her each morning.

Taking a deep breath, he inhaled the mixed floral scents and the body odour that permeated the room. There would be no escaping to the terrace for some cleaner air tonight. He scanned the room for Lady Mary and stifled a yawn. With all these masses of white spinning about the floor he would never be able to identify her unless she was standing directly in front of him.

He leaned over to his grandmother. 'Please tell me they have begun serving something more fortifying here than that insipid lemonade.'

'I wish I could—but that is what flasks are for, my boy,' she whispered, patting her reticule.

From the corner of his eye he spied Lady Morley, heading their way. Before he was able to summon an excuse to avoid having to speak with the woman his grandmother came to his rescue.

'Oh, look—I believe I see Lady Cowper,' she said. 'Will you excuse us, Beatrice?' Without waiting for a reply she tugged on Julian's arm and they began walking towards one of the patronesses who ruled Almack's.

'Now you see why I avoid these evenings,' Julian said, studying the crowd in front of them and trying to determine the least dangerous route to Lady Cowper. 'They can be most trying.'

'Chin up, my boy, I believe this night is about to become quite interesting.'

He glanced down at his grandmother. Why did he have the feeling she was privy to something he was not?

They approached the affable Lady Cowper, and the ladies exchanged pleasantries. Then she turned her full attention to Julian. 'What a pleasure to see you, Your Grace. It has been some time since you've been in attendance.'

'Yes, I suppose it has.'

'It appears we have caused quite a stir this evening,' his grandmother commented, glancing around.

'Yes, in fact I believe your arrival has surpassed tonight's latest sensation.'

His grandmother stepped closer and lowered her voice. 'Really, Lady Cowper? Do tell.'

'That American author Vandenberg is here, with his daughter. I understand the man is entertaining, and his daughter is quite accomplished.'

Julian's heart skipped a beat, and he fought the urge to scan the assembly room for her.

His grandmother's eyes widened a little too much. 'Really? They are here tonight? I would enjoy making the man's acquaintance. *A Traveler's Tale* is a most enjoyable read.'

'I am certain Madame de Lieven can introduce you. She has sponsored the family.' She leaned in close and lowered her voice. 'We were astonished when she promoted the Americans. However, I find they comport themselves surprisingly well.'

'Americans are not the provincials some imagine them to be,' Julian stated firmly, feeling an inexplicable need to come to their defence.

Both women stared at him in surprise, before Lady Cowper narrowed her gaze. 'Surely you're aware that we have seen very few American women in our circles? It was difficult to determine how they would behave.'

His grandmother began to cough, and Julian would not have been surprised if she had dramatically thrown herself on the floor to enhance the effect.

'My word, do you require assistance?' Lady Cowper asked with true concern.

His grandmother shook her head and the coughing miraculously stopped. 'A glass of lemonade should help ease the tickle in my throat,' she said, patting her chest. She grasped Julian's sleeve and gave it a subtle tug, leaving him no choice but to walk with her to the refreshment table.

He handed her a glass and held back a laugh when she poured in some clear liquid from a small silver flask. He wasn't certain what she had added, but as long as it was potent he didn't really care. Selecting a glass, he held it out to her, and she added a generous splash. The smell of gin reached Julian's nose as he raised the glass to his lips. If his father had been alive now the man would have had an apoplexy, knowing the matriarch of their family carried gin on her person. However, if it would help Julian survive an evening in the marriage mart he would not admonish her.

'Do you see her?' his grandmother asked as her gaze trailed over the room.

He had known she was up to something! He took a long drink. 'To whom are you referring?'

'Oh, I think you know.'

'What exactly are you plotting?'

'Why do you believe I am plotting anything?' she asked, arching an inquisitive brow.

'I am not dim-witted,' replied Julian, and he arched his brow in return.

'No, you are not.'

'That was not an answer.'

'What was the question?'

He momentarily closed his eyes. When he looked back at her the glass in her hand was empty. 'I'm trying to decide if it is wise to give you more lemonade.'

She reached behind him and took another glass. 'You do not need to attend to me all evening. You should look around. You might find someone of interest.'

Julian eyed his grandmother in annoyance. Why did the women in his life seem to have this need to meddle in his affairs? He stood near her, refusing to give any indication that he was in search of a wife. However, this time when his gaze travelled across the room he easily spotted Miss Vandenberg amid the whirl of white. He was transfixed as he watched her attempt to move gracefully through a quadrille with that idiot Lord Boreham.

'Are you going to dance with her?' the pest at his side whispered.

He glanced down at her. 'I have no desire to dance this evening.'

'Forgive me. I thought you had found something that held your attention. I must have been mistaken.'

'You most certainly were,' he replied, his eyes inexplicably drawn back to the dancing couple.

She lowered her voice even further. 'If that is Miss Vandenberg, Madame de Lieven will know if she has been given permission to waltz.'

Julian stared at his grandmother, aghast. 'I have never waltzed here, and I do not intend to do so now.'

However, if they did waltz together he would have her

undivided attention. She would not be able to leave the conversation when it was convenient for her, as she had each time they'd spoken in the past.

A smile tugged at his lips as he watched her walk off the dance floor.

When the quadrille ended Katrina returned to Mrs Forrester and Sarah, who were standing near one of the white gilded columns. She was grateful for the reprieve.

'You appear to have both feet intact,' Sarah teased. 'Perhaps Lord Boreham has taken dancing lessons.'

Fanning herself to cool her heated body, Katrina smirked. 'No, I have simply become adept at hiding my pain.'

'Did you hear about the caricature that was printed of him recently?' Sarah asked, staring questioningly into her glass of lemonade.

Most of these satires mocked political figures and the Prince Regent. Katrina knew there were others that were drawn of certain members of the *ton*, but since she was fairly new to London, and not well acquainted with too many people, she never paid much attention to them. However, now she was intrigued. 'What does it look like?'

Sarah glanced over at Lord Boreham, who was standing a few feet away with a group of young bucks. 'In it he is sprawled on the ground at the entrance to the Palace of Westminster. I do not recall the caption, but the image was memorable. A number of the dandies standing with him now were having a good laugh over it last evening.'

Although she was not fond of the marquess, Katrina felt sorry for him. It must be mortifying to have someone you didn't know make a mockery of your life.

'Katrina, if you persist in moving your fan so rapidly I fear the lady behind you will discover her peacock-feathered cap flying away!' advised Mrs Forrester.

Katrina slowed her hand. 'Pardon me, but it is so warm in here. I'm looking forward to stepping through the next dance just to create a breeze.'

'A waltz would do nicely,' Sarah said.

Katrina leaned in closer. 'I cannot believe we need permission to waltz here. I have been waltzing all over Europe, and now someone of no relation to me must give their consent.'

'Well, I find it unusual that men cannot wear trousers here,' Sarah said, scanning the stocking-clad calves of the men around them. 'What an odd rule.'

'Perhaps the patronesses are using their influence as an excuse to admire finely formed legs,' replied Katrina. 'What I don't—'

'Madame de Lieven, how wonderful to see you,' said Mrs Forrester, a bit too enthusiastically.

Katrina raised her fan to hide her laugh and turned. Her eyes widened when she saw the Russian Ambassador's wife on the arm of the Duke of Lyonsdale.

'It is lovely to see you, ladies,' Madame de Lieven said, inclining her head. She introduced Mrs Forrester and Sarah to the Duke, and then turned to Katrina. 'I understand you are already acquainted with His Grace?'

Katrina could feel the weight of his attention as she lowered herself into a curtsy. 'I am,' she muttered.

'Ladies,' he said, in that deep voice that reverberated through her body. 'I hope you are enjoying yourselves this evening.'

Mrs Forrester replied rather quickly—perhaps because she was wary of what Katrina or Sarah might say. 'Thank you, we are. I believe Almack's is an experience one must have in order to fully appreciate it.'

That was vague enough. Katrina bit her lip to keep from laughing.

'And what do you appreciate the most?' he asked them, with a knowing look in his eye.

'We've been discussing the fine dancing,' replied Mrs Forrester.

'And the fashionable attendees,' said Sarah as she glanced down at the Duke's muscular calves, encased in white stockings.

When Katrina coughed to cover her laugh, he narrowed his eyes at her. 'And, Miss Vandenberg, what have you come to appreciate this evening?'

Don't say finely formed legs!

Katrina knew he suspected their discussion had not been innocuous. Could she ignore a duke in the middle of Almack's and not lose her voucher? Probably not. She lowered her hand and stared directly into his green eyes.

He arched his brow.

She glared momentarily.

His lips twitched.

'I have been enjoying honest discussions with my friends.' She saw in his eyes that he understood what she implied.

Madame de Lieven cleared her throat and they both turned her way. 'Miss Vandenberg, His Grace has requested a waltz with you, and I have happily granted his request.'

Katrina stared at her and prayed she had remembered to close her mouth. 'How kind of you,' she managed to utter. Who was *she* to speak for Katrina? And that insufferable man knew she could not turn him down now.

'I believe the waltz is next,' Madame de Lieven noted, appearing pleased with herself.

Lyonsdale held out his arm and sent Katrina a challenging look. 'Then it is wise for us to proceed to the dance floor,' he said.

She glared at him while politely resting her hand on

his sleeve. They excused themselves and strolled through the crowd of people who parted for them. Watchful eyes followed their every step.

'I assure you I do not bite,' he whispered into her hair.

She chewed her lip to stop herself from telling him to go to the devil. Stepping on to the dance floor, he spun her around elegantly and placed his gloved hand on her back. Heat ran from his hand through her entire body. It was becoming difficult to breathe normally. A momentary sense of panic made her wonder how quickly the waltz would end. Maybe she could fake an illness in the middle of it?

He pulled her closer. She pushed her body further away.

'I have the distinct impression that you would rather be elsewhere,' he said. 'May I ask why?'

'No, you may not. I am still angry with you, lest you had not noticed.'

'I thought you might be. Does your anger preclude us from speaking?'

'It does. Angry people should not converse. It leads to further ill will.'

'Is that an American rule of conduct? What is the case when only one of the party is angry?'

'Then that person should remain silent. Usually the harshest statements are made in anger.'

He leaned his head closer. 'And you are angry with me because you feel I have deliberately deceived you?'

'Yes.' She would not give him the satisfaction of knowing she was also angry because he had previously ignored her.

'You say angry people should not converse, and yet here you are speaking to me. I really am becoming puzzled with your logic.' He inhaled slowly.

Katrina jerked her head away from his.

He had the nerve to grin at her. 'I am simply stating the inconsistency of our situation.'

'Do not patronise me,' she chided. 'And stop sniffing my hair. It is disconcerting.'

'For you or for me?'

'For me,' she replied in a low, forceful voice. 'If sniffing my hair leaves you disconcerted that is another reason you should stop doing it.'

'But there lies the rub. You see, where you are concerned I cannot help myself. I have become quite fond of lemons, by the way.'

'They can be sour and leave a bitter taste in your mouth.'

His gaze dropped to her lips. 'Yes, that is true. But they can also be refreshing, as well as tart.'

'Perhaps you would do better to seek out something bland, like lavender or orange blossom. I've noticed a great many women in London favour those scents. I am certain if you try you can find an alternative place for your nose,' she suggested with false sweetness.

His lips twitched. 'Oh, I can think of a few places my nose would care to be.'

The insufferable man! She was not as naïve as he might think.

'I am not speaking with you.' She raised her chin, annoyed that he had taken the upper hand in their discussion.

'So you said. You dance very well, by the way.'

'Do you always ignore other people's wishes?'

'Usually. They never seem to mind.' He gave a small shrug as he guided her gracefully into a turn. 'In any event, I was not ignoring your wishes. You stated quite clearly that you were not speaking with me. I, on the other hand, have never said I am not speaking with you. In fact I believe you are the one ignoring your own wishes. *You* are continuing to speak with *me*.'

She shifted her attention to the dancers behind him and let out an exasperated breath.

He leaned down slightly. 'That still might constitute speaking. It is a confirmation of your annoyance with me.'

Sliding her gaze back to him, she wondered how many more minutes she would have to be in his company. He sent her an amused look. Could she kick him during the dance without anyone seeing?

'Now, Miss Vandenberg, you do not want the entire assembly to know that you are cross with me. It might reflect poorly on you. I suggest you pretend to enjoy being in my arms.'

That was the problem. Being in his arms was distracting, and it was making her feel all…fluttery. She forced herself to appear bored.

He appeared smug.

Blast it all!

'Do you think every unmarried woman in this room wants you?'

'Well, since I am one of only two eligible dukes in England who are able to eat with their own teeth, yes, I believe that to be true.'

'I suppose that would matter were I English, but, you see, to me your title has little appeal. In fact, to me, your title is inconsequential.'

'How so?' he asked, tilting his head to the side.

'The other ladies in this room are shopping for a title and prestige, but I am not. I intend to return to America when my father is finished with his business here and I have no intention to marry you or any other Englishman. So, you see, your title holds no interest for me.'

Julian almost stumbled on the wooden floor. He didn't know how to respond. *His title was impressive!* There wasn't an available woman in the room who didn't want to be married to him. Except, it seemed, the woman in his arms.

Over the years there had been times when he'd wished he could find someone who would see him for the man he was and not his title. Now that he had his wish, he wasn't certain he liked the result.

Annoyed with the turn in their conversation, he knew he needed to regain the upper hand. He leaned forward and took a deep breath. Miss Vandenberg shot him a frustrated glare.

It was much too easy to get a reaction from her, and Julian wasn't ready to think about why that pleased him. Any reservations he'd had about asking her to waltz had gone the minute he held her in his arms and she began to speak. He wondered if she smelled like lemons everywhere...

'Please stop,' she whispered.

'The dance? I think people would notice, don't you?'

'Sniffing me.'

'Oh, that. If it truly bothers you I will find it within me to stop.'

'I would appreciate the effort.'

There was a brief silence. 'I do need to thank you, though.'

'For rinsing my hair with lemon juice? I assure you it has nothing to do with you.'

'No, not that. I want to thank you for sending my grandmother your father's book. It was quite kind of you.'

'It was no bother.'

'All the same, you made an old woman very happy.'

'Then, for her, I am pleased I arranged it.'

He thought he saw the faintest hint of a smile. 'Tell me how you knew it was the Dowager Duchess of Lyonsdale I was referring to in our conversation. It might have been my maternal grandmother.'

'Do you realise how commanding you are? Phrasing

requests as questions is much more polite.' She lifted her brows expectantly.

He, the Duke of Lyonsdale, had just been schooled in manners again by this American. It was absurd.

'It's a habit born of my title. In any event, I will heed your well-meaning lesson and try again. Would you please explain your exceptional deductive skills to me?'

This time a smile definitely tugged at her lips, and Julian found his question well worth the effort.

'I enquired about you and discovered the Dowager lived in your home. I assumed she was the lady in question and had the book sent there.'

'And how did you explain the request to your father?'

'I've been handling my father's correspondence while we have been abroad. I told him we had encountered each other at Hatchards, and that you told me your grandmother's tale of woe.'

'He did not question our introduction?'

She leaned closer to him. He could feel her breath on his ear, and he wanted to close his eyes to savour the sensation.

'I have a secret, Your Grace. In America, formal introductions are not an absolute necessity. Americans frequently meet each other in similar fashion.'

Leaning back, she met his gaze with a good-humoured twinkle in her eyes. Her voice had been low and husky. The heat from her breath had travelled through every part of him.

He lowered his lips towards her ear, wanting to prolong this playful turn in their conversation. 'What else do Americans do?'

The music of the waltz ended, and Julian was forced to let her go.

'I suppose you will have to continue to wonder,' she replied with an impish grin.

He held in a smile, wishing he could spend the remainder of the evening in her company.

Chapter Nine

Many a quizzing glass was raised as Katrina and the Duke walked through the parting attendants. Katrina could hear the whispers following them. Their sparring had been much too entertaining. She needed to remind herself that he was an arrogant man who had avoided her until their accidental encounter at Hatchards. Now, instead of leaving her when the dance was over, he was escorting her off the floor. Spending more time in his company would not be wise.

She began to slide her hand from his arm. 'I see my father is waiting for me. Thank you.'

The Duke held her hand in place, keeping her at his side. 'Would you be so kind as to introduce me?'

Would he act like an arrogant aristocrat towards her father? She slowed her steps before leading him to where her father was standing, not far from the dance floor. After introducing them, she waited for Lyonsdale's next move.

He gave a polite nod of his head to her father. 'I'd like to thank you for sending your book to my grandmother. Your kind gesture made her quite happy.'

'It was my pleasure. I am always delighted to hear someone has enjoyed my efforts.'

'I hear all of London is enjoying your efforts. I understand you are here in preparation for the Anglo-American Conference? I imagine your days are filled with information-gathering. Hopefully you will also have opportunities to explore more of London. I fear evenings such as this do not show us in our best light.'

The inconsistency in his behaviour was baffling, and it was difficult to form a clear picture of his character.

'And what would you recommend to the worldly traveller?' she asked.

He turned his head towards her. 'Vauxhall Gardens and Drury Lane for entertainment, Tattersalls for quality horses, Hyde Park for beauty and fresh air, and Gunter's for ice.'

He really did have lovely hair. It appeared thick and had some wave to it. And she realised she had memorised every detail of his chiselled features and square jaw.

Her father cleared his throat, drawing Lyonsdale's attention away from her. 'I believe you could easily write a guide to London and earn a few pounds, Your Grace.'

'I fear spending most of my life here has given me a skewed perspective on what others would find entertaining. Perhaps I presume too much?'

'I do not think you presume too much at all,' her father continued. 'Your very thorough list has intrigued me.'

Katrina tilted her head, taking in Lyonsdale's comfortable yet elegant stance. 'What would you recommend above all else? If you had only one day in Town, where would you go?'

There was a substantial pause, as if he was trying to recall what he found enjoyable. 'I would go to the British Museum and see the Elgin Marbles.'

She tried to recall ever hearing the name. 'I'm not familiar with them.'

'They are a collection of artefacts from Ancient Greece. You should try to see them before you leave.'

She found it a surprising answer, coming from a man so consumed by his work. 'And that is what you enjoy in London above all else?'

His lips rose into a hint of a smile. 'At the moment they are my preferred attraction.'

Her father cleared his throat again. 'I believe I was correct in my initial assessment, Your Grace. You could compose an admirable travel guide.'

Lyonsdale shifted his intense focus from her. 'Thank you, sir. I will keep that in mind in the event that I find I am a bit light in the pockets. However, I doubt it would be as entertaining as I hear your book is.' He smiled pleasantly. 'Please excuse me. I shall take my leave. It has been a pleasure.' He tipped his head to both of them and turned away.

She sensed her father's weighted stare.

'Let us find you some lemonade,' he suggested when Lyonsdale was far enough away. As they began walking towards the refreshment table he lowered his voice. 'This will not end well, my girl.'

'There is no story here, Papa. Do not look to write one.'

'That dance said differently. The man is a duke.'

'I am well aware of that.'

'Then you know you can have no future with him. He is destined to choose one of his own to marry.'

'His choice of a bride does not concern me. You know I do not wish to find a husband here. I will not be attached to a man who will commit himself to me in the eyes of God, only to cast me aside when it's convenient for him to do so. I know all about how Jerome Bonaparte deserted his wife because she was American. I have no desire to have that done to me.'

'Those might be your feelings at the moment, but feelings can alter when attraction comes into play. I have seen it happen before.'

'There is no attraction here. There is no game to be had.'

'You fool yourself if you think so. This room witnessed quite a display of mutual attraction this evening. I would not be surprised if you find yourself in the papers tomorrow. I am only saying this to caution you. Guard your heart, my dear.'

'It was a waltz. Two people have to grant each other their undivided attention. What you witnessed was a dance.'

'What the entire room witnessed were two people so absorbed with one another they did not notice when the music ended,' he said, handing her a glass of lemonade.

'Of course we did. We stopped dancing.'

She could not deny that she was attracted to Lyonsdale, but it wasn't as if he was irresistible. Ignoring the pull, she refused to scan the crowd to see who was receiving his attention now.

As Julian reached his grandmother's side he followed her gaze to the couples who were assembling on the dance floor.

'You were waltzing,' she commented, sipping her lemonade.

He lowered his head to keep their conversation private. 'We are not discussing this.'

'I am simply making an observation.'

'Well, please do not.'

'She is rather a pretty thing.'

'I said we are not talking about this.'

'Talking about what?' his mother interjected as she joined them.

'We were discussing the headache Julian has suddenly

acquired,' replied his grandmother as she smiled into the rim of her glass.

Julian straightened and pressed his lips together to keep from laughing.

'But you never get headaches. How long have you had this one?' his mother asked anxiously.

'Only a short while, I assure you,' he replied, locking his fingers behind his back.

'Is it severe?'

'Not at the moment, but that could change.'

'Do you require a physician?' she asked in a panicked voice, studying his face.

'A physician is not necessary.'

'Very well. I know I need not remind you that you must dance with someone else this evening. We cannot have people believing you have designs on your one partner.'

Julian knew his mother was right. He had only danced once this evening, and he was certain people were speculating about his attendance. If he singled out Miss Vandenberg as his only partner, people would assume he was courting her.

Studying the room, he finally spotted Lady Mary, moving elegantly through a quadrille. He would ask her to dance. It was time he put some effort into conversing with her.

Moving his gaze from Lady Mary, Julian momentarily caught the eye of the amusing Miss Vandenberg...

An hour later he collected Lady Mary for their dance. When he took her hand in his there was no consuming need to pull her into his arms. Was this what bedding her would feel like? Putting on his usual bored expression, he began to dance. He studied her small features, her round youthful face and thick auburn hair. Nothing inside him stirred.

'Is there something wrong, Your Grace?'

'No. Why do you ask?'

'You appear perplexed.'

'Not at all,' he replied, blinking away his thoughts.

They danced in silence for quite some time, and Julian tried to think of something they could discuss.

'Your family—are they well?'

'Yes, thank you. And yours?'

'Very well.'

The minutes ticked by.

He tried again, 'I expect your ride here was pleasant?'

'Yes. The roads were very smooth. We encountered very few delays.'

'Excellent.' Julian clenched his jaw.

Again, there was silence.

'Have you been enjoying your time here this evening?' Lady Mary finally attempted to keep the conversation moving.

'Yes, thank you. And you?'

'Yes, very much. I always enjoy a ball or an assembly. It is agreeable, seeing so many friends in one place.'

How was it possible that she could speak of enjoyment without really smiling? And why did her eyes appear so lifeless?

'What other things do you find enjoyable?'

'Well, I enjoy needlework, playing the pianoforte, helping my mother entertain, and riding through Hyde Park.'

Not once did he see a spark of excitement in her. 'But what is it that makes you truly happy?'

She looked confused. 'Forgive me. I do not understand.'

'If there was one thing you could do for enjoyment, what would it be?'

'It would be difficult to pick only one thing. What would *you* choose?'

Chapter Ten

The next morning Katrina was still not fully awake as she sat in the dining room, having breakfast with her father. She took a bite of her toast, and her eyes alighted upon a few sentences in the *Morning Chronicle*.

The crunchy bread got stuck in her throat and she began to cough.

There was an account of an '*eligible Duke*' dancing with a '*foreign lady*' at Almack's. Speculation was that the '*eligible Duke*' was looking for a bride, and the '*foreign lady*' was attempting to gain a title.

Her father handed her his napkin. 'I was wondering when you would see it. All the newspapers have something to say about your dance. Apparently London has been eagerly awaiting any indication that Lyonsdale is interested in marriage, and if an eligible man attends Almack's it's assumed he is in search of a bride. One newspaper speculates that there might be a romance forming between you.'

'But he was there to escort his mother and his grandmother.'

'I doubt he would tell you if he was looking for a bride.'

Katrina pushed the paper away, feeling unsettled by the

Julian fought the urge to close his eyes in exasperation. 'I do not know. I wanted to know what you would choose.'

Lady Mary gave a false smile. 'Well, we have that in common. I am not certain what I would choose either.'

attention. 'Then why dance with me? Obviously I cannot be under consideration.'

'That didn't stop the rumours that you are searching for a title.'

'I've danced with a number of titled gentlemen while we've been here. He is not the first one.'

'Yes, but you have not danced with an unattached man of his rank. A duke who never dances the waltz and suddenly does so with you will cause people to speculate.' He narrowed his eyes at her. 'Why do you think he asked you?'

That very question had kept her up most of the night, and she still had no answer. She would eventually return to New York, and he would remain in England—probably married to some dull daughter of another duke. Glancing at her toast, Katrina dropped it onto her plate. Her appetite was gone.

The moment Julian entered his breakfast room he knew something was amiss. Apart from the servants his mother was there alone, and there was already a glass of what he assumed was sherry in her hand. Just as he was about to take his first sip of coffee she slid the newspapers closer to him.

'Have you read them yet?' she asked.

'No. Why?'

'Because you are in all of them. You and that *American*.'

The servants didn't need to witness this discussion. He signalled for them to leave and searched for the gossip column in the paper closest to him.

'What do they say?'

'That you danced with her.'

It was too early to deal with his mother's irrational ranting. He pushed the paper aside and took a sip of his coffee. 'It was only a dance.'

'They are saying you are looking for a bride.'

'That should make you happy.'

'Having every Mayfair mother attempt to shove their daughter your way—hardly. They say she is looking for a title.'

'Miss Vandenberg? They obviously have never spoken to the lady.'

'Careful, Lyonsdale. She may seek to trap you.'

'Miss Vandenberg is the last woman in all of London who would trap me.'

'Then you have no designs on her?'

'Of course not. As I said, it was just a dance.'

And it was. Wasn't it?

Later that morning Katrina was composing a letter to her cousin John when she heard a carriage roll to a stop outside her home. Peering through the linen curtains of the drawing room, she tried to see who it was.

As she shifted her body and tilted her head further Wilkins knocked on the open door to inform her that she had a caller. He seemed to be standing a little taller. When she picked up the card from the silver salver she blinked twice at the Dowager Duchess of Lyonsdale's name.

It could not be a coincidence that she was calling on Katrina the very day the papers had printed gossip about Katrina and the woman's grandson. If only she had time for a glass of Madeira.

When the slight old woman slowly entered the room, Katrina dropped into a curtsy and felt the weight of the Dowager's studied gaze.

Drawing on her diplomatic experience, Katrina smiled politely. 'Your Grace, I am honoured by your call.'

The Dowager's eyes were sharp and assessing. With a slight lift of her chin, she held herself with a commanding air. 'Good day, Miss Vandenberg. I wanted to call on you to thank you for your generous gift.'

At least she hadn't demanded Katrina leave the country.

'Would you care for some tea?' Katrina offered, gesturing towards the settee and chairs near the fireplace.

'Tea would be lovely.' The Dowager perched her small, erect frame on the settee. 'Shall we wait for your mother?'

Katrina sat in one of the bergère chairs and nodded to Wilkins for tea. 'My mother passed away many years ago.'

The Dowager's eyes narrowed. 'My mother died when I was an infant. I have no memory of her.'

'Nor I. Mine died two days after I was born.'

A look of understanding passed between them.

The Dowager cleared her throat. 'I assume your father has hired a companion for you, while you are in London?'

Katrina shook her head. Her Great-Aunt Augusta, who had been more a mother to her than anyone, had passed away ten months before. She would have accompanied them to London. Having someone else living with them in her place would have been too painful a reminder of her loss.

'He offered, but I declined.'

'That sounds rather lonely. Surely you have someone to chaperon you when you are attending your social engagements?'

'I do not mind solitude. And the wife of the American Minister has been kind enough to chaperon me on most occasions. Other times I have my maid, who has been with me for many years.'

'I assume having other Americans around you has eased your adjustment somewhat?'

'It has.' Katrina could tell she was being measured by the Duke of Lyonsdale's grandmother. She just wasn't sure why.

'I find it surprising that your father will be involved in negotiating a treaty between our two countries. I doubt anyone here would ask Byron or Scott to do such a thing.'

'My father is a barrister as well as an author. He has presented cases to our Supreme Court and performed services for President Monroe.'

'I see.' The Dowager was silent as she openly took in her surroundings. 'Will your father remain with the American delegation in London after the negotiations are complete?'

'As yet he has not been asked to do so.'

How long did it take to make tea?

The Dowager nodded thoughtfully and clasped her hands on her lap. 'You must convey my appreciation to your father for the book he sent me.'

'I will let him know when he returns home today. Are you a great reader?'

The Dowager inclined her head. 'In my youth I read often. I fear that with age my eyes are not what they once were. Most days I have my maid read to me. It is easier on my eyes.'

Finally Wilkins entered with the tea tray. 'Will there be anything else, miss?'

Katrina had taken note of the Dowager's slight frame. 'Yes, Wilkins, I believe a nice log on the fire will do, on such a dreary day.'

The Dowager's body appeared to relax slightly as the cosy fire warmed the room.

'How would you care to have your tea?'

'With some milk and four lumps of sugar, please.'

Before she caught herself, Katrina's brows rose in surprise. Her Great-Aunt Augusta had enjoyed her tea very sweet, as well. Preparing the cup brought back fond memories of the times when she'd used to sit with the woman who had raised her. She had been her mother's aunt, and of a similar age to the Dowager. There was something in the Dowager's eyes that reminded her of her aunt.

'An extra sweet or two never hurt anyone,' the Dowager explained, with the faintest hint of a smile.

Katrina grinned and inclined her head. 'My Great-Aunt Augusta would certainly have agreed.'

'Then your great-aunt had exceptional taste,' she said with a sparkle in her eye. She accepted the Wedgwood cup from Katrina. 'I understand you are acquainted with my grandson?'

Knowing this was the true intention behind the unexpected visit, Katrina focused her attention on pouring herself tea. 'I am.'

'I assume you have seen the papers today?'

Katrina placed her cup on the table in case the Dowager's words left her with shaking hands. 'Yes, I have.'

'What are your feelings on the speculation, Miss Vandenberg?'

'His Grace showed a polite courtesy in asking me to dance. There is nothing more to it. The papers seek to sensationalise the mundane to sell copies. In truth, my only concern is how my actions reflect on my father and his work here.'

The Dowager's features softened and she took a sip of her tea. 'You'll have to acquire a thick skin to live among us. The papers have something to say about everyone. Do not let what they print concern you.'

'Thank you, but I believe my actions will not warrant comment in the future. I am not an outrageous creature to garner their attention.' And for that Katrina was grateful.

Her comment seemed to appease the Dowager, and the remainder of her visit was spent discussing their shared love of reading and Katrina's tour of the Waterloo Battlefield.

By the time the Dowager left, Katrina knew her to

be not only elegant in manner, but kind-hearted as well. She had extended an invitation to Katrina to call on her at Lyonsdale House, and even informed her that on Monday afternoons at two she was always at home to receive calls. She had also informed Katrina there was no need to bring a chaperon.

It would be rude not to return the call, and if Katrina was honest with herself she was curious to see Lyonsdale's home...

Chapter Eleven

Katrina stood at the front door of Lyonsdale House and studied the wavy grain of the polished wood. While this door was similar in size to the door of her own London home, this building was much larger. All she needed to do was lift the brass knocker. And yet she couldn't manage to raise her hand above her waist.

The Dowager had invited Katrina to call on her. She'd even specified a time that would be most convenient for her. And, while it wasn't exactly a normal calling hour, it did show she had been sincere in her invitation. Didn't it?

If Katrina didn't knock soon, the posy of violets in her hand would be reduced to a wilted mess. She glanced down and wondered if she should have brought them. Her Great-Aunt Augusta had always enjoyed it when Katrina had brought her flowers from the garden. It had seemed to brighten her spirits. But this woman was a dowager duchess. Maybe it simply wasn't done. She was about to toss the bouquet into a row of nearby boxwoods when the door suddenly opened.

Standing before her was a slim, grey-haired man that Katrina assumed was Lyonsdale's butler. He eyed her with a speculative gaze, before his focus dropped to the flowers in her hand. 'May I help you, miss?'

Katrina straightened her shoulders and gave him a polite smile. 'Yes, thank you. I was wondering if the Dowager Duchess of Lyonsdale is receiving.'

His gaze dropped once again to the flowers. 'Do you have a card?'

There was little question that she should have tossed the flowers. It was too late now. The man had made it a point to let her know he had seen them.

There was almost a look of recognition when he read her card. 'This way, miss,' he said, allowing her to step foot inside the hallowed hall of Lyonsdale's grand home. 'I will inform Her Grace that you are here.'

Katrina's footsteps echoed down the hall as she was shown into an ornately decorated drawing room. Gold cherubs flew along the gilded mouldings that ran along the high ceiling, and life-size portraits of past generations stared down at her from their lofty positions on the crimson silk walls. The room smelled of almond oil, no doubt from the freshly polished doors and furniture.

Not certain where to sit, Katrina decided on a bergère chair in the grouping of seats closest to the door. She stared at the portrait of an austere gentleman across from her, who wore a ruffled collar. From his perch on the wall, he didn't seem to like her flowers either.

She was beginning to believe the butler had forgotten about her when she was greeted by the warm smile of the Dowager.

'Miss Vandenberg, this is an unexpected surprise.' The Dowager took a seat opposite Katrina and her gaze dropped to the flowers. 'What do you have there?'

Katrina handed her the posy that had reminded her of home. 'These were growing in our garden. They were so lovely I thought I'd share them with you.'

The Dowager's eyes grew misty. 'My son would pick

violets for me when he was a small child. They bring to mind such cherished memories. Thank you.'

At least she hadn't committed another *faux pas*. 'You are most welcome. I'm glad they give you pleasure.'

Their conversation was interrupted when the butler entered the room, carrying a tea tray.

'I have grown accustomed to enjoying a cup of tea around this time,' the Dowager said. She handed the flowers to her butler. 'Reynolds, do see to these and bring them back here.'

The Dowager poured tea into two of three Sèvres porcelain cups, remembering that Katrina liked it with milk and only one lump of sugar.

Reynolds returned with the flowers in a small gilded vase, and the Dowager signalled to him to place it on the table closest to her.

'Have you had the opportunity to see more of London since we last spoke?' she asked, stirring her four lumps of sugar into her tea.

'I went with the Forresters to see the new exhibition at the Royal Academy yesterday. The paintings were lovely. I especially enjoyed one of fairies by a Mr Henry Howard.'

'Are you fond of art?'

'Yes, very much so.'

'Then I must introduce you to the Duchess of Winterbourne. Olivia is a lovely woman, and I believe the two of you might share some interests.'

There was something unidentifiable about the Dowager that continued to remind Katrina of her great-aunt. Both women had the ability to fill her with a sense of comfort.

She was about to respond when the sound of heavy footfalls drifted in from the entrance hall. Both she and the Dowager turned towards the doorway and found Lyonsdale standing on the threshold. He was dressed in a bottle-green tail coat, brown waistcoat, and buckskin breeches. And he appeared to be just as startled as Katrina to find themselves staring at one another.

'Do come in, my boy,' the Dowager said with a bright smile. 'I believe you're acquainted with Miss Vandenberg?'

There was a slight hesitation in his stride, and he narrowed his gaze at his grandmother. 'Of course. Good day, Miss Vandenberg,' he said, executing a perfect bow.

The sound of his voice left her with flutters low in her abdomen. 'Good day, Your Grace.'

The Dowager motioned to the chair next to Katrina. 'Would you care to join us? A nice cup of tea might be just the thing after your long committee meeting.'

Katrina found it difficult to determine if she wanted him to stay or if it would be better for him to leave them.

'I would not wish to interrupt your discussion.'

Horrid, fickle man!

'Nonsense. Miss Vandenberg and I were just beginning our visit. There is nothing to interrupt.'

He inclined his head and took the seat next to Katrina. Her heart turned over unexpectedly.

'You are back early today,' the Dowager continued.

'No, I return home at exactly this time each Monday when the committee is in session.'

So this was one of the ways a duke occupied himself during the day. 'Is this a Parliamentary committee?' Katrina asked.

He accepted the tea and shifted his gaze to her. 'It is.'

'What does your committee meet about?'

'We are investigating the effects of working conditions on child labourers.'

'You are?'

He lifted his chin, as if he was anticipating derision. 'I assure you it is a valid issue, and one that needs to be addressed.'

It wasn't necessary to point that out to her. She was simply surprised that a man of his substantial wealth had any interest in the children of the poor.

'I agree. It's commendable that your committee has taken up the cause for those who are frequently neglected.'

'We have just begun our interviews. Our aim is to ensure these children are neither exploited nor harmed.' His gaze drifted to the flowers. 'I see the violets are multiplying,' he commented to his grandmother. 'This is the first time you have seen fit to display them outside your rooms.'

The Dowager gave Katrina a warm smile. 'These are from Miss Vandenberg. She was kind enough to bring them to me.'

He did nothing to hide his surprise. 'You have brought my grandmother flowers?'

'I have. I found them beautiful and wished to share them with her,' she stated, annoyed with herself for feeling the need to explain her actions to him.

'I would have assumed you would favour orchids or some other rare, exotic bloom.'

'I am partial to simpler things. I do not need the world to confirm a pedigree for me to appreciate beauty.'

He studied her over his teacup, and she found the room was growing rather warm.

'They match your eyes.'

'I beg your pardon?'

'The violets— they are the same colour as your eyes.'

It was impossible to pull her gaze from his—that was until the Dowager gave a discreet cough.

'Miss Vandenberg, would you care to see our library?' she asked. 'With your fondness for books, I am certain you will find something of interest to borrow.' She turned to Lyonsdale. 'With your permission, of course.'

'That is a fine idea. Please, by all means, Miss Vandenberg. My library is at your disposal.' He sat back in his chair and took a sip of his tea.

Katrina now had an excuse to remove herself from his presence. Maybe it would relieve her of the restless feeling that hadn't gone away since the moment she'd laid eyes on him.

'That's very kind of you.'

'Capital,' the Dowager replied with a broad smile. 'I shall wait here while you escort her.'

'Me?' he spluttered, and appeared to be thinking up an excuse as to why he wasn't available.

'It is your library,' his grandmother explained. 'You know it far better than anyone else in this house. Besides, I've had a dull ache in my legs all day. I do not expect you will take long.'

If Katrina hadn't been paying such close attention to him she might have missed his hesitation before he turned back to her.

'Shall we, Miss Vandenberg?'

They entered the hallway in silence, walking side by side. After a few moments she turned to him. 'You do not need to remain with me while I make my selection. I am certain I will be able to find my way back to the drawing room.'

'Are you attempting to remove yourself from my company?'

'Not at all. I simply assume you have pressing matters that require your attention.'

'I find I can think of nothing at the moment that is more pressing than helping you obtain something for your enjoyment.'

This time when he spoke his voice was warm and friendly.

She had provided him with an excuse. If he chose not to take it, it was no longer her concern.

'Your grandmother called on me recently,' she said, as a way to explain her presence in his home.

'I assumed she must have.'

'She is a lovely woman.'

'That's debatable.'

'Come, now—she is quite affable.'

He shook his head. 'That is one word to describe her. I can think of others.'

'You are very fortunate to have her.'

Their arms inadvertently brushed against one another, and he placed some distance between them. After a few more steps he moved his hands behind his back as they continued down the long hall.

'If you had a grandmother like mine you might have a different opinion on the matter.'

'I did not know either of my grandmothers. They passed away before I was born.'

He lowered his head and looked at her with regret. 'Please forgive me. I should have thought before I spoke.'

He might not appreciate his grandmother, but she did. She gave him a reassuring smile. 'No apology is necessary.'

They strolled through an ornately carved archway and entered a long wood-panelled extension of the hall. To their right, tall windows with blue damask silk draperies brought muted light into the room. The opposite wall was covered with life-size portraits of men in various poses and attire.

Katrina paused and looked over the portraits of the men who were staring down at them. She advanced further and their superior gazes followed her.

'Who are they?'

He appeared to stand taller, if that was even possible. 'May I introduce you to the Dukes of Lyonsdale?'

Her eyes widened as she spun around. '*All* of them?'

He let out a soft laugh at her obvious amazement. 'We are missing one. However, every man in this room has held my title at one time. My ducal title is one of the oldest in England.'

In Katrina's dining room at their country home in Tarrytown her mother's portrait hung on the wall behind the chair where she had sat. Her father said it reminded him that she was still somehow with them. He also carried a miniature of her mother on his person. The only other portraits of her family were one of her father and one of his parents. Lyonsdale had many, many more.

Near the doorway they had walked through hung the portrait of a man with dark curly hair, wearing armour. His sword was raised in the air as he sat upon his steed. From his expression she gathered he would be happy to use that sword on her if she moved the wrong way. He was an intimidating sight.

Lyonsdale approached her. 'That is Edward Carlisle, the First Duke of Lyonsdale. He was awarded the title by King Henry the Seventh for service to the crown in battle.'

'Which battle?'

'The Battle of Bosworth.'

Well, that explained nothing. She continued to study the designs on the man's armour.

'The Battle of Bosworth took place during the War of the Roses.'

He might just as well have been speaking Italian.

'You *have* heard of the War of the Roses, haven't you?'

She shook her head while she looked up at the superior expression of the First Duke. 'Do you know when he was given the title?'

'Of course—in the year 1485, not long after Henry was crowned King.' He placed his hands behind his back and rocked on his heels.

Lyonsdale knew what his ancestor had been doing

in 1485. She knew little of her family's history past her grandparents. A bubble of laughter escaped her lips.

He appeared affronted. 'What have I said that you find so amusing?'

'All I know of my family is that my great-grandfather came to America from Holland and was proficient in building ships. That is how my father came to inherit our shipyard in New York.'

There was no telling if his shocked expression was at the lack of information she possessed or her ancestor's occupation.

'Surely you know more than that?'

'No. That is all I know,' she said with a shrug. 'My father may know more.' She knew nothing of her mother's family. It had never occurred to her to ask.

Lyonsdale appeared to be catatonic. He wasn't even blinking.

'Would you like to tell me about the others?'

It took him a minute to answer. 'What others?'

She gestured to the portraits with her hand. 'The other Dukes.'

He snapped out of his stupor and let out a deep breath. 'I believe you are simply being polite.'

'That's not true. Tell me more about your family.'

They walked from portrait to portrait and he recounted numerous accomplishments spanning hundreds of years. It was an impressive group of men. Had they all been in a room together it would have been difficult to choose one who stood out from the rest.

When they reached a gap between two of the portraits Katrina stopped. 'Where is this one?'

Lyonsdale cleared his throat and crossed his arms. 'The Fifth Duke was a disgrace. He was too concerned with his own pleasure and did not live up to the responsibility of his title. His portrait is not fit to hang with the others.'

Now, *this* sounded interesting. She stepped closer and lowered her voice to a conspiratorial whisper. 'What exactly did he do?'

He leaned his lips close to her ear and his warm breath fanned her neck. Her eyes fluttered at the sensation.

'I'll. Never. Tell.'

When he pulled his head back the cool air was a shock.

The proper thing to do would be to end this discussion, however much she wanted to know what the man had done.

'Was it something truly dreadful? I'll wager it was.'

He arched a regal brow, which gave him an expression closely resembling that of the Sixth Duke, who was looking down at them with disdain.

'Miss Vandenberg, it is not polite to poke into other people's affairs.'

She gestured to the empty wall. 'He is dead. He will never know.'

He spun on his heels and walked towards the far end of the room. 'I meant *my* affairs,' he called out over his shoulder.

She hurried to catch up with him. 'I was not talking about you. I was talking about the Fifth Duke. What was his name?'

'His history is my history. His actions reflect who I am. Hence it is my affair. His name is inconsequential.'

'That's a peculiar name.' She tried to hold back her smile but it didn't work.

He stopped abruptly and turned to her. Their eyes met and a smile tugged on his lips.

It felt like an odd little victory.

'I believe you were interested in my library?'

'I was... I am.'

What did one have to do to be removed from a portrait

gallery? Was he a gambler? A rake? Perhaps he enjoyed his brandy a bit too much?

'I can keep a secret.'

His dubious expression was the only response she was to receive.

Past his shoulder she spied Lyonsdale's own portrait. His face was fuller and younger.

'You appear astonished to find me here,' he said.

'Is it a requirement that none of you smile for your portraits?'

'The responsibility of this title is not a jovial matter. The portraits should imply that.'

She let her gaze drift to the men who were still watching them. 'I suppose... But none of you appear at all pleased with your illustrious accomplishments.'

'Would you have us laugh in our portraits?'

'No, but a hint of a smile would be refreshing. You are an impressive collection of English noblemen. However, I fear dinner would be a dour affair if you all were present.'

He looked insulted, which she found amusing. 'I believe, Miss Vandenberg, we were heading to the library.'

'Lead on, Your Grace. I will humbly follow.'

'You are a sauce-box. You are aware of that, are you not?'

It proved impossible to hold back her laugh.

She was about to respond when she froze at the sight of the library before her. The long oak-panelled room held more books than Katrina had ever seen in any home. All four walls were covered from floor to ceiling with rows of books, and at the far end two walls of bookshelves jutted into the middle of the room. She wished she might remain in this room for days.

'It may prove difficult to make your selection if you do not step inside,' he called out from inside the room, with a trace of laughter.

Warmth spread across her chest, up her neck and across her cheeks. Avoiding his gaze, she crossed the threshold and was met by the scent of old books and leather.

'This is lovely.' Her voice died away in the hushed stillness of the room.

'Thank you. You may explore it to your heart's content.'

'I'd caution against making such an offer. You may find me curled on the floor, surrounded by books in the early-morning hours.'

'One can only dream, Miss Vandenberg...one can only dream.'

Smiling at his teasing comment, she navigated around a grouping of well-used chairs and highly polished tables. As she walked along, scanning the shelves, she felt the heat of his presence behind her.

'Are you a great reader?' she asked. 'Or do you rarely frequent this room?'

'In my youth I would spend many agreeable hours here. That large chair by the fire was a particular favourite spot of mine. It is from there that I read about gods and adventures and pirates and kings. Unfortunately now my duties in Westminster keep me too busy to read for pleasure.'

That made her pause and turn to him. 'There is always time for a good book. Even if that time is before you close your eyes at night. A well-told story feeds the soul.'

'Spoken like the daughter of an author.'

He didn't have a true measure of her if that was what he thought.

'Spoken by a woman who knows the value of literature,' she replied, poking him in the chest. 'You should consider my words.'

'I consider all your words—much to my vexation.'

What man said that to a woman?

'You think I'm vexing?'

He crossed his arms and raised his chin. 'I think you provoke me to see the world differently.'

'Forgive me. I do not wish to inconvenience you,' she snapped, spinning around to prevent herself from saying more.

He took her arm and gently turned her to face him. 'Do you seek to purposely misread me? If so, you should be commended. You do a fine job.' He was wise enough to redirect their conversation. 'Now, tell me if you have any notion of which subject matter might interest you.'

The heat from his hand on her forearm warmed her entire body. She glanced about, needing to recall the purpose of their excursion. Intrigued by his ancestors, she was curious about the battle he had mentioned.

'Would you have any books on your country's history?'

'Are you certain I cannot interest you in a gothic novel?' A teasing glint sparkled in his green eyes. 'Perhaps one with a dungeon?'

She held back a smile and faked eagerness. 'Do you have any?'

'I honestly couldn't say,' he said dryly.

'Well, it matters not. I am interested in a historical read.'

He let go of her arm. 'Follow me. I will show you where to look.' He led her behind the last row of shelves. 'Is there anything about our history you have a particular interest in?'

It wasn't necessary for him to know that she wanted to learn more about his family. She was certain that would make him strut about for the remainder of their time together. He had mentioned a King Henry. She could start there.

'Since we have no monarchy in America, I'd like to read about yours.'

He slid the brass and oak library ladder towards her. 'You should look on the upper shelves.'

* * *

Julian picked up a book on Greek mythology and began skimming the contents while he waited for Miss Vandenberg to make her selection. He had read this book before, many years ago. From what he could recall he had enjoyed all the fantastical tales. Maybe he would read a few pages this evening, before he turned in for the night.

He should allow her to peruse his collection without hovering around her like some lovestruck youth. It would be the polite thing to do. But Julian had no desire to be polite.

'What do you know of King Henry the Eighth?'

She really did have a lovely voice. When he lifted his head, his reply caught in his throat as he found himself at eye level with the delicate curves of her breasts.

Her creamy skin was flushed with a warm glow as his gaze fixed on a small birthmark on the upper swell of her left breast. How he wished he could spend hours exploring that one small spot. How many birthmarks did she have? Did she have them in other enticing places?

The catch of Miss Vandenberg's breath broke his concentration. He quickly raised his gaze to meet her amused expression.

'Well?' she prompted.

That birthmark had caused the blood to rush from his head to his groin, and Julian had no recollection of their conversation. She rolled her eyes and lowered herself to the next step down. Her breasts were now out of his direct line of vision. He wasn't certain if he was relieved or disappointed.

'I asked what you know of King Henry the Eighth. There are a number of volumes of books on him here.'

Books. They had been discussing books. Would she think it odd if he banged his head against one of the shelves? Probably. He snapped the book on mythology closed.

'He ruled England during the sixteenth century and altered the course of our religious practices. You may find it interesting that he had six wives.'

Her shocked expression made him laugh. '*Six?* How could one man have six wives?'

'One died by natural means, he beheaded two, divorced two, and the last outlived him.'

'He beheaded his wives?'

'Two of them, yes.' He backed away from the ladder to give her room to step down. Curious as to the book she had chosen, he held the tome that was still in her hand and read the title. 'Excellent choice,' he informed her.

'Why would any man behead his wife?'

'It is said he found them…unfaithful.' This really was not a discussion one should have with a young, unmarried lady.

She stepped closer to him. 'So he killed them? I have heard of many instances of wives being unfaithful here. Are they still beheaded for it?'

'If that were the case there would be quite a few ladies missing.'

'I really cannot begin to comprehend you English.'

'And what puzzles you so?'

'Your ideas on marriage and what constitutes a good one.'

'And what constitutes a good marriage to an American?'

'Love, fidelity, friendship…respect.' She tilted her head to the side and a loose blonde curl caressed her long neck. 'Have you ever been in love?'

A duke did not fall in love. Duty came before personal interest. Everyone knew that. He shook his head.

She nodded, as if she understood. Since she was an

American, she would never have to concern herself with duty. This woman would be able to marry for love.

As an unmarried gentleman, he knew he should tread lightly in conversations of marriage. Yet she had been the one to broach the subject first. It would be poor form to end a discussion she was clearly interested in.

'Have you ever been in love?' he asked.

A wistful look crossed her beautiful face. 'I have not fallen in love yet, but I have witnessed it enough. Have you not seen two people so in love that it appears their hearts will stop beating if they are not together? That is the love I believe my parents had and what I wish for myself. I want to wake to thoughts of one gentleman and close my eyes to dream of him.'

'The sounds rather consuming.'

'I believe love is consuming—in the most wondrous of ways.'

'Now you are waxing poetical, Miss Vandenberg.'

'Laugh if you will. But I shall live my life in America, in a marriage of love and fidelity, happy to keep my head.'

The thought of her married to someone else and living far away disturbed him. He could not fathom why it should bother him. He did not believe her silly notions of love. He certainly did not want her to love *him*!

'And you, Your Grace—what is your idea of a perfect marriage?'

He had no idea. A knot formed in his stomach. His marriage had not been perfect. Even in the best of times it had felt awkward. His grandmother said she had been happy with his grandfather, but the man had died before Julian was born.

'I do not know,' he replied honestly.

'Maybe some day you will discover what it means to be happily married.'

'I doubt that.'

'For that I am truly sorry.'

She proceeded to walk past him, and he moved his arm across the aisle to block her passage. It was mere inches from her breasts. He didn't want her to leave. Not yet.

Their eyes locked and he lowered his head towards her, taking in her lemon scent. She was unaware of how captivating she was when she smiled.

'You think I'm vexing,' she said softly, with those tempting lips.

He lowered his head closer. 'I think you're enchanting.' Just one taste was all he needed. 'Katrina…' he whispered, testing the sound of her name.

'I don't know your name,' she said, their breaths mingling.

'Carlisle.'

'What Carlisle?'

'Julian Henry Michael Charles Carlisle.'

'That's quite a long name.'

'We English like to impress.'

When their lips finally touched he closed his eyes.

Almost instantly she pulled back and ducked under his arm. Reaching the end of the row, she paused and gave him a devilish grin. 'As impressive as your name is, I do not believe it is impressive enough to warrant a kiss from me.'

By the time he walked out from where they were hidden, he caught sight of her walking out through the library door. Crossing his arms and leaning against the bookcase, Julian chided himself at his own stupidity. Dreaming about her was one thing, but actually knowing the feel of her lips and the taste of her mouth would be a mistake. He suspected that if he ever did kiss her thoroughly, she would be impossible to forget.

Chapter Twelve

People from various classes and backgrounds were strolling around the British Museum as Katrina and Sarah made their way from one marble statue to the next.

'I don't see what all the fuss is about. I understand they are quite old, but most of them are broken,' Sarah mused.

Suddenly both women stopped at a marble sculpture of a nude man reclining.

'On the other hand,' Sarah continued, 'I'm beginning to see what merit there is to these works.'

They both tilted their heads slightly, taking in the statue's details.

'Do you think it is accurate?' Katrina whispered. 'Even the size?'

Sarah gave a gentle tug on her arm. 'If we have seen one naked man today, I am sure we will see others.'

Heat began to creep up Katrina's face and she lowered her head. Still, the prospect of actually seeing what was inside a man's breeches was too great a temptation. She turned her head one last time before Sarah pulled her forward.

'I noticed the beautiful bouquet in your drawing room earlier,' Sarah said with a smile. 'I presume the roses were from Monsieur DuBois? He is very handsome, and he was attentive to you last night at the musicale.'

Katrina lifted her shoulder. 'He is passable.'

'Come, now, with his dark eyes and comely features, you must admit he is fine on the eyes.'

Katrina shrugged again.

Sarah looked surprised. 'He is not to your liking?'

'He is…in some respects. DuBois is pleasant company, and we have things in common…'

'But?'

Katrina wished she could explain it—especially to herself. Monsieur DuBois was a lovely man. She enjoyed his company. When they had first met in Paris, months ago, she'd fancied herself smitten with him. However, things had changed since she had arrived in London. Lyonsdale had tried to kiss her.

'He doesn't make my heart race.'

'I wasn't aware you thought requiring a physician was desirable,' Sarah said, laughing.

'I believe a man should make you feel something. When he kisses you it should feel like…'

'When he kisses you it should make you feel as if you can't quite catch your breath.'

'Exactly.'

'So kissing him does not make you feel like that?'

Katrina shook her head. 'We shared one small kiss in Paris. My breathing never altered.'

There was no reason that Sarah needed to know the kiss hadn't exactly been a small one. At the time she had thought it a great passionate adventure to be held in his arms and kissed deeply. Now she was trying to recall why she had thought it was so wonderful. Perhaps because it had been her first kiss. Lyonsdale had merely bushed his lips against hers and she had felt as if she would melt into the floor. There was no telling what would have happened if she had allowed him to actually kiss her.

'I think the next time you find yourself alone with Du-Bois you should kiss him again.'

'Sarah!' she chided, looking around.

'No one can hear. My mother is in the next gallery,' her friend replied dismissively. 'Perhaps he was trying not to offend your delicate feminine sensibilities.'

'Sarah, he is *French*.' Katrina rolled her eyes. 'And I am not going to kiss him again. Let's concentrate on the exhibition.'

'I think our discussion is infinitely more interesting,' Sarah countered, trudging behind her to the next group of statues.

Julian wasn't surprised that Hart had already moved on to the next gallery. When he finally caught up with him he found his friend lounging against the large doorway with his arms crossed, staring into the second room displaying the Elgin Marbles.

'You know, you might not grumble every time I mention coming here if you actually took the time to look at the pieces,' Julian commented, approaching his side.

'I believe the attendees are much more stimulating subjects.' Hart motioned with his head to the other side of the room. 'I have been watching them for the last ten minutes. They really are quite entertaining.'

Julian looked across the room and froze. This could not be happening. He had thought he might be making progress. He hadn't thought of her once since early morning. Fate truly was playing tricks on him.

Miss Vandenberg looked fetching in a small navy bonnet and a navy pelisse over a pale green dress, and she appeared to be enjoying the time she was spending with Miss Forrester.

'I understand you waltzed together.'

Julian was uneasy with the mischief in his friend's eyes. 'How do you know that?'

'I read the papers, like everyone else—albeit later in the day. What do you say you introduce me?'

'No.'

'I promise to behave.'

'No.'

'Windsucker.'

'Dolt.'

Hart tossed the lock of hair out of his eyes. 'Well, I think you're going to have to do something. It seems the lady knows you are here.'

The moment their eyes met every part of Julian's body reacted to the sight of her. When she gave him a small smile he managed to nod in return.

'Capital! You've been acknowledged. Now, go and speak with her.'

What could he possibly say to her when all he could think about was taking her to some remote area of the museum? Trying to kiss her had been highly improper. What if she was angry with him for his boldness?

He was at war with himself. Part of him wanted to go over to her and remain with her for the rest of the day. The other part of him knew that spending any more time with her would make him miserable with unfulfilled longing.

'Are you going to stare at her all afternoon?' teased Hart.

'The thought did occur to me.'

Katrina could actually hear the pounding of her own heart. She had spied Lyonsdale standing near the doorway and simply wanted to observe him. But he had caught her staring, and Katrina had been so embarrassed she had lowered her head so he wouldn't witness her blush. Now, because they had made eye contact, he would feel obligated to say hello.

With a confident stride he crossed the gallery with his companion and stopped a few feet in front of her. 'I hope you ladies are both well,' he said, inclining his head politely.

She struggled with the urge to finish the kiss he had started. 'Yes, thank you, and you?' she said, twisting her finger around the braided handle of her reticule.

'Quite well, thank you,' he replied, and then introduced Katrina and Sarah to his friend, Lord Hartwick.

'Have you both been enjoying the exhibition?' Sarah asked.

'He has,' replied Lord Hartwick. 'I must confess broken statues do not hold my interest—especially when most of them are of men.'

Lyonsdale eyed his friend sharply, and a silent communication passed between them before Lyonsdale turned back to Katrina. 'Has any particular piece caught your eye?' he asked.

Why was it that the only sculpture she could remember seeing was that of the nude man? Was Lyonsdale as muscular as the man carved out of marble? From the way the cut of his coat accentuated his frame, he appeared to be. There had to be another piece of art she could remember seeing...

'The horse's head,' she blurted out, grateful she had thought of such an innocuous piece.

'It is quite lifelike, is it not? I enjoy the friezes myself.'

Their almost kiss had muddled her brain. Katrina was beginning to picture *his* head upon the statue that had so intrigued her earlier. That odd flutter was back, low in her abdomen, and the air was growing thin. If she didn't distance herself from him immediately she was certain to make a cake of herself.

'Well, it was nice to see you again. I believe we will leave you gentlemen to your leisure and continue on.'

When Lyonsdale inclined his head and was about to turn away, his friend cleared his throat. Katrina caught the questioning look that crossed Lyonsdale's face.

Lord Hartwick tipped his head. 'I believe, ladies, that you could not have a better guide than His Grace. Perhaps you would be interested in having him explain the Marbles to you?'

Katrina eyed both men hesitantly. How could she possibly say no without insulting Lyonsdale? But if she spent any more time with him in a room full of barely clad statues she might tug him behind one and kiss him till he had trouble breathing as well.

'It is very kind of you to offer, however, we would not want to keep you longer than necessary with our pace,' she said, feeling Sarah's eyes on her.

'I assure you it would be of no inconvenience. Although I can understand you wanting to take your time with the exhibition,' Lyonsdale said, glancing at his friend.

'Well...thank you again for your offer,' she said, linking her arm through Sarah's. Hopefully the air was cooler in the adjoining gallery. 'Perhaps we will see each other again.'

When Miss Vandenberg and her friend were a good distance away, Julian rounded on Hart. 'What in the world possessed you to do that?'

'Well, pardon me for trying to extend the encounter.'

'Next time do not lend me your assistance.'

'Next time I won't. You are on your own, Romeo.'

'Do not call me that.'

Hart shook his head. 'You must be aware that the two of you produce an interesting display when you're together. It's like nothing I've witnessed with you before.'

'What display?'

'When the two of you stare at one other, one might expect you each to drag the other behind some grand statue in this room.' Hart glanced around. 'Possibly that one over there.'

Julian's eyes narrowed. 'She declined your offer to have me show her the Marbles. What in the world could possibly make you think she wants me?'

She had also refused his kiss, however, he was not about to state that fact. Her eagerness to leave just now told him how insulted she must be by his improper advance. He had allowed his passion to overtake him. Guilt churned in his gut.

'Oh, we are not playing the two young simpering misses, are we? If there is one thing I know, it's the look of a woman who wants to be taken. Now, don't expect me to give you an exact recounting of the number of times she glanced at you and the way her breathing increased when you drew close to her.'

None of this could be true. 'How do you know her breathing increased?'

'Her lovely little breasts rose most rapidly.'

Julian's right hand curled into a fist. 'What were you doing staring at her breasts?' he said through his teeth.

'Pardon me—have we met?' Hart crooked his lip. 'I'm curious. Have you called out her name yet when you're with Helena? If you have, please tell me she noticed.'

Julian tugged at the cuff of his sleeve. 'You'll be pleased to know I have ended my association with Helena.'

A broad smile broke out on Hart's face. 'You have been keeping secrets from me. Not at all sporting of you. Did she turn some tables?'

'She threw a candlestick at me, but I managed to save my head. She was offended that the pearls I gave her weren't diamonds. Apparently a duke should give diamonds when he ends a liaison. Did you know that? I didn't. Glad I never did give her any, though.'

'So now you are free to pursue the lovely Miss V?'

'She is an unmarried woman. I'll not ruin her.'

Hart eyed him closely. 'Perhaps you should marry her, then.'

'What? *You* are talking about marriage? *You* who repeatedly defile the sanctity of such a union all over Town?'

'Well, I am not talking about *me*. You are too honourable to have her any other way, and you have a disturbing need to get leg-shackled again. Why not now? Why not to her? Once you get over this obsession with her you can find amusements elsewhere.'

'She is an American.'

'She is hardly running around in animal skins.'

'So I should throw away centuries of the Lyonsdale bloodline to marry an untitled woman who isn't even English? How do they even raise their children in America?' Just the idea of it was making him sweat.

'Do you believe that if you marry her you will create green dwarf children with pointed ears? She is pretty, appears intelligent, and she comports herself well. I am sure her children will follow suit. If anything, she is the one who would be making a sacrifice. After all, your children could resemble you.'

'I am a duke. It's not done.'

Julian's eyes drifted to the doorway and he clenched his jaw. He wanted her—more than anything. But it was his lot in life that he could not have her.

'Very well. However, it makes no sense to me why you would want to remain this frustrated.'

'I am *not* frustrated,' Julian replied, more loudly than he had intended.

Hart grinned in triumph.

Spinning on his heels, Julian cursed his friend as he walked away.

Later that evening Julian sat at his desk and stared at the blurred writing on the paper in front of him. He should have been focusing on memorising the words he had written, since he would be delivering them to a chamber full of his peers in a few days' time. Instead he was continuing to mull over Miss Vandenberg's reaction to him at the museum. It had been apparent that she couldn't wait to leave his side. She was an unmarried woman, and he had tried to kiss her. Of course she had been insulted by his actions. Hart's assessment of their encounter had been all wrong.

Julian was not in the habit of apologising for anything. This time he needed to make an exception.

A low knock on his door broke the silence of the room. His mother stood in the doorway, dressed for her evening engagements. He motioned for her to enter and she took a seat across from him.

'You are working late, I see,' she said, adjusting her gloves.

'I am memorising a speech.'

'I hear you are expected to give an address this week. I hope the vote is in your favour.'

'Thank you.'

She shifted a little in her chair and glanced down at her hands, folded in her lap. 'You have brought nothing but honour to this family. I am very proud of the man you have become.'

'Thank you,' he replied, taken aback by her unusual praise.

'I'm aware that you do not appreciate me pestering you to find a suitable bride, but I only do so because I'm interested in what is best for you.'

'And you believe what is best for me is Lady Mary Morley?' He sat back and crossed his legs, knowing it was time to begin showing an interest in the girl.

'I do. She is from a prominent family, and she has been trained in how to comport herself as a duchess.' His mother leaned forward in her seat. 'Lady Mary is graceful, accomplished, and she appears robust. Since she is but seventeen, she should have many years ahead of her to bear you a number of children. She will be an asset to you—not a hindrance. Surely you must see she is an ideal choice?'

On paper, she was—but she wasn't someone who could stir his soul and make him ache when he had to leave her. She wasn't Miss Vandenberg.

He looked at his mother's hopeful expression and knew she believed she was guiding his actions for the benefit of the Lyonsdale name. And they both knew the family's reputation meant everything. He recalled what Miss Vandenberg had said in the library about the bond between her own parents. Was it possible he could eventually have that with Morley's daughter?

'Were you eager to marry my father?'

His mother's eyes widened momentarily before she caught herself. 'I beg your pardon?'

'When you were told you would be marrying, were you eager to do so?'

Julian didn't miss the uncomfortable expression that crossed her face. 'I do not recall. I am certain the thought of becoming a duchess in one of the most prominent families in England was pleasing. But I honestly do not recall being eager for anything in my life. I find such strong emotion rather base and vulgar.'

'Were you happy being married to him?'

She shifted again on the chair. 'I do not understand why you are interested in such things. People in our position do not concern themelves with happiness. We strive for contentment, and I was content being married to your father.'

Julian rubbed his chest, relieving some of the tightness that was gripping his ribcage. He glanced at the portrait of his father, visible beyond his mother's right shoulder. Had he ever heard his father laugh? Was that what being married to the wrong woman did?

He shook his head as he buried those questions in his subconscious. 'Was there something else you wanted to see me about?'

She took a breath and appeared relieved at the change in subject. 'Actually, there was. I heard from Lady Jersey that Finchley is reconsidering his vote. I thought that might be of interest to you.'

'I appreciate you taking the time to inform me. I shall speak with him tomorrow.'

'I understand he has been known to dine at White's.'

Julian wished that he could tell if she was interested in his affairs because she truly wanted to help him, or because she wanted another accomplishment of his to place in the family annals. It would have been nice to believe she did it out of a fondness for him.

'Thank you, Mother.'

She turned away. 'I am glad I could be of assistance.' When she'd reached the doorway, she turned back to him. 'I trust you to make the right decision. I will say no more about Lady Mary and defer to you.'

He watched her turn into the hallway before he sat back in his chair. Staring once again at the portrait of his father, he studied the pair of solemn green eyes that looked back at him. Since he was young, Julian had looked upon the life his father had led as a blueprint of the way a duke conducted himself. Once he'd died Julian had clung to the actions that had defined his father. There was no guidebook that came with becoming a duke. One went by example.

Had his father ever regretted marrying his mother? Had he been he content living with a woman who showed no affection and would rather jump into a pond than have an intimate conversation? Would he ever have admitted it to his son?

This was the life he was destined to lead. His mother had said that people in their position didn't concern themselves with happiness. Looking upon his father's solemn portrait, he was certain the man would have agreed. It was time that Julian stopped holding out hope for what could never be.

But then his thoughts turned to a pair of fine blue eyes. Simply thinking about Miss Vandenberg made him smile. She amused him, exasperated him, and excited him. She deserved an apology for his actions. He only hoped that this time when he saw her, he would be able to control his desire.

Chapter Thirteen

The next afternoon rain fell in sheets and thunder shook Katrina's house while she wrote letters home to her family and friends. Her concentration was broken when Wilkins presented her with the unexpected sight of Lyonsdale's card. A fluttering feeling settled low in her abdomen as she rose from her writing table and brushed out the wrinkles of her blue and yellow muslin gown. She needed to compose herself before he entered the drawing room.

'Good day, Your Grace,' she said, dropping into a curtsy. 'My father is not at home, but at the Chancery. I can relay a message to him if you wish.'

The sight of him in her home was making her babble.

'Actually, Miss Vandenberg, I came to call on you.'

Certainly she had misheard what he'd said. She glanced at Meg, who wasn't doing anything to hide her surprise at seeing the Duke of Lyonsdale in the cosy drawing room. When Katrina finally caught her maid's eye she gestured for her to return to her seat and continue mending.

Awkwardly Lyonsdale cleared his throat. He appeared to be waiting for something—her manners and proper etiquette, probably. He had her so flustered she couldn't even recall proper protocol.

Walking to the settee and the chairs by the fireplace,

she gracefully lowered herself into one of the chairs. 'Would you care to sit?'

'Thank you, I would.' A faint smile softened his features as he sat across from her, looking very masculine on the delicate settee.

When he accepted her offer of tea, she nodded her request to Wilkins. Her butler eyed Lyonsdale, before giving her a crisp nod and leaving the room without closing the door.

She turned her attention back to her guest. 'I'm surprised you have ventured out on such a dreary day. I must confess I've not heard many carriages go by all morning.'

He shifted restlessly on the settee. 'I had some important matters to attend to. While the roads are a bit treacherous, they are passable.'

The unlit fireplace seemed to hold his interest. When he looked back at her, the tension was palpable.

'I needed to see you to offer you my apology.' The words came out stilted, as if he hadn't said them often. He should have apologised for ignoring her weeks ago.

'Why are you offering me your apology?'

He leaned closer and they both stole a glance at Meg. Thankfully her maid appeared occupied with her mending. He licked his lips and Katrina almost slid off her chair, remembering the brief feel of those lips brushing against hers.

'I need to apologise for what occurred in my library,' he whispered.

There were many things this man could apologise for, and he was choosing to apologise for their almost kiss?

She was mortified that she had believed him to be as attracted to her as she was to him. It would be horrid to hear him admit he hadn't intended to kiss her. Dear God, maybe *she* was the one who had moved her lips up to his!

'Let us not speak of it again,' she whispered back.

His brow wrinkled. 'I fear I have offended you, and that was not my intention.'

'You have not.'

'Are you certain?'

This was torture. Did he have to go on? 'I assure you there is no need to speak of it.'

He lowered his chin and licked his lips again. 'Miss Vandenberg, I feel a need to be frank.'

'Please do not.' Could not the floor open up and swallow her, just this once?

He kept his voice low. 'I did not wish to insult you, but you stir something inside me.' A pained look crossed his face.

The breath she was holding was released with a whoosh, and she held her stomach to steady the butterflies inside.

'You wanted to kiss me?'

'I thought that was very apparent.'

'But you just apologised.'

'Because I insulted your honour with my action.' He rubbed the back of his neck and eyed her sideways. 'You pulled away from me in my library. Did you want me to kiss you?'

How could she answer that and not sound wanton?

'Did you?' he prodded.

She was struggling to find a response when Wilkins arrived with the tea tray. He placed the tray on the table between them and quietly left the room, once again leaving the door open.

'Oh, look! The tea is here,' she said.

'So it is.' He shifted in his seat and then straightened. 'How fortuitous,' he said dryly.

It was taking quite a bit of effort to hide her relief. 'Tea?'

'Yes.'

'Milk and sugar?'

'Neither, thank you.'

Katrina glanced at him in surprise.

'I don't enjoy my tea sweet,' he offered.

'Apparently,' she replied, handing him his cup.

He looked over at Meg and then back at her, and then placed his cup and saucer on the table. He kept his voice low. 'Aside from offering my apologies to you, I also have another reason for calling on you today.'

'Which is…?'

'While I was out this morning I saw this and thought you might enjoy it.' He held out a wrapped package she hadn't noticed he had been holding when he entered.

'You know I cannot accept it,' she said, pouring a splash of milk into her own cup.

'Please—think of it as a way for me to extend my thanks for the book you sent to my grandmother.'

'Or a peace offering?'

Amusement sparkled in his eyes. 'If you like.'

She hesitantly placed her cup on the table and took the package. As she unwrapped it her eyes widened. '*Frankenstein*. I want to read this.'

'I thought you might. You were looking at it the day we met at Hatchards.'

Her hands fell to her lap, still holding the book. 'You remember that?'

He leaned in closer and lowered his voice. 'I also remember your maid's love of gothic tales, so you might want to consider hiding it from her.'

Thunder boomed in the distance.

'That is probably a wise suggestion.'

'I thought so.'

'Have you read it?'

He shook his head and leaned back. 'No. However, I purchased a copy for myself as well and thought to begin it tonight.'

This time thunder shook the room, and Katrina glanced

at the closest window. Rain poured down the panes, obstructing the view of the street. 'It does appear to be an ideal day to read such a tale. It would be a shame not to take advantage of this atmosphere. Would you like to begin reading it now?'

'You mean together?'

'Certainly. Unless I am keeping you from a pressing engagement?'

'I'm intrigued by your suggestion. How do you propose we begin?'

'I suppose each of us could read silently, if you find that acceptable?' It might prove difficult to concentrate on the words if she had to listen to his deep voice read them.

He nodded, and then his eyes widened as she lifted her delicate chair and placed it next to the settee.

'I do not believe I have ever witnessed a lady moving furniture before. You *do* have other servants, do you not?'

'Of course. But I am fully capable of moving this chair, and it would have delayed our enjoyment if we'd had to wait for them.' She settled herself into the chair and smiled over at him.

'You do realise you could sit here on the settee with me? There is room for both of us,' he said.

Thunder boomed again. 'No, I do not believe that would be a wise idea.' He smelled heavenly—like clean soap and leather.

'You are next to me now.'

But this way there was no risk of her caressing his arm or making a cake of herself in any other way. 'I am already settled quite nicely here. Please—won't you open to the first page so we may begin?'

Lyonsdale arched his brow, appearing every inch the aristocrat he was. 'So I shall be the one to hold the book?'

'You are the man. I thought it was your chivalrous obligation to hold the book while I read.'

'But I am a duke, so I thought you would be holding the book for *me*,' he said with amusement in his eyes.

'Yes, but I am an American. We believe that every man is created equal.'

His gaze raked her body. 'But you are not a man.'

'You've noticed.'

'It has not escaped my notice.'

Katrina found the room suddenly quite warm, and she smiled at him through her lashes.

He gave an exaggerated sigh. 'Very well. I will be your chivalrous bookstand.'

She handed him the first book of the three-volume edition. 'I will be very grateful.'

'Will you show me how grateful?'

'What did you have in mind? I could make you more tea?'

'Not exactly what I was thinking.'

'I shall have biscuits sent up.'

By the time Wilkins arrived with a plate of biscuits Katrina was leaning over the armrest of the settee, her chin almost resting on Lyonsdale's shoulder. The Duke was actually reclining back on the sofa in a most inelegant pose, with his legs crossed. Their heads were almost touching and they were reading from the same book, completely unaware of the butler's presence.

The two engrossed readers remained that way for over an hour. When they finally stopped reading for the day Lyonsdale closed the book and stared straight ahead, chewing his lower lip. It was proving impossible for Katrina to take her eyes off that soft skin.

'I must confess I have never read anything quite like that in my life,' he commented, still appearing very relaxed in his reclined pose.

He twisted his head towards her and she rushed her gaze up to meet his. There was a twinkle in his green eyes, and she was positive he had caught her pining for his lips.

'Have you?' he asked.

'Hmm…' she managed to utter thoughtfully, not having any notion of what he'd said.

Lyonsdale grinned. 'I asked if you'd ever read anything like this. I certainly haven't.'

'No, I've haven't either. Thank you for purchasing it for me.'

The rain still pelted against the windowpanes and the room echoed with the soft ticking of the mantel clock. He leaned his head closer to her.

Oh, dear, he was going to kiss her!

Katrina's breath caught in her throat and she spun her head towards Meg.

Her wonderfully discreet maid still appeared engrossed in her needlework.

'Meg, perhaps you would like to get some tea for yourself,' she called out.

Raising her head from her mending, Meg shifted her gaze between her mistress and the Duke. She had been Katrina's maid since Katrina was fifteen and Meg twenty-six. They had been together almost ten years, and Katrina knew her well enough to see that Meg wasn't certain if she should leave Katrina alone with Lyonsdale.

Katrina gave her an encouraging nod and Meg placed her mending aside and slowly stood.

'I will not be long,' Meg said, curtsying and leaving the room without closing the door.

When Katrina turned back to Lyonsdale she noticed his satisfied grin. 'I simply sent her for some tea because she has been sitting by that window for hours. She needed a respite.'

He raised both his hands. 'I did not say a word.'

'Would you care for more tea?'

His gaze dropped to her lips. 'What I really want is to kiss you before your maid returns.'

Pointing her finger at him, Katrina let out an exasperated breath. 'I did not send her away so you could kiss me.'

His brow wrinkled in confusion. 'You truly do not want me to kiss you?'

She should never have sent Meg away. Lyonsdale was much too charming. Kissing him would be a great mistake. They had no future together. What if his kisses made her lose her breath? What would she do then?

With the tips of his fingers he gently raised her chin. 'Tell me now, before your maid returns. Will you allow me to kiss you?'

Oh, how she longed to know what his kisses would feel like. Losing her ability to speak, Katrina simply nodded her head. His lips curved into a slow smile as he traced her lower lip with his thumb. Then he lowered his head and kissed her softly.

The simple touch of his lips against hers left Katrina wanting more.

Julian knew from the moment he stroked Katrina's tempting lower lip that stopping at one kiss would be close to impossible. As it was, it took all his effort not to pull her on top of him after one innocent kiss. Shifting his head, he nipped her mouth until her lips parted. She tasted like sweet tea and something wonderful.

With her hand tentatively resting on his chest, she hesitated a moment before deepening the kiss. This was heaven.

She was kissing him back, gently exploring his mouth. His cravat was growing tight, along with his breeches. He needed to stop, but it was painful to think he had to release her from his arms. Reluctantly, he pulled his head back.

Her eyes were still closed, and her lips held a faint smile. He was about to kiss her again when her lashes fluttered open, revealing eyes that were his favourite shade of blue. Transfixed by the sensuous sight she made, Julian knew at that moment that he never wanted Miss Vandenberg to kiss anyone else.

'I thought you said just one kiss,' she uttered breathlessly.

'Forgive me. I will strive to do better next time,' he teased.

'I believe you are much too confident in your charms.' She smiled as she lowered her hand from his chest and placed it on her lap.

'Perhaps I am.' He picked up a loose tendril of her hair and rubbed the silky lock between his fingers before hooking it over her ear. 'It was a pleasure reading with you.'

'I enjoyed it thoroughly.'

That smile of hers warmed him even further. 'How long do you anticipate remaining in London?'

She gave a slight shrug. 'It is difficult to tell. A few months, I suppose. Hopefully the negotiations between our two countries will progress smoothly.'

The notion of her leaving and his never seeing her again was burning like acid in his gut. Soon he would approach Morley about his daughter. Then his life would be spent devoted to his responsibilities in the company of a woman he was indifferent towards. Deep down he knew he would never feel as happy as he did at this very moment with Miss Vandenberg. He didn't want the feeling to end. Not now, anyway.

'I have a proposition for you.' Even before the words were out of his mouth he couldn't believe he was actually going to ask her. He needed to spend less time in

Hart's company. 'Would you consider finishing the book with me?'

'You mean continue to read it together?'

'Yes. I realise it is highly irregular. But you were the one to originally suggest it. You once told me you have no intention of marrying an Englishman. And a man in my position must marry a woman from the highest levels of English Society. But you must admit we do enjoy each other's company. I see no harm in spending some more time together before our lives change course.'

She bit her lip. 'Even as an American I know it would not be proper. My reputation would be ruined.'

'I assure you we would see each other in secret. No one would ever know.' He took her hand in his and placed it over his heart. 'On my honour, I would not do anything to jeopardise your reputation.'

She leaned towards him and a mischievous sparkle lit her eyes. 'Then it would be our secret?'

He liked the idea of sharing something only with her. It felt…intimate. 'Yes. It would be our secret.'

This was an ideal solution to his problem. It would be easier for him to proceed with marrying Lady Mary if thoughts of Miss Vandenberg weren't floating through his head all the time. He'd wager that familiarity would lead to boredom. The more time he spent with her, the more quickly he would realise she was not that remarkable. It made perfect sense.

There was just one more thing that would make this arrangement perfect. 'And when we are alone together you can call me Julian.'

She eyed him sideways and he thought she was going to refuse, until another mischievous smile crossed her lips. 'Very well, Julian. Then you must call me Katrina.'

He knew in his bones that from this moment on she would always be Katrina to him.

Her body appeared to dance with excitement as she shifted in her seat. 'Do you promise not to tell a soul?' she asked.

They grinned at each other like two children conspiring to steal all the Christmas treats.

'I promise. And you? You must also promise not to share this with anyone.'

'My lips are sealed,' she said through a smile. 'Fortunately for you I have a strong desire to know how this story ends.'

Chapter Fourteen

Three nights later, Katrina noticed two things about the Whitfields' impressive entrance hall. The first was that her drawing room could easily fit inside it. The second was that the large black and white marble floor resembled one large chessboard, which was appropriate since the happenings of the *ton* always appeared to be a strategic game.

She had not seen Julian since he had called on her and proposed their secret pact. It felt like weeks, although she knew it had only been days. He'd said he would call again when he was not busy with his affairs at Westminster. She did not want to interfere with his duties, but if this continued it would take them over a month to finish reading the book.

Sarah tapped her wrist. 'Do not look to your left,' she whispered into Katrina's ear. 'Lyonsdale is standing by the staircase and has eyed you very intently from your slippers to your hair. You cannot tell me that man does not have an interest in you.'

Katrina's heartbeat quickened and she had an urge to adjust her hair. Reliving his kiss, she refused look at him, certain she would blush. Surely Sarah would be able to tell they were now more than passing acquaintances.

'Sarah, you have to stop. Someone might overhear you.'

'But do you not want to know that his eyes are still on you?' Sarah looked at Katrina with a wrinkled brow. 'Why will you not even acknowledge him?'

At this moment she couldn't acknowledge him. If she did, everyone around her would know they shared a secret. It would be impossible to hide it in her expression.

Katrina was saved from responding by the appearance of Madame de Lieven, who glided up to them on the arm of Mr Armstrong. It was the first time she could recall being happy to see the woman.

'Miss Vandenberg, Miss Forrester—how lovely to see both of you again. You remember Mr Armstrong?'

Katrina recalled the hawk-like features of the youngest son of Lord Greely. 'Of course. How do you do, Mr Armstrong?'

'Quite well. I had the opportunity to speak with Wellington at length earlier.' His chest was puffed out a bit more than usual. 'I am acquainted with him, don't you know?'

Katrina watched him raise his quizzing glass and observe the room. When his quizzer rested on her, Katrina raised her chin until he lowered the glass.

'Pray tell, Miss Vandenberg, have you found the time to explore Town yet? I am certain it's like no place you have imagined,' he said.

'I find London most diverting,' she replied politely.

His lips rose in a superior smile. 'I notice you were extended vouchers to attend Almack's. You dance very well for an American.'

How exactly should one respond to a comment like that? She was never certain. Glancing to her right, she noticed Sarah's attention was on her slippers, her pursed lips giving away her amusement.

'I understand you know how to waltz?' Mr Armstrong continued.

Oh, no. No. No. No. Why couldn't she have talked with him later in the evening, when her waltzes might have all been claimed?

'I do,' Katrina replied slowly, glancing at Madame de Lieven. She caught the knowing glint in the woman's eye.

'I believe that's the beginning of one now. If this dance isn't claimed, would you do me the honour of dancing with me, Miss Vandenberg?' He held his arm out to her.

She wanted to flee. If she waltzed with him she would have to spend time with him for longer than any human being should be required to be in his company. However, if she declined his invitation she would be forced to sit out every dance. That would lead to a very dull evening.

She had no choice but to take his arm. If only he were Julian.

Julian stood near the threshold of the ballroom and watched Lord Greely's whelp escort Katrina onto the dance floor. Even in the low light coming from the chandeliers above he had no difficulty tracing her graceful form as she moved through the waltz. She was a vision in white organza and blue silk. He could watch her all night...

'I would not wait too long to pursue her. She will be taken if you do,' Hart commented casually.

Julian took a sip of what he was certain was watered-down Madeira and wished he had borrowed his grandmother's flask. 'I don't need your advice.'

'Apparently Armstrong has no objection to the lady's nationality. Maybe he likes leprechauns...or would the children be wee beasties? I cannot recall.'

'What do you suppose he is up to?' Julian wondered out loud as he narrowed his gaze.

'Isn't it obvious? The man appreciates a pretty face and a lithe form. He might even enjoy dancing.'

'I've never trusted him,' Julian said, eyeing the couple over the rim of his glass.

'Really? You don't trust him with all things or with your Miss V?'

'She isn't mine, and I have never trusted him about anything. He is a sycophant and always has been.'

'You are aware there is a bet placed in White's about the two of you.'

'Me and Armstrong?'

'No, you dolt. You and Miss V.'

Julian's heart began to pound. He had only called on her that one time, and he had taken pains to walk to her house in the pouring rain with a rather large umbrella. How could someone know of their secret arrangement?

'How was I not aware of this?'

Hart shrugged. 'Do you really care? There are plenty of bets placed about me. I pay them no heed.'

A tic formed in Julian's jaw. 'What does it say?'

'The bet is on how long it will take for you to enter into a liaison with her.'

Julian had a sudden need to crush something—or someone. He consciously relaxed his hold on his glass. At least the bet was not about *if* he was having a liaison with her already.

'Who placed the bet?'

Hart resumed watching the dancers and crossed his arms. 'Don't recall. They really are stunning together... all that golden glory. I imagine their children will be very attractive. Unless, of course, they do take on the appearance of green beasties.'

'You're an ass.'

'So you have said—time and again,' Hart replied with amusement. 'Shall we play some cards? I have a hunting box in Scotland that Lord Middlebury must be missing. I am feeling generous and may lose it to him.'

* * *

Helena stepped to the edge of the dance floor and studied the woman who had captured Lyonsdale's attention. Could this be the woman who had somehow persuaded Lyonsdale to waltz with her at Almack's?

Elizabeth, the Duchess of Skeffington, approached her side. 'I am amazed we are listening to a quartet this evening. And the wine is positively insipid. It appears, Helena, that the Whitfields are not as prosperous as they once were. I would not be surprised if young Whitfield is hunting an heiress this very night.'

When Helena made no reply, her friend continued. 'That is a lovely gown she is wearing. I believe by the cut it's French. It certainly cannot be American-made.'

Helena shifted her gaze. 'To whom are you referring, Lizzy?'

'Oh, forgive me. I thought you were watching Miss Vandenberg—the woman dancing with Mr Armstrong.'

'Why would I concern myself with someone dancing with a mere third son?'

'Because she is the woman Lyonsdale waltzed with at Almack's. I was watching them that night. He appeared quite taken with her. I assumed you had heard. It was on everyone's lips the next day.'

Of course she had heard about his waltz. She paid attention to every bit of gossip in the papers. One never knew when it might be used to one's advantage. However, Lyonsdale had danced with the woman only once, and she had assumed it was for political reasons.

'You never said anything to me.'

'As I said, I assumed you had already heard. You know how much I loathe gossip. It was astonishing to see, though. He appeared to be smiling that night. I don't believe I have ever seen him do so with a woman.'

The American was still turning about the floor in her

waltz. Her hair was the colour of straw, and her lips were too thin. The gown she wore covered a form that did not possess breasts or hips that would bring a man to his knees.

'Who is she?' Helena asked her friend.

Lizzy's eyes brightened. 'She is the daughter of Mr Peter Vandenberg, the American author who is here on diplomatic affairs. One would think London was full of bluestockings, with all the talk of his book.'

They stood in silence, each watching Miss Vandenberg.

'It's fascinating,' Lizzy continued, 'that when Lyonsdale chose to waltz it was with an American. That's rather…humbling.' Lizzy eyed Helena over her fan. 'I've not witnessed you and Lyonsdale conversing tonight.'

An unwelcome flush crept up Helena's neck and she forced herself to appear relaxed. Was it possible that he had ended their affair because of a provincial colonial? What did it say about her that he had replaced her with an American? She stole a glance at the men and women standing around them. Were they discussing it behind their fans and casting judgement?

'Surely you haven't been watching him all evening,' she said to Lizzy, pushing her nails further into her gloved fist.

She needed to ensure no attachment was forming between Lyonsdale and the American woman before she found herself the subject of gossip in the papers for her smug brother to gloat over.

Chapter Fifteen

For a ball consisting of weak beverages and a poor choice in musicians, Katrina found there was quite a crush. Apparently the Whitfield name meant something to the *ton*. She excused herself from Sarah and Mrs Forrester to find a bit of a reprieve in the ladies' retiring room. When she crossed the threshold, she was relieved to find the delicate gilded chairs were empty and the sole occupant was a maid, who remained by the door.

Walking towards a wall hung with mirrors, Katrina peered at her reflection. She had a rosy glow, which sadly was the result of heat and not from the joy of dancing with her various partners. They hadn't exactly been horrible partners. They just weren't Julian. If she had been dancing with him her glow might have been from an amusing conversation—or from the way her body seemed to catch fire whenever he was near.

She missed him. She assumed he was keeping his distance so as not to cause speculation. It was an honourable action, but she didn't have to like it. How she wished he would ask her to dance. Then she could listen to that amusing deep voice that warmed her like a cup of chocolate.

Katrina was so absorbed in her thoughts that she almost didn't notice a woman in a Pomona-green silk gown walk up beside her. She was stunning, with perfect delicate features and a thick head of dark hair. The woman studied her own reflection and adjusted the curls near her temples before shifting her grey eyes to Katrina.

'Aren't you that American woman?'

Would there be one ball, one fête she would attend where she wouldn't have to face at least one ignorant comment about Americans?

Katrina held back a sigh, anticipating one of those conversations. 'There are a few Americans in London. Which one do you believe me to be?'

'The author's daughter,' the woman replied, raising her chin.

'By author, do you mean Peter Vandenberg? If so, I am indeed his daughter.'

The woman eyed Katrina critically, from her slippers to her hair. *Did she not realise Katrina could see her?*

'And who might you be?' Katrina asked.

'Oh, I am Lady Wentworth. I am a very dear friend of the Duke of Lyonsdale. I understand you danced with him recently at Almack's?'

That statement had not been uttered by chance. Katrina's muscles tightened like a bowstring. 'His Grace and I did share a dance.'

'He is a handsome man, is he not?'

'I suppose.'

If one liked men who had wavy dark hair, moss-green eyes, chiselled features, and cut a fine form.

Lady Wentworth let out a soft, disgustingly lovely laugh. 'Surely you agree? It's a pity you're American, and therefore could never become his duchess. I can assure you whoever he does marry will be quite fortunate.'

Her lips rose in a sly smile. She leaned close to Katrina's ear, and her hot breath scorched her neck.

'He knows how to do delicious things to make a woman quiver with need.'

She stepped back, looked Katrina directly in the eye, and cocked an arrogant brow. Katrina's stomach rolled and pitched. She would not give this horrid woman the satisfaction of knowing how her words had filled Katrina with a sense of betrayal. Could this be why Julian had not called on her?

After weeks of pretending that English aristocrats didn't bore her to sleep, Katrina had become quite adept at hiding her emotions. She smiled sweetly back at the witch beside her. 'One would imagine that since he is neither married nor publicly displaying a mistress he has yet to find a woman who makes him feel the same in return.'

There—that felt better.

Katrina forced her lips into the brightest smile. 'Do enjoy your evening, Lady Wentworth.'

As if she didn't have a care in the world, Katrina turned and breezed out of the room. Unfortunately the reality was that her world had just become a colder place. She would only be in London for a few months. It shouldn't matter to her that this woman was sharing Julian's bed—but it did.

She needed time away from the ballroom and the sight of Lady Wentworth.

Earlier in the evening she had a pleasant conversation with the Duchess of Winterbourne, who had mentioned there were some lovely landscapes hung along this long, deserted hallway. Now was the perfect time to view them.

The sound of confident footfalls had Katrina praying that the pompous Mr Armstrong had not found her. Turning her head, she was startled when Julian took her arm and tugged her through one of the open doorways into an oak-panelled room.

The sight of three large stuffed birds glaring at her in the moonlight from the round table beside them made her jump, and it took her a moment before she shifted her attention to the man standing a few feet in front of her. Lady Wentworth's comment echoed in her mind, and it occurred to her that all Julian had to do was look at her to make her insides quiver. She had to remind herself he was not the man for her.

'Are you trying to ruin me?' she demanded, placing her hands on her hips. 'What possessed you to drag me in here?'

He stepped closer, creating a cushion of heat between them. No man deserved to look that good in unremarkable formal black evening clothes.

'Of course I'm not trying to ruin you. My committee meetings have been consuming my days. I wanted you to know I have not forgotten about our promise.'

Once more she heard Lady Wentworth's voice.

'Please do not feel obligated to continue to read with me. You're a very busy man, and I'm certain you'd prefer to read the remainder of the book at your leisure.'

He lowered his gaze towards his shiny black dress shoes. 'On the contrary, I would rather read it with you.' As he looked back up at her through his thick lashes a look of confusion crossed his face. 'Do you no longer wish to read with me?'

He was not courting her. She had no claim on him. How could she tell him how she felt without sounding jealous? *Which she absolutely wasn't.*

'Do you really think this is an appropriate place to have a conversation? We should not even be in here together.'

'I had no choice—you would not so much as look at me.'

'I was trying to avoid speculation about us.'

Julian narrowed his eyes and tipped his head back. 'We have spoken before in public. I do not think it would shock people if we were to do so again.'

'And how would you have informed me that you want us to continue reading together with people around us?'

The faint, distant strains of the quartet drifted into the room through the closed door as he flashed her a devilishly handsome smile. 'That is why this is an ideal location for our discussion.' Sliding his hand around her waist to the small of her back, he pulled her to him. 'I cannot stop thinking about you and our kiss.'

Neither could she, and that was a problem. Before she fell asleep she thought about it, over and over. Even at odd moments in the day she would think about the feel of his lips and the taste of his tongue. She had wanted that kiss to go on for ever.

She placed her hands on his solid chest, intending to push him away. Her arms wouldn't move. How she longed to press her body further into his.

A look of what might have been tenderness softened his features. 'You are most unexpected.'

It would be so easy to lose herself in him, but according to Lady Wentworth he was one of many English aristocrats with philandering ways. She would not be one of his conquests.

He lowered his head to hers and his soft breath caressed her lips. This time she pushed against his chest, and he immediately let her go.

'I will not kiss a man who shares his affection with another.' It was said in such a rush she wasn't certain she had been coherent.

He jerked his head back and crossed his arms, his biceps bulging under the sleeves of his coat. 'Are you referring to me?'

She put her hands on her hips. 'Yes—you were the one who looked as if you intended to kiss me.'

'I did want to kiss you… I *do* want to kiss you. However, I'm not sharing my affection with anyone.'

Now it was Katrina's turn to narrow her eyes. 'Not even with your paramour?'

He let out a bark of laughter. 'My what?'

'Your paramour…or mistress. Or do you call her something else?' Katrina huffed. 'I would appreciate it if you would not find so much amusement in what I'm saying.'

'Forgive me,' Julian said, quietening down and trying unsuccessfully to stop smiling. 'I can truly say I have never met any woman quite like you.'

'Simply answer the question, please.'

'What was the question? Oh, yes—well, I don't call her anything because there is no one else.'

'But I thought… That is to say, aren't you…?' Katrina chewed her lip, feeling foolish. She knew she hadn't mistaken Lady Wentworth's insinuation. But who was she to believe? A horrid woman she didn't know or Julian—Julian who felt deeply about honour and duty?

'Do you really think we should be discussing this?' he asked, lowering his head and prompting Katrina with his eyes. 'You know gently bred ladies should not even be aware of such things?'

'Well, I am. I lived in Paris and I have witnessed open displays of indiscretion.'

She had even stumbled upon Comte Janvier and Madame Broussard in a garden once. The Comte's trousers had been down around his knees and Madame Broussard's skirt had been lifted so high Katrina knew exactly what occurred between men and women. However, it wasn't necessary for Julian to know the extent of her knowledge gained from that tableau.

'Are you are telling me there is no one you are sharing your affections with?'

'I have had women in my life in the past with whom I have shared my affections, but no longer. Now I find the only woman I want to share my affections with is you.'

Katrina's heart hammered against her ribs and the room grew unbearably warm. 'Only me?' she let out with a breath.

Slowly and seductively his lips rose into a smile. 'Only you.'

Staring into her eyes, Julian felt overwhelmed by his feelings for her. He lowered his gaze and found his attention riveted to her smooth skin and that enticing birthmark on the upper swell of her left breast. He hardened at the thought of trailing his tongue from that birthmark down to the nipple he knew was hidden under the white organza of the bodice of her gown. He wanted to suck on that nipple until he heard her groan—or moan.

Bloody hell, what would she sound like?

'I wish I knew what you were thinking,' she said, biting her lip.

'There are times when you make it very difficult to be a gentleman.' He pulled her close and crushed his lips to hers. Her mouth was warm and sweet. Best of all, she was kissing him back with as much passion as he felt coursing through his own veins. He could kiss her all night… Until she moved her lower body against his and his trousers tightened even more. Then the image of sliding himself inside her would not leave his brain.

'Say my name,' he said, trailing kisses along her jaw and having the oddest desire to hear his name on her lips.

'Julian…' It came out more like a moan as he softly bit her neck.

As much as he knew he shouldn't, he slid his hand up her waist over the soft fabric of her gown until he cupped her left breast. The weight of it fitted perfectly into his palm, as if she were made just for him. He gave it a gentle squeeze and felt her breath catch in his mouth. Her nipple hardened into a tight bud in his palm. With his eyes closed

he broke the kiss, to trail soft nips down the long column of her neck. As he reached her collarbone he pulled on the neckline of her gown and kissed his way along the small swell of her breast, paying special attention to that beguiling birthmark.

Her fingers were digging into his shoulders, and it felt so good. When he swirled his tongue around her sweet, hard nipple she let out a throaty groan that nearly had him laying her down on the table that was next to them. He sucked on it and she softened in his arms. Every subtle response from her body increased his desire to drive deep inside her. The air was quickly leaving the room. It was torture that she was an unmarried woman he couldn't have. This was an urgency of passion such as none he had ever felt before. He needed to know she wanted him just as much as he wanted her. Even if he knew he could not take her.

He began to edge her skirt up and cursed his gloves, which would prevent him from feeling how wet she was. He let go of her gown and kissed her once more. Her eager response matched his. The pressure of her body moved against him, causing friction. He needed to stop before he disgraced himself.

It took a tremendous amount of discipline to pull his head away from her soft breast and step back. When he did, they were both panting hard.

She was a vision, with her lips still wet from his kiss and her left breast exposed. Much to his disappointment she adjusted her bodice and returned to looking like a very proper lady faster than he would have preferred. His body, however, was not showing any signs of softening. He closed his eyes and silently counted off the British monarchs in chronological order.

'Is anything the matter?' she asked. 'You appear to be in pain.'

He laughed at her innocent comment and cracked open one eye. 'I thought you'd lived in Paris.'

Her brows drew together in confusion, and then her expression cleared in some form of understanding. 'Is that why you stopped?'

'I stopped because had I not, I would have had to find some explanation for the state of my trousers for the remainder of the evening.'

He wasn't certain she understood. She opened her mouth to say something but suddenly the door opened—and Miss Forrester walked into the room.

His heart stopped in panic and he felt as if he had run a very long race.

It appeared she hadn't spotted him as she addressed Katrina. 'I cannot believe you are hiding...'

Her eyes darted to Julian and her lips parted. It was remarkable how quickly she composed herself and focused all her attention on Katrina, completely ignoring him.

'Considering how easy it was for me to gain entrance to this room, it might be wise for me to remain to lend you an air of respectability, should anyone else see fit to come in here,' she offered.

Katrina did not appear to be alarmed by Miss Forrester's presence. Hopefully this meant Miss Forrester could be trusted not to reveal their encounter. As much as he liked Katrina, he still had no desire to be forced into marriage. His heartbeat began to slow down.

Katrina's attention remained on Miss Forrester. 'Why were you searching this hallway?'

'Because my mother was concerned that you were taking an inordinately long time in the retiring room and I offered to fetch you. Lucky for both of you I did. I remembered how interested you were in those paintings the Duchess of Winterbourne mentioned, and thought

you might be hiding from the remainder of your dancing partners.'

Katrina rubbed her forehead. 'How many dances have I missed?'

'Just one.'

Miss Forrester's presence had alleviated the pull on Julian's trousers and it was now safe for him to return to the ball. He would leave it to Katrina to find an explanation for her friend. But before he was able to excuse himself, the door opened again. This time Hart stepped inside.

If this kept up she was sure to be ruined!

Even in the moonlit room there was no mistaking the amused glint Julian saw in his friend's eye as he glanced from Miss Forrester to Miss Vandenberg and finally to Julian. Hart casually leaned his back against the door and crossed his arms. His smirk was not appreciated.

'I say...this *is* interesting.'

Miss Forrester stepped forward, as if to block Hart's view of Katrina. 'Miss Vandenberg and I entered the room just a few minutes ago. We were unaware that His Grace was already in here.'

Hart bit his lip and nodded sagely. 'I see—and what exactly drew you two ladies to this remote location?'

'Taxidermy.'

'Pardon?'

Miss Forrester raised her chin and crossed her arms. Apparently she was standing her ground. 'I said taxidermy.'

Hart rubbed the smile off his lips. 'I see. And what specimens drew you to this room, exactly?'

She waved her hand carelessly behind her. 'Birds.'

'So you have an interest in ornithology?'

'Ye-e-e-s,' she replied, drawing out the word.

'And what particular species were you interested in seeing?'

'Well, whatever species His Lordship has, of course.'

'Of course.' Hart tossed back the lock of hair that fell near his eyes.

He was having too much fun at Julian's expense. Hopefully he could convince Hart not to tell their friends about this.

Miss Forrester took a step forward, crossed her arms, and tipped her head to the side. 'And you, my lord. What brings *you* to this far corner of the ball? There is nothing of interest here.'

'On the contrary—I have an interest in birds as well,' he said through a smirk.

She looked as if she was about to reply.

Hart held up his hand. 'I assume you are finished with your studies in this darkened room, so we will say it's been a pleasure and allow you ladies to return to this evening's entertainments.'

Miss Forrester grabbed Katrina by the hand and pulled her towards the door. 'That's very kind of you. Good evening, gentlemen.'

Katrina glanced back at Julian one last time with a regretful look before she was dragged out through the door. He didn't even get a chance to say goodbye to her, or to kiss her one last time for the night.

Hart closed the door and locked it. Why hadn't Julian thought to lock the door earlier? Perhaps it was because he'd never needed to do so before. This was the first and only time he had ever stole away with a woman at a ball.

'You and I need to have a talk,' Hart said. 'And I know just the place to have it.'

They walked two doors down to the Whitfields' billiard room, and Hart racked up the balls without saying a word. Julian grabbed two cues from the rack on the wall, grateful for the short reprieve. Once the balls were set, they flipped Hart's lucky coin to see who would go first. Julian won.

He leaned over the Whitfields' billiard table and released his cue. He watched the balls scatter.

Shaking his head, he turned to Hart. 'How in the world did you find us?'

'As luck would have it I was supposed to be meeting someone there shortly. It appears you and I need to begin coordinating our appointments.'

Julian narrowed his gaze. 'That won't be necessary. What you witnessed was a mere coincidence.'

Hart walked around the billiard table, analysing the best angle for his shot. He looked as if he was trying to hold back a smirk. 'I see. We can move forward with that story if you like. But I will say it is fortunate it appears you have gained another ally in Miss Forrester.'

Julian rested his hand on top of his cue and watched Hart line up his shot. 'Why do you believe it is a good thing to have Miss Forrester as an ally?'

Aside from the fact that she wouldn't gossip about what she'd found when she had walked into the room.

'To gain the support of your lady's friend is always a good thing. Just think of all the ways we could use her.'

Julian sent him a stern look.

'I mean you. All the ways *you* could use her.'

'I will not be using anyone. Nor will you. And Miss Vandenberg is not my lady. It was an accidental encounter, nothing more.'

'If you say so,' Hart said, taking his shot.

Hart never agreed so easily. This was not a good sign.

Chapter Sixteen

The late morning sun warmed Katrina's garden as she sat on a wooden bench with her box of watercolours. Peering closely at a teacup filled with violets, she concentrated on trying to recreate this small reminder of home. As she swirled her sable-haired brush through the purple and blue paint Julian's comment about the colour of her eyes when they'd sat together with his grandmother drifted into her thoughts. It made her smile.

Glancing down, she realised she'd muddled the colours together into an unusable mess. There had to be a way to shove him out of her mind. She closed her eyes, took a deep breath of the floral-scented air, and listened to the birds chirp around her. If she tried hard enough she could imagine she was sitting in her garden back home in Tarrytown, overlooking the sparkling Hudson River.

It was peaceful there.

It was quiet.

'Have you managed to fall asleep like that?'

Katrina opened one eye and met Sarah's quizzical gaze. And just like that her peaceful bubble burst.

'What were you doing?' Sarah asked, taking a seat on the bench across from her.

Katrina cleaned her paintbrush in a glass of water. 'I was resting my eyes.'

'It is lovely here in the shade,' Sarah said as she untied the cinnamon silk ribbon of her straw bonnet and casually tossed it beside her. 'And what a charming bunch of violets. I have little skill with a paintbrush, much to my mother's displeasure.'

'Skill or patience?'

'Both, I suppose. How long will that take you to complete?'

Katrina shrugged and continued to add petals to the paper. 'I find the process soothing.'

Or at least it had been until Sarah began rhythmically tapping her foot on the gravel.

'Is there something you wanted, Sarah?'

'I was hoping you would accompany me to Bond Street.'

'We were shopping only yesterday.'

'I've reconsidered those slippers. You remember? The ones with the fine needlework?'

'I have no wish to move along with the crowds today. Could it possibly wait for another day?'

'I suppose it could, but— What is that?'

Katrina looked up to find Wilkins, walking towards them on the garden path, carrying a large vase of purple and yellow flowers. As he drew closer, she realised they weren't exactly flowers.

'Pardon me, miss. These came for you, and I was wondering what you would like me to do with this unusual arrangement?'

'Aren't those weeds?' Sarah asked, as she narrowed her eyes at the objects in question.

'I believe so, Miss Forrester,' he replied. 'Thistle and ragwort, if I am not mistaken. Would you prefer I place the stems in the garden for you, miss?'

Although they were indeed weeds, the arrangement had been created with obvious care. Katrina thought the contrast of purple and yellow to be rather striking. But why would someone send them to her?

'Did they arrive with a note, Wilkins?'

He handed her a folded piece of paper sealed with a blob of red wax.

True beauty resides in the most unexpected places.

When she read the message she knew they could only have come from one man—the only man who had ever told her she was 'most unexpected'. She folded the paper and brought it to her lips to cover her smile. He was clever. She would give him that. And, as much as she tried, it was difficult to remain unaffected by Julian.

When she directed Wilkins to place them in her bedroom he stared at her as if she belonged in Bedlam. The moment he was far enough away, Sarah jumped up and sat next to her.

'Who are they from? Did Mr Armstrong send them?'

'No, he did not. They're from an acquaintance.'

Sarah eyed her with open curiosity. 'If someone sent me weeds I do not believe I would be smiling. Unless—' Her eyes widened with realisation and she snapped her lips shut. She waited until Wilkins had disappeared through the terrace door before she continued. 'They are from Lyonsdale.'

Katrina looked away. 'What would cause you to believe so?'

'Because you only smile like that when he is near. What did the card say?'

'It is of little importance.'

'Why will you not tell me?' Sarah said, fisting her hands on her lap.

Katrina turned back to her friend. 'There is nothing to tell.'

'After finding the two of you together, I wish you would admit you fancy him.'

She could not allow herself to think such thoughts. If she thought too much about how she felt about him heartache would be her only reward. 'What good would it do? We have no future together.'

'The Duke's questionable taste in botanicals paints a different picture. Has he called on you?'

Katrina rubbed the tightness in her chest. She hated lying to Sarah, but she and Julian had promised not to tell anyone about their secret agreement. 'Of course not. The man is a duke and I am American. I possess no title and have no impressive heritage. And, I have heard rumours that he is carrying on a liaison with Lady Wentworth.' *Now* Sarah would stop pestering her about him.

'You are prettier.'

Katrina sent her an incredulous look. It was an admirable attempt on her friend's part, but Katrina knew how beautiful Lady Wentworth was.

'Well, you are more amiable, and probably much more intelligent.'

That made Katrina laugh, and she was grateful to have found such a good friend.

'Why do you believe he sent those...weeds?' Sarah continued.

Katrina shrugged and returned her focus to the violets. His cheeky gesture had made her smile.

'You cannot convince me you are indifferent to him, and he is obviously quite taken with you. Let me help you with this.'

'Oh, no,' Katrina said, pointing her paintbrush at Sarah. 'Do not do a thing. Do you understand, Sarah?'

'But I can help you. As you are aware, my presence

will add an air of discretion to your encounters, and it will also protect you in the event that you discover his taste in most things is consistent with his taste in botanicals. Please let me help you.'

'I said no. Do not misinterpret a fond regard for romance.'

'But he kissed you!'

'What?' Katrina glanced around in panic, her heart racing.

'At the Whitfield ball. You cannot tell me he did not kiss you. When I entered that room you looked like a woman about to swoon.'

She needed to stop the pounding of her heart. 'I do not swoon. I never swoon. And, more importantly, we did not kiss. There was no kiss.'

'Well, there should have been! You need to be around him more.'

'Sarah!'

'I am simply stating my opinion.'

Chapter Seventeen

The Forresters' barouche rolled through Richmond under a canopy of trees as a soft breeze blew. The coachman guided the team of four to a raised mound where trees and shrubs dotted a grassy lawn that sloped off in all directions. Sarah chose a shady area under an old cascading willow tree as the perfect spot for a picnic.

If Katrina had to spend a day without being near Julian, at least she was in a pretty place.

After setting a large wicker hamper on the white cotton blanket, Sarah's footman returned to the barouche.

'This really was a fine idea, and at this early hour I'd be surprised if we encounter anyone else for hours.' Katrina began unpacking the food from the hamper. 'I can't recall the last time I was on a picnic. Whatever made you think of this?'

Sarah gave a careless shrug. 'It came to me the other day when I was in Hyde Park. I was told this is an ideal place to pass the time. Spending the day away from London is a nice reprieve from all the calls we must make and the dull visitors we must receive.'

'Whatever would I do without you?'

Sarah's lips turned up in a mischievous grin. 'Trust me when I say you would be lost without me.'

* * *

Not far away, two riders were racing through a clearing at top speed. The coat-tails of the rider in front flapped in the wind behind him. A satisfied smile rested on his lips. The second rider clutched his horse tightly with his muscular thighs. His slightly long black hair whipped into his eyes as he angled his body lower, attempting to outrun his opponent. His face was set in an expression of pure determination, and he was oblivious to the scenery around him.

Julian kept his eyes fixed on the grove of trees that marked the finish line. 'You'll never outrun me!' he yelled over the pounding of hoofbeats.

'This race isn't over yet!' Hart yelled back as he pulled his horse directly to the left of Julian's.

Julian's horse was ahead by a neck when they reached the trees. As he pulled in the reins he spun his horse around and laughed. 'And that, my friend, is how you win a race.'

'You don't say? I would not have noticed you had won if you had been remiss in mentioning it.'

'That is why I knew it was my duty to do so.'

Julian had forgotten how much he enjoyed flying through the fields at top speed. He was glad Hart had suggested this outing. He could have called on Katrina today, but he had been shaken by the intensity of his need for her when they'd been alone at the Whitfields' ball. His carelessness at not locking the door had almost cost her her reputation. Fortunately Hart valued discretion. The next time he was alone with her, if they were not careful, they might not be so lucky.

'You realise I held back?' Hart said, breathing hard. He tossed his head to move the lock of hair that fell over his eye. The lock slid down again.

'Yes, you have the appearance of a man who took his time,' Julian replied, smirking.

'I do, don't I? In any event, it was a fine race. Let's find a spot in the shade to rest the horses. I do believe I have a flask somewhere on me.' Hart searched their surroundings and smiled. 'Maybe we could beg refreshment from those fair ladies sitting in the shade,' he said, gesturing with his head.

There was a large willow tree with a thick covering of branches swaying slightly in the breeze. It wasn't until a strong gust of wind blew the branches aside that he spied the women sitting under it. How was it possible that Katrina was sitting not far from him on the park-like grounds of Hart's estate? She was wearing a straw bonnet, a white and blue striped gown, and a blue spencer—and she was stunning.

Watching the men approach lazily on horseback, Katrina wondered why she had chosen this particular bonnet to wear today. She was certain there was a better choice in her wardrobe somewhere.

'I do believe that is Lyonsdale and Lord Hartwick,' Sarah said softly, smiling at the men as they rode closer. 'What a strange coincidence that they're here today as well.'

Katrina watched her friend with suspicious eyes. 'You couldn't possibly have known…could you?'

'How could I have known they would be here? It isn't as if I am a friend of either His Grace or Lord Hartwick. You look quite fetching, by the way. Your face has a bit of a pink glow.'

Katrina glared at her friend.

'I am simply stating my opinion,' continued Sarah.

By the time the men reached them Katrina could hear her heart pounding in her ears. She watched Julian pull his mount to a stop under the tree. The footman approached as well.

Sarah motioned him away. 'You may stand with the carriage. We will not be requiring your assistance.'

'Ladies, what a pleasant surprise,' Lord Hartwick said with a tip of his head. 'I was not aware that you were acquainted with this place.'

'This is our first foray here, my lord. It's quite picturesque,' Sarah replied in an overly pleasant voice.

Julian arched his brow at Katrina and she lifted her shoulder in a slight shrug. To her, he appeared to be a suspect in this 'chance encounter' as well.

'This is one of my favourite places,' Lord Hartwick said. 'The view from here is rather stunning. Have you had an opportunity to study the landmarks, Miss Forrester?'

'Why, no, I can't say that I have.'

Lord Hartwick jumped down from his horse and held his hand out to Sarah. 'Would you be interested in having me point them out to you?'

One might think there was a fire on the blanket, watching the speed with which Sarah stood. 'That is most kind of you, Lord Hartwick.'

Katrina suppressed the urge to trip her as they brushed the cascading branches out of their way and walked to the look-out with his horse trailing behind.

Julian slid out of his saddle and tied the reins to a branch. Patches of sunlight danced along his brown coat through the leaves.

He gestured towards the blanket with his hand. 'May I?'

She nodded as she took off her least favourite bonnet.

After he had accepted a glass of Madeira, he stretched out his legs. 'I only decided on this adventure last night. How did you arrange this?'

Katrina wondered why she had never noticed that his

legs were so long and powerful. She raised her gaze to meet his. 'I didn't arrange this. I assumed you did.'

They both turned to find their friends occupied with viewing the scenery through the trees. 'You do realise you are on his land?'

It would take a great deal of control not to trip Sarah at some point today. 'I was not aware. Sarah never said...'

'They believe they are quite clever.'

'I believe they are two people who should never be left alone together. In some ways they are far too much alike. Does he know?'

He appeared affronted by her question. 'About our arrangement? No, I vowed not to tell anyone. Does she know?'

Katrina shook her head. 'It was difficult not to tell her, but I too have kept our secret.'

He looked back at their friends. 'I wonder what they would say if we told them we might have been alone in your home if it weren't for their assistance.'

'I believe my picnic would come to a rather abrupt end.'

'And I believe my friend would suddenly remember an important meeting back in Town.'

The sight of Julian's soft lips curving into a smile left her mouth dry. While she had been attracted to him before, knowing what his kisses did to her was a complete distraction now. Did those kisses have any effect on him as well? Would he want to kiss her again?

She took a sip of Madeira. 'While we are waiting for them to stop pretending they are interested in the view, I was wondering if you might offer some assistance in a matter that has been troubling me.'

A look of concern crossed his face. 'Of course.'

'Recently I received a substantial bouquet of thistle and ragwort. Unfortunately the sender was remiss in signing the card. I don't suppose you would have any idea who in London might send such a thing?'

His brow creased, but he had a hint of a smile. 'Someone sent you weeds? How unusual. Does that happen often?'

'Never. I found the colour combination quite striking, and I wish to show my appreciation to the sender for their thoughtfulness. But, alas, I don't know who to thank.' She smiled innocently.

His gaze dropped to her lips. 'And how would you show that appreciation?'

'I don't believe it would be proper to divulge that to anyone but the sender. A pity, that...'

'Yes, a pity.' He shifted slightly. 'You can give me an idea, though?'

'No. I don't believe I can.' Katrina averted her eyes as she tried not to smile.

He leaned towards her. 'Not even a hint?'

She shook her head and took another sip of Madeira.

Julian swallowed hard.

She bit back a smile. Perhaps he did want to kiss her again. There had to be something they could talk about that did not conjure up thoughts of his lips on her skin. Her breasts began to tingle and she almost spilled her wine.

'Do you ride here often?' she asked, all in one breath.

It took him a moment to answer, as if his thoughts had been far from where they were. 'I haven't in an age. Although Hart and I have enjoyed racing up this mound for many years.'

'I assume from the familiar way you refer to him that you are great friends?'

He nodded. 'We are. I have known him all my life. Our family estates border one another, and we attended Cambridge together. And you and Miss Forrester—are you great friends?'

'I feel we are becoming so. I was introduced to her years ago in Washington, and now we share a similar circumstance in a foreign land. She has a good heart, and we have similar tastes in amusement.'

'Is Washington your home?'

'While I've spent considerable time there, my home is in New York. We have a residence not far from New York Harbour, where my father owns a shipyard, but we also own a home further north in Tarrytown, along the Hudson River, away from the hustle and bustle of town.'

It appeared as if he wanted to say something, but he wasn't sure how to put it into words.

Katrina tilted her head and studied his uncomfortable expression. 'Is there something you want to ask me?'

'I understand he is a widower. I was wondering... That is to say...'

'Do you wish to know about my mother?'

He nodded. 'Forgive me, I am certain it is a subject you do not wish to discuss.'

'There is no need to apologise for your interest. My mother died long ago.'

An unsettled expression crossed his face as he turned away. 'You have my condolences.'

'Thank you.'

She had never known her mother. From what she could tell from her father, her parents had loved each other deeply. That was what she wanted in a marriage.

She studied Julian's chiselled profile. He was an honourable man. He was easy to speak with and he made her laugh. Would she find a man like him when she returned to America? Her heart grew heavy, and she reached for more wine.

'You mentioned you have known Lord Hartwick since you were children. I cannot imagine you so young. What were you like?'

He appeared to consider her question thoroughly. Then his lips curved and his eyes sparkled. 'I wanted to be a pirate.'

That was an unexpected revelation. 'If I promise to keep your secret, will you tell me if you were successful?'

He smiled. 'I did have a swordfight in a boat. Do you suppose that counts?'

'I suppose. Did it have a crew?'

'I presided over a crew of one. My first mate attempted a mutiny, hence the swordfight. Apparently he was tired of rowing.'

'Your first mate didn't happen to be Lord Hartwick?'

Julian laughed and shook his head. 'Actually, it was my brother, Edward.'

That was a new revelation. Why had she never seen his brother at any of the social engagements she had attended?

'I was unaware you had a brother.'

'I did. He was killed in a riding accident nine years ago—a month before my father died.' Pain and loss were reflected in his eyes.

She held out her hand to offer some comfort. He threaded his fingers through hers and then stared at their intertwined hands as if he had never seen his hand placed with another.

'Were you very close?'

A sad smile crossed his lips. 'We were born only ten months apart and were inseparable.'

'You are very fortunate to have had him in your life, even for a short while. I always wanted a brother or a sister to share in my amusements. And I have a sneaking suspicion the two of you might have enjoyed a bit of mischief together.'

His eyes crinkled at the corners as a full smile brightened his previously melancholy demeanour and he let go of her hand. 'We might have found ourselves in trouble a time or two. I recall one autumn we decided to hide in piles of leaves and startle the gardeners as they worked on tidying up the gardens around our estate. I don't believe they found it as amusing as we did.'

'Did you receive a scolding or did news of your antics never reach your parents?'

'My parents were unaware. However, my grandmother informed us that if the gardeners refused to clean up the leaves Edward and I would be forced to do it ourselves.' He rubbed his hands on his thighs, as if he was eager to recount another amusing tale. 'There was also one summer when a vast number of frogs were mysteriously finding their way into my mother's bedchamber.' He let out an uncharacteristically loud bark of laughter. 'To this day I can still recall the sound of her screeches each time she discovered one.'

How was it possible that this reputable duke was more mischievous as a child than she had ever been? The very thought of his very dour mother jumping around her bedchamber made Katrina laugh.

It surprised Julian that there wasn't any hollowness in his chest as he discussed Edward. In fact, in an odd way, he felt closer to his brother now than he had in a long time.

A dragonfly landed on his sleeve and fluttered its wings for a few moments before it flew away.

His brow furrowed. 'Are you eager to head back to America?'

'It's not easy to be away so long from what is comfortable and familiar.'

'I suppose it isn't,' he agreed, out of politeness. All his life everything around Julian had been familiar—everything except the way he felt being with this woman. Being around Katrina made him feel somehow different, somehow more alive.

'I say, Miss Forrester, may I open that bottle of wine for you?' Hart asked as he and Miss Forrester joined them on the blanket.

Julian dragged his gaze away from Katrina. 'Did you enjoy the scenery?'

'Miss Forrester and I took note of every building we were able to see from here—twice.' Hart poured some wine and handed the glass to Katrina's friend. 'I say, Miss Vandenberg, is that pigeon pie?'

'It is, my lord. Would you care for some?'

'Yes, please,' Hart said, sending her one of his charming smiles. 'And you do not have to "my lord" me, Miss Vandenberg. Hartwick will suffice.'

Julian was uncertain if he liked them being on familiar terms. But it was not as if he thought Hart would seduce her. He knew his friend would never betray him. And it most certainly was not that he thought Katrina might prefer gregarious Hart to him.

After the four of them had finished eating most of the delicious food that had been packed into the basket, Hart took off his coat and reclined on the blanket, placing his hands behind his head. 'That was the finest picnic fare I have ever eaten.'

Had his friend forgotten entirely how to act around proper unmarried women?

'Hart, ladies are present. Put your coat back on,' chided Julian.

Hart tilted his head back. 'I am comfortable this way. We are on a picnic, far from prying eyes. Ladies, are you offended by my shirtsleeves? Honestly, it isn't as if I were attempting a seduction.'

In exasperation, Julian threw a strawberry at Hart's head.

'Hey, what was…? Oh, I love strawberries.' He bit into it.

'You will apologise for that last remark.'

'About strawberries? But I really do like them.'

'Not *that* comment, dolt!'

Miss Forrester snorted.

Hart jerked his head around. 'Did that sound come out of such a delicate lady?'

'Apologise,' scolded Julian, losing his patience.

'Fine!' Hart spun around and stood. 'Ladies, I am terribly sorry I have offended you with my shirtsleeves and my glib tongue. It is not often that I find myself in such estimable company, and I will try my best to refrain from offending you in the future. However, I feel I must state that chances are great that I will offend in some way.' He bowed down low with great flourish.

The women exchanged a glance and laughed. 'You are forgiven, Hartwick,' said Miss Forrester with a wave of her hand. 'Keep your coat off if you wish. I assure you Katrina and I will not be offended. It is not such an unusual sight back home.'

Hart turned to Julian. 'America sounds like a place I would enjoy immensely.' He reclined back on the blanket and crossed his hands behind his head.

It was difficult for Julian not to kick him.

Katrina bit into a strawberry and studied Hart's relaxed pose. 'Why do you suppose it isn't proper for a lady to see a man in his shirtsleeves?'

Hart flipped onto his stomach and rested his chin in his hand. 'I was wondering that very thing myself.'

Miss Forrester, who was sitting next to him, raised her wine glass. 'It isn't as if we would swoon at the sight of a man's arms. At least *I* would not.'

'You need to take a closer look at my arms,' Hart stated.

'I see your arms now, Hartwick, and I find myself amazingly upright,' she replied.

Katrina turned to Julian. 'Do you suppose someone

thinks a woman might lose control of her actions if she
sees a man's broad shoulders and muscular arms?'

'Not *all* arms are muscular,' commented Miss Forrester.

Julian shrugged, tying not to think of spending time
with Katrina in a state of undress. His blood pounded
through his veins. 'We could test your theory.'

*Bloody hell! When had he lost the ability to think be-
fore he spoke?*

Hart choked on his Madeira. 'Capital idea, Julian. Why
don't you take your coat off as well?'

Miss Forrester smiled brightly. 'Yes, do, Lyonsdale.
Apparently Hartwick, while finely made, simply is not
causing Katrina and I to question our moral fibre.'

Hart narrowed his eyes at her.

'Well, I did acknowledge that you were finely made,'
she amended. 'However, to test the theory properly we
need more than one subject.'

Both Miss Forrester and Hart stared at him.

'You want me to remove my coat?'

'It was your idea,' Miss Forrester pointed out.

'His Grace never does anything improper,' Hart muttered, refilling Miss Forrester's glass.

Katrina thought that Julian had done nothing *but* act
improperly with her since the moment they'd met. However, she was not about to voice that thought. She had
seen men in their shirtsleeves before. Why was the mere
thought of Julian in his making her feel different? Suddenly she was very eager to see him remove his coat.

He looked over at her. 'What is your opinion on the
matter, Miss Vandenberg? It is your question we are ad-
dressing.'

She rubbed her lips. 'Hartwick in his shirtsleeves is

having no effect on me. I suppose if we are to be scientific on the matter we need you to remove your coat as well.'

He smiled at her and her stomach flipped. 'I am glad to hear he has no effect on you.'

'Yes, yes…we know. I have no effect on the ladies,' Hart said impatiently, with a wave of his hand. 'Just take your damn coat off.'

'Tut-tut, Hartwick. There is no need to resort to such language,' Sarah said in amusement.

'Very well,' Julian said.

Reluctantly, he stood and removed his coat.

The air left her lungs as she watched his brown coat fall away, revealing a broad chest behind his yellow waist-coat and a pair of strong, curved shoulders. Maybe the English were correct. Maybe women should not see men in their shirtsleeves.

'I am sorry,' Sarah said. 'It appears we still have no answer as to why men need to remain in their coat-tails.'

'Wait, Miss Forrester,' Hartwick said slowly. 'Miss Vandenberg hasn't given us her opinion.'

What could she say? *Could you remove your waistcoat and shirt as well?*

She scratched the back of her neck and bit her lip. 'You look very nice without your coat.'

He looked triumphantly at his friend.

'Just because she gave you a compliment it doesn't mean you look better than I do. Miss Vandenberg is being polite and doesn't want to hurt your feelings.'

'This is not a comparison of who looks better, Hart-wick,' Sarah said. 'We are trying to determine if seeing a man in his shirtsleeves causes us to act irrationally.'

'Are you sure, Miss Forrester, that you have no desire to act the least bit irrationally?' Hartwick asked, wig-gling his brows.

'No, Hartwick. I have no desire to do so at all.'

Katrina shifted her gaze to Julian's yellow silk waistcoat and bit her thumb. She had a longing to slide her hands over his firm chest to his broad shoulders. Her gaze edged to those inviting lips of his…

'I have already showed you the view of the river, have I not, Miss Forrester?' Hartwick called out.

'Yes, but I suppose one can never fully appreciate such a lovely view unless one sees it for a second time.'

Julian was staring at Katrina, making her feel incredibly warm.

'We *can* hear you,' he bit out.

Sarah laughed, and Hartwick cleared his throat. 'Would you like us to leave the two of you alone?' he asked.

'That would be highly improper, Hartwick,' Sarah said, 'since His Grace is in his shirtsleeves.'

'Sarah! Honestly…' chided Katrina, narrowing her eyes at her friend.

Julian turned to Hartwick. 'So when I finally do something improper *this* is how you react?'

Hartwick raised his hands in surrender. 'We are only trying to be accommodating. So, I think we have determined the reason why it's improper for men to be seen in their shirtsleeves by ladies.'

Katrina turned to Hartwick. 'No, we have not. Sarah and I are completely composed.'

'Well, *I* am anyway,' muttered her traitorous friend.

'What other rules can we test today?' asked Hartwick eagerly. 'Is there some article of clothing you are not supposed to remove in our presence? I am open to suggestions.'

'You rake!' replied Katrina, laughing. 'Are you trying to get us to show you our ankles?'

'Your hair,' Julian said suddenly.

All three turned to him, and he shrugged.

'A lady's hair is usually pinned up.'

Hartwick sat up. 'That's the spirit. We are in our shirt-sleeves and you owe us a boon. I think Julian has a fine idea. You ladies should take down your hair and Julian and I will see if we can resist you.'

Sarah eyed Hartwick. 'Suppose you lose your senses and your over-amorous nature overcomes you?'

'That's what Julian is here for. He is forever proper.'

'*He* is sitting here in his shirtsleeves,' Katrina pointed out sceptically as she eyed him up and down.

'Oh, please… He has so much restraint that even if his life depended on it he would never touch you. *He* is the epitome of the proper English aristocrat,' Hartwick said, with sarcasm in his voice.

Julian turned to his friend. 'You speak as if being responsible and acting honourably is a bad thing. Maybe you would find yourself in less trouble if you tried it.'

Katrina peered through the lowest hanging branches towards Sarah's barouche. 'What do you think the footmen will say if they see us like this?'

'Do not fret. No one can see us,' replied Hartwick as he chewed on a long piece of grass.

'Why do I believe you have said that before?' Katrina muttered.

'Why, Miss Vandenberg, I am offended,' Hartwick said, bringing his hand to his chest. 'I think there is a bit of fire in you.'

She turned to Julian. 'Was that a compliment?'

The enticing man with the broad shoulders shrugged. 'It's difficult to tell.'

'Of course it was a compliment. A lady with a bit of fire in her is much more enjoyable than a milksop.'

'You thought I was a milksop?'

'No. As I said, you have a bit of fire in you. Miss Forrester, on the other hand, is infinitely boring.'

Sarah shook her head. 'You are only saying that because I did not swoon when you removed your coat.'

'No. For that, I think you may need spectacles. But we are getting away from the point. I believe Julian challenged you ladies to take down your hair?'

'It was hardly a challenge. I was simply curious.'

'I am trying to help facilitate your request,' Hartwick replied impatiently. 'Perhaps you could persuade the ladies. They seem to trust you more than me.'

'I can't imagine why,' muttered Katrina.

Sarah cleared her throat, catching their attention. 'I believe we are testing theories today. Katrina, please remove the pins from your hair.' Sarah began to arrange her own hairpins on the skirt of her cinnamon-coloured gown. 'We can easily re-pin each other shortly.'

Hartwick laughed out loud. 'Well done, Miss Forrester.' He made a show of studying her. 'Now, what colour is that, exactly?' His eyes dropped to his mud-splattered boots and he smiled. 'Oh, I know. You hair is an earthy colour.'

'It is chestnut, Hartwick,' Sarah said, shaking out her hair. 'A gleaming, glossy chestnut. Which you would realise if you weren't so self-absorbed,' she teased.

'*I* am self-absorbed? How many times today have you admired your slippers?'

'What has that to do with anything? I like my new slippers.'

'Apparently so. Julian, have you seen anyone look at their feet…?'

The moment Katrina removed one pin from her hair Julian was transfixed. He watched as little by little ringlets of golden silk cascaded past her neck, down her back, and over the slope of her breasts.

Many nights he had pictured her in his bed with her

hair down, and he had wondered how long it was. Would it cover her breasts if she rode him? Would it bounce against the small of her back as he took her from behind? Now he knew that the ends of her hair curled against the lower curves of her breasts. His mouth began to water as he imagined the feel of her hair against his cheek as he slid his tongue along those breasts...

Before he was aware of what he was doing, he slid his fingers into the soft strands. Everything around them fell away, and the only thing that mattered was the woman next to him. He kissed her softly and she placed her hand on his chest. He deepened the kiss, certain she must feel his heart and soul pounding against her hand.

'I thought you said he was always proper?' Miss Forrester's voice broke the silence.

'He was until he met your friend,' Hart replied.

'Maybe it's your influence.'

'I've tried for years to get him to follow his desires. This is none of my doing.'

'I don't believe they should be doing that, even with us in attendance.'

'It is just a kiss.'

'That is *not* just a kiss, Hartwick.'

'No. I suppose you are correct, Miss Forrester. That definitely is not just a kiss.'

It was the last thing he wanted to do, but Julian managed to pull his head back. Katrina buried her face in his shoulder and he rubbed his cheek against her soft hair.

'We can hear you.' His voice sounded strained, even to his own ears.

'We know,' Hart said, taking a sip of wine.

It had taken all his restraint to leave his hand on Katrina's jaw and not move it to any other part of her body. He was finally able to position one of his legs to hide the strain in his breeches. How could he have kissed her in front of Hart and Miss Forrester? How could the simple act of her taking down her hair have made him so excited? When could he get her alone to continue what they'd started?

'Don't you think it would be a good idea to show Miss Forrester the view?' he suggested to Hart.

His friend smirked at him. 'I have already done so.'

'Perhaps she hasn't seen all that this hill has to offer.'

'I believe I have seen quite a bit of what this hill has to offer,' Miss Forrester said dryly, raising her glass to her lips.

'Do the two of you have something important to tell us?' Hart said, as he crossed his legs in front of him and rocked his boots from side to side. 'You have kissed each other in front of Miss Forrester and me. Should I be requesting pistols at dawn to defend Miss Vandenberg's honour?'

Julian was about to chastise Hart, but Katrina spoke up first. 'Don't be nonsensical, Hartwick. You of all people should understand. It was simply a kiss.'

What did she mean, it was simply a kiss? Had it not been her lips he was kissing? Had she not felt that…that… *thing*?

'So there is no impending announcement you wish to share with us?' Hart asked.

'Heavens, no,' exclaimed Katrina with a light laugh.

Julian studied the woman whose lips were still wet from his kiss. She had moved away, putting distance between them. Did she have to sound so relieved that she would never need to marry him?

To hell with being cautious—he needed to see her alone again.

Chapter Eighteen

Walking among the rose bushes planted along the back wall of her garden, Katrina glanced up at the late morning sky. Earlier in the day, dark clouds had hung low. Now the sun's rays were peeking through, and the air was heavy with the scent of fragrant blooms.

Reaching out with her cutting shears towards a red velvet bud, Katrina winced as she pricked herself on a thorn. How could something so beautiful be so dangerous?

Drawing her hand back, she sucked on her finger. That was the third time she'd pricked herself today. A wise person would know when to stop. There was no sense in risking further injury.

As she stepped onto the gravel path that led to the house a dragonfly flew past, reminding her of the one that had landed on Julian's sleeve during their picnic. All too soon he would be a distant memory. He would marry a woman born to be a duchess—someone who had the family name and connections she did not. And she would return to America, hopefully to find a man who made her feel all the things Julian did. She had to believe that was possible, otherwise when their secret arrangement came to an end it would devastate her.

Wilkins met Katrina as she reached the steps of the terrace. He extended a polite bow. 'You have a caller, miss.'

When she read Madame de Lieven's name on the card she resisted the urge to hide back among the roses. But, after directing Wilkins to show her guest into the drawing room, Katrina removed her apron and went to make herself presentable.

When she entered the drawing room a short while later she found Madame de Lieven seated on the settee by the unlit fireplace, examining the blue Sèvres porcelain urn on the small table next to her. She looked up as Katrina took a seat across from her. They exchanged the usual pleasantries, and it wasn't until the ladies were in the middle of tea that Madame de Lieven broached the expected subject of Mr Armstrong.

'I understand he has sent you flowers?' she said, eyeing a very elaborate floral display of white lilies and pink roses.

'Yes, he has.'

'Why have I not heard that you have been seen together?'

Katrina gave a noncommittal shrug, not sure how to respond to end the questioning.

Madame de Lieven took a long sip of tea and then placed the cup down slowly onto the saucer in her lap. 'He is a man of means, with impressive connections. He will make you a fine husband. When will you see him again?'

'I couldn't say.'

'I will arrange something.'

Was this what it would be like to have Lady Morley for a mother?

Katrina placed her own cup and saucer down on the table. 'That is very kind of you, but as I have already mentioned I have no wish to find a husband here in England.'

'Nonsense. I think you are not as averse to the idea

as you might like me to believe.' She stood and adjusted her gloves. 'It was a pleasure to see you again, Miss Vandenberg.'

'Thank you for your kind visit.' The words were brittle on her tongue, but they came out smoothly.

She walked her guest down to the front door, but before she was free of Madame de Lieven for the day the woman turned with one final question.

'Will you be attending the Hipswitch garden party?'

Having an inkling of what was to come, Katrina took a resigned breath. 'I am. My father will likely be in meetings. I plan to attend with Mrs Forrester and her daughter.'

Madame de Lieven tied her bonnet. 'I'm certain Mr Armstrong will be pleased to hear it.'

Katrina watched her walk down the steps and into her awaiting carriage. It wasn't until the carriage had begun to roll down the street that Katrina closed the door and banged her head gently against the wood. Why hadn't Madame de Lieven focused her attention on Sarah? She would be remaining in London much longer than Katrina, and therefore her potential ties to what was happening in the United States were greater. Unless the woman believed she had more time to forge a friendship of sorts with Sarah and would be hunting her down next.

Hopefully, arranging the flowers she had managed to collect would pull her thoughts from speculating on how bad the Hipswitch garden party was sure to be.

A rustling sound from inside the nearby dining room caught her attention, and she walked to the doorway to see what it was. As she crossed the threshold she was startled by Julian's presence inside the room. He was wearing a navy tailcoat, a white silk embroidered waistcoat, and buckskin breeches tucked into a pair of shiny top boots.

She blinked a few times, trying to make certain that

he was real and not a figment of her wishful imagination. 'What are you doing here?'

'That is a fine way to greet your guest,' he said with an impish grin.

She stepped closer to him and closed the door behind her. 'You are skulking in my dining room. What did you expect me to say?'

He took her hands and pulled her even closer with little resistance. 'I'm not skulking. I came to read with you and was told Madame de Lieven was here. I informed your butler that I would wait for you in here.'

'You asked to wait in my dining room?'

'It is the closest room to your front door. I did not feel it wise to proceed further into your home.'

'You cannot stay. My father is working in his study. If he were to see you, how would we explain your presence?'

'I have an ideal solution. Come for a drive with me. We can read in the carriage.'

He nuzzled her neck and her legs grew weak.

She tilted her head, exposing more of her skin for his kisses. 'Someone will see.'

'We will be in a closed carriage with the drapes drawn.' His soft kisses were turning into nips. 'I promise no one will see us.'

'They'll see me entering it with you. That will never do. You should return another day.'

Turning him away was not what she wanted, but they had no choice. They were sure to get caught.

'I have Hart's unmarked carriage parked in the mews. I'll leave now and have the driver stop in front of your house. No one will know I am inside.'

'I don't know—'

His warm hands cupped her face and he kissed her deeply. Would there ever be a time when his kisses did not affect her so? He pulled back and studied her closely, as if he were looking for a reaction. What that reaction was, she couldn't imagine. A wisp of hair had come loose by her left temple, and she blew at the strand with a puff of air.

'Come for a drive with me before I have to leave for Westminster.' That devilish smile of his was not helping her resolve. 'You know you want to.'

'You are not as charming as you think,' she replied through a reluctant smile.

'Yes, I am.' He laughed low and cradled her neck in his hands. 'The longer we remain here, the greater chance there is for discovery. Now, go and retrieve the book and meet me in the carriage.'

There were times when anticipation and excitement could cloud one's judgement. For Katrina, this was one of those times. 'Very well. I will go with you.'

He held her gaze as he kissed the inside of her wrist. A tingle spread up her arm and down her side. If he continued in this fashion she would be tempted to suggest they lock the door and remain in the dining room all afternoon.

It appeared he had read her thoughts, and he straightened in an overly confident manner. 'I will show myself out. And Katrina…' he adjusted his cuffs '…do hurry.'

She stepped away from the door and his sleeve brushed against her arm as he walked past. Moments later she heard the door to her house open and close. Her heart raced. She tried to catch her breath. Low in her abdomen her muscles flipped as she imagined kissing him again…

It didn't take her long to gather her favourite bonnet and change into a celestial blue satin carriage dress. Grabbing her copy of *Frankenstein*, she dashed down the stairs and out through the door. An unmarked coach of shiny black lacquer was waiting with its curtains closed. Ignoring her uneasy feeling, she accepted help from the footman, stepped inside, and settled on the bench across from Julian.

His surprised expression was visible in the muted light. 'You have changed.'

'It seemed prudent.'

'There was no need. You look lovely in either dress.'

Warmth spread through her at this compliment. Then the carriage jerked and she was rocked back and forth as the horses began their journey. She wished she could peer outside, to see in what direction they were headed.

'Where are we off to?'

'Nowhere in particular. I have instructed the driver to return us to your home in an hour. However, it may prove a challenge to read the book together if you are not seated next to me.'

The carriage, while spacious, was not overly wide. If she sat next to him their bodies would be sure to touch.

She vaulted across the carriage.

His muscular thigh pressed against hers as she nestled her arm next to his and opened the book.

When Julian had arrived at Katrina's home and had been informed Madame de Lieven was already there he should have walked away. Hiding in the dining room with both the Russian Ambassador's wife and Katrina's father on the premises had been dangerous. However, sitting this close to her now, Julian was glad he had listened to the voice that had told him to stay.

Her warm, soft thigh was pressed against his, and that warmth was travelling over to him. It would not take much for him to harden. His body was begging to lay her down under him and explore every inch of her. Had she not been a virgin, that book she was holding would have been tossed somewhere on the floor by now.

He motioned towards the book. 'Shall we begin?'

She nodded and opened the book to a page marked with a worn strip of deep pink silk. With her permission, he took it out and rubbed it lightly between the fingers of his ungloved hand.

'This is true proof that you are a great reader.'

Her soft laugh made him smile. 'It is a remnant from a gown that once belonged to my mother. My Great-Aunt Augusta gave it to me when I was a child. I've kept it ever since.'

'That was very thoughtful of her.'

'She was all that is kindness. The Dowager reminds me of her.'

Had her aunt smuggled gin into assemblies, faked a malady when she wanted her way, and entertained herself in her later years by inserting herself into situations that weren't any of her business? He wasn't inclined to believe so.

Handing the strip back to her, he looked down at the open book. In the low light he would need to squint to read the words. 'Perhaps this isn't the ideal location for reading.'

'*Now* you decide this isn't wise?'

He took her hand and kissed it. 'I still believe being alone with you in this carriage is the finest idea I've had today.'

'You do realise that if this continues I will find myself finishing this book during my journey home to New York.'

The idea of her travelling home burned his gut. When she left England she would not be returning. Ever. A chasm opened in his chest, and he tried to rub it away.

'You once told me you had no interest in marrying anyone in England, and yet Madame de Lieven appeared eager to inform Greely's whelp that you will be at the Hip-switch garden party. Perhaps you've changed your mind?'

She sighed and shook her head. 'I have not. However, Madame de Lieven can be most insistent in her opinions.'

'Do you truly have no wish to live here?'

'On the contrary—I adore London and the sense of the past that surrounds me. I feel as if I could spend years here and I would still find something new to see. It is the men here who hold no appeal.'

As a man residing in London, to him that was rather insulting—no, it was highly insulting. He raised his chin and pulled his shoulders back. 'All men?'

'Yes,' she admitted without hesitation. 'Rather, not *all* but most—you appeal to me.'

'I'm relieved to hear it.'

'Somewhat,' she amended with a mischievous smile. 'However, I believe we were discussing my marrying an Englishman and not simply liking one.'

'Are you this charming with American men as well? It is a wonder you are still unmarried.'

Instead of offending her, his comment made her laugh.

He eyed her sideways. 'What is it that you find so distasteful about Englishmen?'

She was not destined to be his duchess. This was not a conversation he should be having with her. And yet a part of him wondered why she found him an unsuitable choice for a husband.

'We have different views on fidelity,' she blurted out rather abruptly.

Julian jerked his head back, not having expected that to be her reasoning. 'I wasn't aware we had had a discussion on such a subject. I must make a note to pay closer attention to what you say.'

'Don't be glib. I am well aware of what men of your station do, and I do not wish that for my marriage,' she said with a casual lift of her shoulder.

He leaned closer. 'Really? What is it we do?'

'Men of the *ton* marry women for their impressive ancestry or significant fortunes. When they grow bored with their wives they go about with other women.'

Julian's brows drew together. 'Is this about your earlier notion that I have a mistress? I assure you I still haven't taken one.'

'No. It's about you being an English nobleman,' she stated firmly, looking him in the eye in the dim light.

'And because of that you believe I would conduct myself in such a manner?'

'I have no reason to assume otherwise. You once told me that you do not expect a happy marriage, and you found my ideas on love provincial.'

'Opinions can change.'

She crossed her arms and tilted her head, sceptically. 'So now you will tell me you plan to be a faithful husband?'

He didn't want to think about being married to Lady Mary—not when he was sitting with his body pressed against Katrina. He took a deep breath and held in her lemon scent. Deep down he knew he would think of her every time he took Mary to bed. It was not an honourable notion, nor something he would ever admit to anyone—especially the woman sitting beside him waiting for a response.

Why the hell had he started this conversation with her?

'Well?' She was not letting the matter rest.

He needed her to know what kind of man he was. He needed her to see that he was a man who honoured his vows. 'I've already been married and, although the union was arranged by my father, I was faithful.'

It came out in a rush, and he turned his head away from her. He rarely spoke of Emma. It was difficult to take a steady breath.

Katrina fell back against the plush upholstery, her properly erect posture forgotten. 'You were married?' It came out as a whisper. 'We spent all that time together and you never told me.'

'I assumed you knew. Everyone in London is aware that I was married.'

'Well, no one told *me*.' She appeared to wait for him to continue.

He never intentionally discussed Emma. The subject of her death was too personal and much too painful. He tried to scrub the image of her lying dead out of his mind. It had haunted him most nights—at least until he'd met Katrina. That hadn't occurred to him until now.

He looked into her expectant eyes. An unwelcome lump was forming in his throat. 'My wife's name was Emma. She was the youngest daughter of the Duke of Beaumont. Our fathers arranged our marriage while I was away at Cambridge. She died while giving birth to our stillborn son.'

He leaned forward and rested his elbows on his knees. It was easier to move away from Katrina than to continue to look into her eyes.

'To this day I am sorry for her loss and the loss of my child.' *But his regret would never bring them back.*

She brushed the hair by his temple in a comforting gesture. 'I am sorry for your loss too.'

Not knowing what else to say, Julian gave a quick nod.

Katrina continued to stroke his temple. 'My mother died shortly after giving birth to me. My father feels her loss even to this day.'

Julian squeezed his eyes shut and scrubbed his hand across his face. There was comfort in the closed confines of the gently rocking carriage and muted light. It felt…safe.

'I never held him.' The statement left his lips before the thought had fully formed in his head.

The soft pressure of her hand on his back was an unexpected gesture. 'Did anyone ask if you wanted to?'

He shook his head and bit his lip. The lump in his throat was making it difficult to swallow. 'They only asked if I wanted to see him.'

'Did you?'

He nodded as tears that had never been shed rimmed his eyes. The physician and Emma's maid had been so focused on tending to her, they hadn't had time to clean his son. He'd been so small—and so still.

'I should have held him. No one held him.'

She rested her head lightly against his shoulder and a hot tear began to trickle down his face.

'A father should hold his son,' he choked out, 'even if just once. I named him John, after Emma's brother. They had been close, and it seemed only right. I had them buried together. My mother tried to insist John should have his own coffin in the family crypt, but I thought it best for them to be together. She said it was unseemly and that she was certain my father would have felt the same.' He finally looked over at Katrina and saw the shimmer of unshed tears in her eyes. 'What would you have done?'

She slid her fingers through his. 'I think Emma would have wanted to be with John.'

He'd thought so too. The crushing weight of indecision that had plagued him since her burial eased for the first time. He had needed to know he had made the right decision in honouring their memories. He'd needed someone he respected to say it to him. It had eaten away at his conscience for too long. And he knew Katrina would always be honest with him.

She rested her head on his shoulder again. 'I believe deep down we know what the right course of action is. We just need to listen to what our heart tells us. I'm sorry to have caused you to relive such painful memories. I should have realised.'

He kissed the top of her head and took a deep breath. The lump in his throat was dissolving. 'Do not apologise. I needed to hear that you believe they were laid to rest in a proper fashion.'

A comforting silence stretched between them as the carriage rocked them gently through the streets of London. The distant sound of voices and the rolling of the carriage wheels on cobblestones felt oddly comforting.

'I'm certain you're grateful you accepted my invitation today,' he said dryly after some time.

She lifted her head up and offered him a reassuring smile. 'There is no place I would rather be.' She tugged off a white kidskin glove and wiped the wetness from his cheek with the pad of her thumb.

His heart gave an odd flip.

'It's never easy to lose someone we love,' she said, running her thumb along his forehead.

It took him a few moments before he realised she was referring to Emma. 'I did not love her,' he said. 'I liked her enough, but I didn't love her.'

Love was something he knew nothing of. He had not been born to fall in love. He wasn't even certain he would know what love felt like. And yet… How would he define his feelings for the woman next to him? It wasn't love, but what was it?

'I believe I have taken you on a melancholy journey away from our original conversation.'

'I've forgotten what we were discussing,' she said, sitting up.

'We were discussing fidelity. And I think for all your notions about people prejudging you because you are American you are no better.'

'How so?' she asked indignantly.

'You've tarred and feathered the entire male population of the *ton*, accusing us all of infidelity. You believe my title leaves me incapable of devoting myself to one woman. I am informing you that you are wrong in your assessment of me.'

She crossed her arms over those enticing breasts.

'Do not look chastised.' He sat back and rested his head on the cushion behind them. Their conversation today had been far too grim. 'Have I told you how much I have come to appreciate the smell of lemons?' he commented casually.

Even in the muted light of the carriage he could see her faint smile. 'You might have mentioned it a time or two.'

The smile fell from his lips. 'I fear one day I will miss that smell.'

Silence stretched between them, and his heart sank in his chest.

Chapter Nineteen

Katrina was in excellent spirits when Sarah and Mrs Forrester asked her to join them on their shopping excursion along Bond Street two days later. The sun was out and the temperature pleasant, making it an ideal day to meander through the shops. Turning a corner, they noticed a small crowd gathered around the large mullioned window of one particular building. Ever the curious one, Sarah tugged Katrina along to see what was so interesting.

'Oh, it's a print shop,' Sarah said, eyeing the cartoons in each pane of the large window.

'Perhaps we will see someone we know,' Katrina mused as she studied a caricature of the Prince Regent attempting to squeeze his rather large body into a very small corset.

Next to her, an amused Sarah methodically studied each print one by one, letting out a giggle at a few in particular. Suddenly she gave a quick gasp and pulled Katrina out through the crowd. Dragging Katrina to the milliner next door, Sarah pulled Katrina to a stop next to where Mrs Forrester was waiting for them.

'We have a problem,' she announced rather breathlessly.

Mrs Forrester turned a questioning eye to her daughter. 'The two of you have been away from me for only a few moments. What could possibly have happened in such a brief time?'

Katrina caught the look of pity in Sarah's eyes.

Taking Katrina's gloved hand in her own, Sarah leaned closer. 'There is a caricature of you and Lyonsdale in a carriage,' she whispered.

Ice crept up Katrina's spine. *Their secret was out.* It felt as if all the people around them were whispering about her, even though their eyes were still on the prints in the window.

At Mrs Forrester's suggestion they made their way directly to Katrina's home with a stack of the scandalous prints. They had tried to acquire the printing plate, but had been told someone else had purchased it a few hours earlier.

It wasn't until they had entered Katrina's drawing room that she was finally able to study the image.

The illustration showed a carriage with the Lyonsdale crest emblazoned on the door and an American flag flying above, driving through London. Visible through the window was the head of a blonde woman wearing an Indian headdress. Her head was back and her eyes were closed. On top of her was a brown-haired man in his shirtsleeves with his hand on her bare leg, pushing up her skirt. The caption below read *Minding the Savages*.

For the first time in her life Katrina truly thought she might cast up her accounts in front of other people. She dropped down on the settee and let her head fall into her hands. 'How can I show my face in Town after this?'

Crouching down beside her, Mrs Forrester stroked Katrina's back. 'Do not worry, my dear. Anyone who has encountered you thus far has seen you comport yourself as a lady. I am certain this will be forgotten when some new bit of gossip has the tongues wagging.'

The woman was trying to reassure her, but Katrina did not miss the concern in her voice.

'Katrina, I do have to ask—*did* you go for a carriage ride with a titled Englishman?'

She looked into the gentle eyes of the woman who had kindly offered to chaperon her. How could she say she had been secretly seeing Lyonsdale? The woman would never look at her the same way again.

Needing to put distance between them, Katrina jumped up and headed towards the window. It was time to confess everything.

'Mother, it was all my fault,' Sarah blurted out. She looked regretfully at Katrina. 'Please forgive me. I never thought this would happen.'

What was Sarah saying?

Mrs Forrester stared at her daughter with trepidation. 'What did you do?'

'Do you recall when Katrina and I went on that picnic? Well, two gentlemen we are acquainted with happened upon us, and I asked them if they would care for refreshment. They sat with us for a time and then went on their way. It was all very innocent, but our footman or coachman must have told a tale.'

Mrs Forrester rubbed her eyes, as if she could wipe the image of the caricature from her mind. Katrina had already tried that. It didn't work.

The woman took both of Sarah's hands and looked her in the eye. 'Who were the gentlemen?'

'The Duke of Lyonsdale and the Earl of Hartwick.'

Mrs Forrester's loud groan filled the room. 'Sarah, you *didn't*?'

Sarah's hands fisted at her sides as she tried to defend her action. 'The hour was very early. I was certain no one would see.'

But this image clearly showed an exaggerated version

of what had occurred as Katrina drove through Mayfair with Julian. This was not a depiction of the picnic.

She began to tremble, and drops of cold sweat dusted her skin. 'What will I tell my father?'

Mrs Forrester quickly took her by the arm and gently lowered her to the settee. 'Have no fear. I will talk with him first. There might be a way we can avoid a scandal. I doubt the Duke of Lyonsdale has any desire to enter into one.'

Julian's reputation meant everything to him. If his family name suffered because of the implications of the caricature he would hate her for ever.

Her stomach dipped and flipped. Running to the potted palm in the corner of the room, Katrina reached it just in time.

Later that afternoon, in the Palace of Westminster, Julian was taken aback when he entered the Chamber of the House of Lords and a hush fell over the stately room. Appraising faces turned his way, and for the first time in his life he was confronted with critical stares from many of his peers. He had been up late last night and home all morning, finalising the speech he was about to give. What could he have possibly done to warrant such a reaction?

The white-haired Duke of Skeffington toddled up to him. His bloodshot eyes studied Julian over his wire-framed glasses. He was the oldest duke in the chamber, and liked to remind everyone of the deferential treatment he should be given because of it.

He rapped his cane on the floor, narrowly missing Julian's foot. 'Well, boy? Explain yourself.'

They were frequently on opposing sides in this room. His eagerness to hear what Julian had to say was unusual, but it could perhaps be attributed to the man's recent bouts of narcolepsy.

'I will explain myself when it's my turn to address the chamber,' Julian said, ready to push past him.

'I don't give a fig about your speech. I am speaking of you and the American.'

Julian's blood ran cold and every muscle in his body locked. He could not possibly have heard the man correctly. 'I beg your pardon?'

'You have ancestors who were killed by their hands in their war for independence, and now you engage in behaviour such as this? It's disgraceful,' he spat out. 'Your father would have been appalled by your actions.'

He tapped the handle of his cane into Julian's chest before he walked away, unconcerned with a reply.

Julian broke out into a cold sweat. How did Skeffington know about Katrina? He had been so careful. His thoughts turned to their drive through Town. They had been in an unmarked carriage with the curtains drawn. Surely no one had seen them?

More eyes were upon him, and heat crept up his neck. The Duke of Winterbourne came to stand beside him, carrying himself with his usual commanding air. It was a relief to see a friendly face.

'That was quite an entrance you made,' said Winter, casually adjusting his cuff under his robe. 'I imagine Skeffington was gracious enough to offer his opinion on the matter?'

'He was his usual charming self,' Julian managed to say through his bewilderment.

'You surely must have realised that when word got out it would be remarked upon. Both Ardsley and Brendel lost their youngest in our last skirmish with the Americans. Lockwood's two brothers died in America's war for independence. And those are just the men around us. Many men in this room lost family members there, and they place the blame on the colonials. But I do not need to remind you of that.'

He motioned for them to make their way through the crowd and take their seats.

'I do not understand why I am garnering such a reaction now, after dancing with the woman weeks ago,' Julian said.

A look of amused confusion crossed Winter's face. 'You do not know what this is about?'

'Know what?'

'There was a caricature published about you today, my friend. A rather suggestive one about you and an American. The question is, how accurate is it?'

Their secret was out. He needed to see this print. Unfortunately, the session was about to begin.

Bloody hell! How could he answer for something when he wasn't quite certain what he was being accused of?

As the room began to settle down Lord Allyn approached them and nodded a greeting. Julian was expecting his friend to wish him luck today—instead Allyn had a request.

'I'm aware you're scheduled to present your speech today, Lyonsdale. However, with recent events being what they are, I think it best if you refrain from giving it.'

Confused, Julian tried to grasp what Allyn was saying. He had worked on his speech for weeks. He had been asked to deliver it because he was an influential peer, and his speeches were known to sway voters. Now, because of one print, he had become a liability.

'Perhaps Allyn is right,' Winter said in a low voice as he leaned forward.

'Et tu?'

'Listen to him.' Winter pointed towards Allyn. 'This is not an attack on you.'

'Of course it is,' Julian said with quiet emphasis.

'No. It's about certain men who won't listen to you because they will be focusing on the possible scandal surrounding you—a man renowned for your moral character—and an unmarried American.'

Scandal.

Bile rose up in his throat. His family had been untouched by scandal for generations. Would he be the one to let their good name fall? He thought of the Fifth Duke— the one who wasn't fit to have his portrait hung in the gallery. Was that to be his fate?

Clenching his jaw so tightly it might have shattered, Julian shifted his gaze to the row of peers next to him. His pride was crushed. The last thing he needed to see was pity in his friends' eyes.

'Fine. You drafted this speech with me—you give it.' His composure started slipping as he thrust his notes at Winter.

An indecipherable expression passed between his friends, and Allyn gave a brief tip of his head before returning to his seat.

Winter leaned sideways and lowered his voice to a whisper. 'I suggest you find a way to calm yourself before you draw even more attention your way. You are passionate about your work here. You always have been. But you are not the only one of us who can reach these men and change their minds. You are not a party of one man.'

Julian knew that to be true. But he also knew that the career and reputation he had built for himself was the most important thing in his life. It was the legacy he would leave to future generations. How could he have risked all of it for a few stolen hours with a woman? The problem was, it wasn't just any woman—it was Katrina. And, although he was chiding himself for being so incredibly foolish, he knew he would recall every minute of those hours they spent together for the rest of his days.

Oh, God, what had he done? He had promised Katrina he wouldn't do anything to risk her reputation. If only he had been honourable enough to make that so.

His stomach pitched. There was no telling if her reputation was beyond repair until he saw the print.

Katrina rolled off her wet pillow and stared up at what she knew were blue flowers stitched onto the cream silk that hung from the top of her tester bed. But the image was blurred from the teardrops clinging to her lashes and she rubbed her palms over her eyes. That was better. Now, if she could only concentrate on the details of the flowers and not on the image that had been haunting her for the past four hours...

It was no use. Once more she could see the scandalous caricature of her and Julian—a caricature that announced to all of England that she was a lightskirt. How could she show her face in London Society again?

Agreeing to go for a ride with Julian was probably the most foolish thing she had ever done. Now their time together was surely over, and scandal would follow her.

Her heart ached and she wasn't sure it would ever be the same. She was such a fool! How could she have thought her feelings would not become engaged? It had happened so gradually there had not been one particular instance. Had there been, she might have had a chance to resist him.

She smothered her face with her pillow and let out a scream. The problem was she cared too much. She cared that right at that very moment he was probably telling himself he was better off without her. He would never want this kind of attention cast his way.

She thought she heard a knock, but she wasn't certain since she was still squashing the pillow over her head. Tossing it aside, she sat up and looked at her door. There

was another knock, and Katrina groaned at the intrusion.
It was probably Meg, trying to get her to have some tea.
What she really needed was something a bit more fortifying. This would be an excellent time to try the brandy
her father kept in his study. Perhaps if she drank enough
of it she would forget this day had ever happened.

The knocking grew louder. She slid off the bed and
trudged to her door. Opening it slightly, she jumped when
a foot encased in gold silk damask pushed its way inside.

'If you close this door on my new slipper I shall be
vexed.'

Katrina closed her eyes and took a deep breath, preparing herself for Sarah. Opening the door wider, she invited her friend inside and locked the door behind them.

Sarah tugged off her white kid gloves and tossed them
carelessly onto the rumpled bed. Spinning around, she ran
her gaze over Katrina.

Brushing the wetness away from her face, Katrina
avoided Sarah's piercing stare. The last thing she wanted
was to see pity in her friend's eyes.

'You look as if a bear has sat on your head.'

'Forgive me. Had I known you were planning on calling I would have been sure to have Meg arrange an elaborate coiffure.'

Sarah made her way over to the window and sat at Katrina's dressing table. Picking up a brush, she appeared to
study the monogram engraved into the silver. 'If anyone
enquires if I have been here this evening, please inform
them that you have not seen me.'

'Why?'

'Because I was told quite firmly not to disturb you.'

'By whom?'

Sarah tapped the brush in her palm. 'My mother. Luckily your very proper English butler has taken a shine to me,
otherwise I don't know when I would have seen you next.'

Katrina trudged back to her bed and sat on the edge across from Sarah. 'I am not very good company right now.'

'So I can see. I knew you'd take this to heart. But it might not be as horrid as you think.'

'Of course it is. That caricature has announced to all of London that I am a woman of loose morals who let herself be compromised in a carriage!'

'Katrina, those caricatures are meant to be satires. They aren't meant to be viewed in a literal sense.'

'I am aware of that, but the implication is there. It's very humiliating.' She flopped onto her back and covered her eyes. 'And I have tried very hard to act in accordance with all the *ton's* ridiculous rules.'

The bed dipped as Sarah sat next to her. 'Anyone who has met you will know that the drawing is a gross exaggeration of your character.'

'I disagree—many will believe all American women conduct themselves as such.'

'Some people already had those notions before we even stepped ashore. In time, as more and more American women arrive in England, people here will have a better understanding of our true character.'

Katrina raised herself up on her elbows and her eyes met Sarah's soft amber gaze. 'Why is it that I am the one who has garnered all this attention? Madame de Lieven doesn't pester you. The papers do not write about the gentlemen you dance with, and you have never been the subject of a scandalous caricature.'

'You are more attractive than I am.'

'You are simply saying that to try to improve my disposition.'

Sarah's lip twitched. 'Yes, that is true. Everyone knows *I'm* the pretty one.'

Katrina managed to smile before her thoughts turned

back to Julian. 'Lyonsdale cannot be pleased by this. He prides himself on being above reproach.'

'Has he called on you today?'

Katrina shook her head, not wanting to consider the significance of his absence.

'Katrina, that man is taken with you. I doubt a bit of satire will give him cause to announce that he will marry Lady Mary Morley.'

'Lady Mary?'

'Yes. She is the only other woman I've seen him dance with, and I hear she has the approval of his mother.'

Oh, God! Katrina flopped down again. All this time she had been worried about his association with Lady Wentworth. What she should have been worried about was how she would feel when Julian announced that he would marry the very proper, very respectable Lady Mary Morley.

She started sobbing, convinced she wouldn't stop till morning.

Chapter Twenty

As Julian sat in his elegant coach he leaned his head back and took a deep breath. The rocking motion was contributing to the queasiness that had been plaguing him. He closed his eyes, grateful to be away from the prying eyes of Westminster.

Winter had given the speech he'd been supposed to give. Knowing that if he had delivered the same address some of those men would actually have cast their votes in opposition was humiliating. The words 'foolish' and 'disgraceful' were still knocking about in his head.

His stomach pitched again.

Two months ago he hadn't even known Katrina existed. He'd been respected, focused and content. As much as he hated to admit it, his mother had been correct. A man in his position was made for contentment—not some intangible emotion that made him feel as if he were standing on the edge of a cliff not certain if he was ready to jump off.

Katrina had turned his life upside down.

He wanted his orderly life back.

The only way he knew how to get that was to cut his ties with her and pursue Lady Mary Morley. Lady Mary was the ideal woman for a respectable duke.

His chest tightened. He squeezed his eyes shut and tried

to take a deep breath. But if Katrina's reputation was in question he would have no choice but to do the honourable thing. He was an honourable gentleman before all else.

Dammit, he needed to see this print!

His carriage slowed to a stop and he stormed into his home, prepared to contact his secretary and obtain a copy of the print. He stopped when he was informed that Hart was waiting for him in his study. Dealing with Hart was *not* what he needed at the moment.

'Finally!' Hart said from where he sat reclining at Julian's desk, with his ankles crossed, a brandy in his hand. 'I have been waiting here for hours.'

'I am in no mood. Finish your drink and go.' He knocked Hart's boots off his desk.

'That's a fine thank you for all my efforts today. Are you aware that there is a caricature of you and the lovely Miss V?'

'I am. However, I'm warning you. Do not toy with me. I will not be responsible for my actions.'

'Then you've seen it?'

Julian strode across the room and poured himself two fingers of brandy. 'No, I intend to acquire one tomorrow.'

'Luckily for you I've brought one with me to give to you.'

The pounding of Julian's heart echoed in his ears as his gaze was drawn to the paper resting on his desk. He took a long gulp of brandy and moved slowly to get a closer look. When he spotted his crest on the carriage door he saw red. Burning with rage, he let his eyes scan the print illustrated by Cruikshank. He crumpled the paper and threw it across the room.

'I will destroy him!'

'I must confess I never thought I'd see the day your likeness appeared in a print shop window.'

Julian was so enraged he barely heard his friend's words. 'Tell me you have the plate!'

Shaking his head, Hart narrowed his eyes. 'Odd, but when I enquired I was told the plate had already been sold. Perhaps Vandenberg bought it.'

Julian dropped down into a chair. *Dear God, Katrina will hate me when she sees this!* Her reputation was in tatters, and it was all because he had been selfish enough to risk her good name for a few extended hours with her before he committed his life to an unhappy marriage. What kind of man did that make him?

He was a man of honour, and he would fix this.

He turned to Hart. 'I need to borrow your coach.'

Julian sat across from Mr Vandenberg in the man's study and wondered if Katrina's father had poisoned the brandy he had just poured for him. The man was not pleased. That was plain to see from his stern expression and detached demeanour.

'I wondered if you would call here,' he said in a controlled tone. 'The hour is rather late.'

In all his life he had never been uncomfortable sitting across from a man. He was now. 'I was in session today. However, I felt it best to discuss matters before word travels further than it already has.'

Mr Vandenberg sat back in his wingback chair. The amber liquid in his glass held his attention. 'I see. Am I to assume you are here to discuss a certain caricature?'

'I am.' He had never asked for anyone's hand before. He probably should have thought about what to say before he'd entered Katrina's home.

'I have been assured it is not an accurate depiction of events. Is that true?'

His heart dropped at the realisation that Katrina had

been forced to explain her actions to her father. What exactly would she have told him? 'No, sir, it is not. I—'

Mr Vandenberg held up his hand. 'There is no need to continue, Your Grace. I imagine you are here to offer an honourable solution to this unfortunate matter. However, I assure you that won't be necessary. You have no wish to marry my daughter, and she has no wish to marry you. There is a way to address this without forcing you both into a trip to the altar.'

He should have felt relief at the words. Instead, hearing that Katrina didn't want to marry him was like a hard fist into his gut. 'I don't understand.'

Mr Vandenberg folded his hands on his desk and pierced Julian with his gaze. 'If you voice an interest in the upcoming negotiations between our two countries people will assume that the print is a satirical depiction of your interest in the United States and not a bit of gossip about a scandalous ride with my daughter.'

The suggestion ruffled Julian's principles. He sat up taller and pulled his shoulders back. 'That almost sounds like blackmail.'

'Not at all. I am not asking you to voice your support of my country—just to meet with me at the Chancery so we can discuss the issues. You are known to be a fair and honest man. You can make up your own mind if you think we are being unreasonable with the boundaries we are suggesting. Regardless of what you decide, you can express your opinions on the matter openly and present that print as a political satire attacking your involvement with us.'

It was not an unreasonable request. The logic behind it was sound. He hadn't admitted to anyone today that he had actually taken a drive with Katrina. They could each move forward with their own lives and there would be no scandal associated with their names. He could have his reputation back.

'There is one more thing, Your Grace.'

Julian cleared his vision and focused on the man across from him.

'Whatever fascination you have with my daughter, it needs to end now—for both your sakes.'

All Julian could do was nod his agreement. Blackness was swallowing him up as he realised that he would never again know what she was thinking, or receive one of her smiles, or make her laugh.

Their time together was over.

Katrina waited until the front door had closed before she stood up from where she had been perched on the top step of the staircase.

Her father did not even have to look up. 'He has agreed to my proposition. It is done.'

Those three little words sliced into her.

He wasn't going to marry her.

Tonight her father gave him an easy way to avoid scandal—and he had taken it.

'It is for the best, my dear.'

If it truly was, why did her heart feel as if it had been ripped into tiny pieces that would never be put back together? How could this be for the best when the man she loved had just walked away without even saying goodbye?

Chapter Twenty-One

'Men are dogs.'

Surveying a plate of sweet delicacies, while seated at a table on the terrace of Hipswitch House, Katrina wished she could openly agree with Sarah's declaration. Unfortunately she knew that if she did, it would instigate a discussion that would open the wound she was trying desperately to heal.

She had foolishly fallen in love with a man who was more concerned with what the world thought of him than he was with her. If Julian believed she was lacking, then he deserved a life devoid of the love she could give him. She only wished she could feel that way without wanting to dissolve into a puddle of tears each time she thought of him.

Sarah leaned closer from her seat beside Katrina. 'I said men are dogs.'

'I heard you.' Katrina finished her last bite of moist almond cake and eyed a small bowl of trifle.

'Am I to receive no reply?'

The trifle looked lovely. The creamy custard and vibrant red strawberries were calling out to her. One could not take a beautifully made creation such as this and not eat it. It would be an insult to her hosts.

'What would you have me say?' Katrina said, scooping up a large spoonful.

Sarah sipped her champagne and silently watched Katrina savour every last bit of trifle in the bowl. 'Surely you do not intend to eat those Shrewsbury cakes as well?'

Katrina's hand froze midway to the plate containing three biscuits. She did not miss the censure in Sarah's tone. 'I might have thought about it.' She shifted her hand to pick up her glass of champagne instead.

'I am aware that you would be content to sit here and assist Lady Hipswitch in trying all the delicacies she has provided, however, it is a garden party.' She gave the rolling lawns and hedgerows a marked glance. 'I believe it is customary to actually venture into the garden.'

It was safer on the terrace. This was where the desserts were. Katrina liked it here. Julian might be out there somewhere.

'Why would you want to risk the pristine condition of your slippers on grass and soil when you can sit on this lovely stone terrace and admire the view from up here?'

Sarah took another sip of champagne and sighed. 'Because for once I have found myself in a lovely garden during the day, and I am sitting up here when I could be exploring the rose garden or the maze. Haven't you always wanted to attempt to find your way out of a maze?'

Katrina took a Shrewsbury cake. 'I would rather eat biscuits.'

When she went to take another, Sarah grabbed her hand. 'This will not end well if you do not move from that chair. It is a wonder you are not complaining of stomach pains.'

She hadn't eaten that many desserts. Had she…?

Katrina licked her lips and wiped her mouth with a pristine white napkin that now held traces of custard. 'Oh, very well. However, should you ruin those slippers you have talked of endlessly it will not be my doing.'

Sarah stood and opened her white parasol, shading her eyes from the afternoon light. 'I will risk these stunning silk creations just so you do not become permanently affixed to that chair.'

Before Sarah turned back, Katrina grabbed the last Shrewsbury cake and took a big bite.

'I can hear you chewing,' Sarah commented from over her shoulder as she made her way to the terrace steps.

They passed a number of guests who nodded polite greetings while they walked down the stone staircase and scanned the gardens before them.

'Where shall we go first?' Sarah asked.

Katrina's new bonnet shielded her eyes from the sunlight as she looked to her right. An archery competition was taking place in the shade of a large tree, between six stylishly dressed gentlemen in tailcoats, breeches and boots. Ladies and gentlemen stood about in small groups, offering their encouragement. Her heart ached.

Afraid of seeing Julian, she looked to the left and allowed her gaze to roam around the rose garden, which was enclosed with a low boxwood border. It was there that she had spoken to Madame de Lieven earlier in the day. It seemed to be where she was still holding court. Speaking with the woman once today had been enough.

The safest destination was probably ahead of them, where an enormous thick privet hedgerow divided the vast lawn in half and directed the eye to the garden's maze off in the distance.

Katrina waved towards the hedgerow. 'There are paths on either side. Which one should we take?'

Sarah chose the one on the right, and they started down the gravel path as a soft breeze blew against Katrina's cheeks. She kept her attention on the maze instead of on the carefree people strolling around the lawn, afraid she would see Julian or Mr Armstrong.

'You cannot avoid Lyonsdale for ever,' Sarah said, adjusting her parasol.

Katrina ripped a leaf from the hedgerow and tossed it aside. 'I am not avoiding him.'

'You've hidden yourself away in your room for three days.'

'I was absorbed in some good books.' She plucked another leaf.

'Katrina, soon you will return to New York and meet a man who will become so captivated with you that you will consume his thoughts. He will not be afraid to do whatever is necessary to be with you. You will fall in love, and you will forget all about Lyonsdale.'

Just the sound of his name was like a foot crushing the pieces of Katrina's shattered heart.

'And you know this for a fact?' Katrina certainly did not.

Sarah gave her a reassuring smile. 'I do. You will find love, Katrina. Of that I have no doubt.'

She had found love, only her love wasn't returned.

She could not discuss this with Sarah. Not here. Not now. Possibly not ever. How she wished they had never left the safety of the terrace.

They walked side by side in silence as the gravel crunched under their feet. The maze was still a distance away. If she got lost inside it, could she remain in there for ever? Spending the rest of her life trying to find her way out might keep her from thinking about Julian and recalling every moment they'd spent together.

She needed to keep her thoughts from drifting to him. 'Madame de Lieven has been so kind as to inform me that Mr Armstrong is in attendance today.' She plucked another leaf. 'She even saw fit to say that he had accepted today's invitation with the express desire to see me.'

Sarah scanned the grassy lawn to their right. 'It would be easier to avoid him if we knew what colour he was wearing.'

'Men like him should wear garish shades to match their personalities.'

'If only it were proper to run away if we see him approaching.'

Katrina plucked yet another leaf and tore this one is two. 'Whoever drafted these English rules of conduct must certainly have been a man.'

'A very *boring* man,' Sarah amended, adjusting her parasol.

Katrina looked past Sarah and immediately wished she hadn't. Madame de Lieven was strolling with Mr Armstrong, and from the way she was examining the ladies around her, it was apparent she was searching for someone in particular. The woman was much too persistent. Katrina feared that in a moment of weakness she might agree to allow Madame de Lieven to chaperon her on an outing with that windsucker.

She needed to reach the maze—and she needed to do it quickly.

She grabbed the handle of Sarah's parasol and tilted it, obscuring their faces from the guests on the lawn.

As Julian walked down the gravel pathway on the back lawn of Hipswitch House with Hart, he tugged at the brim of his John Bull hat to shield his eyes from the sun. They walked in silence, each consumed with their own thoughts, and Julian stared at the garden's maze in the distance.

He had not attended any social engagements since the day he had been humiliated by Cruikshank's caricature.

He had tried to convince himself it was because he needed to spend time learning the issues surrounding Britain's North American territories. But he knew the real reason he had not ventured out was because it would have been agonising to see Katrina again.

Days had gone by since his agreement with her father—days when Julian had worried over whether he had made the right decision. They might have been married by now. Instead he had sat alone in his study, reading every word of Katrina's father's book and searching the text for anything that might have been a reference to her. He had even tried reading the remainder of *Frankenstein*, but it was too painful a reminder that now he was all alone. Never again would her lemon scent drift towards him as she leaned on his shoulder while they read together.

The nights were worse. He would toss and turn, and dream about losing her all over again. He hadn't had a decent night's sleep in days. If this continued he was certain to drift off in the middle of his next speech. That was why he had decided to come here today. Seeing her from a distance might somehow put his decision to rest.

'Do you have a destination in mind?' Hart asked, breaking into his thoughts. 'Or are we to continue to pace this path all day?'

'There is no need for you to remain in my company.'

Hart tipped his hat to some passing gentlemen they often saw at Tattersalls. 'Winter and Andrew suggested I join them for archery. However, Lady Morley has been enquiring about you for weeks. Fortunately for you, my reputation is not nearly as impeccable as yours. She will never approach you with Lady Mary while I'm near.'

The thought of conversing with Lady Morley made his head pound. 'Perhaps it's time I become accustomed to her company.' He ripped a leaf off the hedgerow of privets that ran along the pathway to his right.

'And perhaps I have a desire to have leeches suck my body dry.'

'I think it's time I offered for her.'

The silence between them was deafening.

'That is what you truly want?'

Julian continued to stare straight ahead of him. 'It's time.' The maze in the distance was getting closer.

From the corner of his eye, he saw Hart shake his head.

'That is not what I asked.'

'I need an heir.'

'And Lady Mary Morley is to be your choice to give you one?'

'She is the perfect choice to become Duchess of Lyonsdale.' A lump settled in Julian's throat, as if blocking the words.

Silence.

'The perfect choice for who? For your mother? For the Lyonsdale Dukes lying in your family's crypt? She certainly is not the perfect choice for *you.*'

Julian stopped and rounded on Hart. 'She is the perfect choice to bear the next Duke. She is the perfect choice to bear my son.' The words tasted false even as he spat them out.

'And what if you only have daughters? Will it still feel as if you made the perfect choice in choosing Lady Mary?'

He needed to speak of something else—anything else. He had regained his political clout. His opinions had weight once again. That was what mattered in life. That was the life his father had led.

'Morley approached me last night at White's. He wanted my views on the fate of the Hudson Bay Company when the Anglo-American Conference convenes. I'm assuming he holds substantial interest in the company and is concerned his investment may suffer.'

'So now you have become a respected voice on the

facts behind the upcoming negotiations between Britain and America? Interesting how you were able to achieve that.'

Julian refused to look at Hart, and instead ripped off another leaf from the hedgerow. 'I find I'm becoming more and more interested in the matters that need to be settled between our two countries. It is in our best interests to try to achieve amiable relations with them. We need the trade, and that last war with them cost us unnecessarily.'

'Perhaps you have found your purpose. Each of the Lyonsdale Dukes is known for something glorious. Improved Anglo-American relations might be your achievement. A bitter irony, it seems.'

Julian glanced over at his friend and caught the mocking glint in his eyes. This time Julian grabbed an entire stem from the hedge and pulled all the leaves off. They fluttered to the ground, unwanted. With each step the sound of crunching gravel was loud over the silence that stretched between them. He closed his eyes and reminded himself that he would forget her.

Hart adjusted his lazy lock of hair. 'She is here. I spotted her earlier today up at the house.'

Julian's dying heart stirred. 'I told you I have no wish to ever discuss her again.'

'I have not mentioned anyone by name.'

Julian glared at Hart, and he was wise enough not to make any further comment.

Hart's attention followed the new group of leaves that Julian was yanking from the hedgerow. 'Hipswitch's gardeners might take umbrage at your pruning techniques.'

Damn the gardeners!

Julian clasped his hands behind his back. Hart would never understand that Julian couldn't even say her name without causing a stabbing pain in his chest. He knew that eventually she would be a distant memory. There would even come a day when he'd wake up and not recall her face. His stomach churned at the notion.

'Well, this should improve that pained expression of yours,' Hart said. 'It's the woman you've been so eager to see.'

Julian closed his eyes. He prayed he would remain composed when he looked at the lovely woman he could not have. Taking a deep breath, he followed Hart's gaze— and froze when he spotted Lady Morley, walking towards them across the lawn with a determined stride.

The maze was not too far ahead. Hopefully he would reach it before Lady Morley caught up to them.

Helena settled onto a bench facing the entrance to the Hipswitch maze and opened her grey silk parasol, sharing the shade with the Duchess of Skeffington. The day had been fruitless so far. The only other eligible duke who wasn't decrepit was a recluse who never came to London. She had no chance of securing him, and the thought of sharing her marriage bed with a wrinkly old man, even if he was a duke, made her stomach turn.

Today she was focusing her quest on finding a marquess. It was possible Lord Boreham had enough funds to be the answer to her prayers. She was rapidly running out of money. She needed to work quickly, but she had yet to see him.

Her friend adjusted her gloves with a satisfied smile on her face. 'I believe Lord Andrew missed his target today because he was distracted by my presence.'

The only reason Lord Andrew had missed the target was because he'd sneezed at an unfortunate moment. When would Lizzy learn that this brother of the Duke of Winterbourne had no interest in her? *The poor, deluded woman.*

'I asked Olivia if she thought her brother-in-law would be attending the Finchleys' masquerade,' continued Lizzy, 'but she informed me she isn't privy to Lord Andrew's schedule and walked off rather abruptly. That was rather rude, was it not?'

'Olivia and Winterbourne barely speak to one another. What would make you believe she would know what his brother does? Lord Andrew has made no advance towards you in ten years. Do you truly believe the man is attracted to you in any way? He barely acknowledges you.'

Lizzy huffed and turned away. 'Have you chosen a costume for the Finchleys' masquerade?'

This was Lizzy's latest way of reminding Helena that she was the one married to a duke. She knew Helena had no association with the Finchleys.

She could go to the devil!

'No, I'm afraid I've not been invited.'

Lizzy's eyes grew wide with false innocence and she blinked. 'Oh, forgive me. I was certain you would have been. The Marchioness is usually so generous with her invitations. The Americans are even invited. I wouldn't have broached the subject if I'd thought an invitation had not been extended to you. That would have been most unkind of me.'

'And you are all that is good and kind,' Helena replied in an overly sweet manner.

'My, you are in a foul mood today. If you'd had a desire to attend all the most sought-after pleasures of the Season perhaps you should have married a man who had a better standing than the one you did.'

'It wasn't as if I had a choice.'

'Well, you should have selected a more discreet place for your romp with Wentworth, then.'

'How was I to know that that area of his father's estate

had a riding path not far away? I thought he would have had more sense.'

'I really did believe when we came out together you were going to be the one who made the best match. You were the most sought-after girl that Season. Well, there is no going back. You should try to improve your station now, at least.'

As if she hadn't been trying for the last five years!

She had done everything possible to marry a marquess or a duke. And all her efforts had exploded in her face.

Lord Blackwood had even had the nerve to laugh at her when she'd reminded him that he'd promised to wed her if she helped him remove Lady Caroline Shaw from his son's life. She'd never understood why he had wanted to separate her from Lord Hartwick, but if Helena had gained the title of marchioness and the wealth she deserved she really wouldn't have cared. And now Lyonsdale had left her. She was running out of available wealthy men with prominent titles.

Miss Vandenberg strolled past them, deep in conversation with her friend. As they entered the maze Helena wondered for the hundredth time what it was about her that Lyonsdale found attractive.

'I assume there is no opportunity to reconcile with Lyonsdale now that he is pursuing the American?'

Helena snapped her head towards Lizzy. 'What are you talking about? That caricature was merely a political satire. Everyone has heard how involved he has become in the details of the relations between our two countries. There is nothing between them.'

'That is not what Blackwood said when I spoke with him at Carlton House last night.'

If Lizzy mentioned dining at Carlton House one more time, Helena would be shoving her down a flight of stairs the next time the opportunity presented itself.

'And what *did* he say?'

Lizzy's mouth curved into a satisfied smile. 'He said he found it vastly entertaining that after spending time in *your* bed Lyonsdale preferred an American. He said that if there was any truth to the notion that Lyonsdale would make her his duchess, then every member of the *ton* would finally say what he has always known to be true…that, as pretty as you are, you do not have the character of a real lady.'

Helena's grip strangled her parasol handle. *Lord Blackwood should die a slow and painful death!*

She would not be made into a mockery by Lyonsdale's perverse interest in Vandenberg's daughter. She would rather die than be the subject of the derision of the *ton*. Who would want her then? As it was, she was much older than the girls most men sought for a bride. And Wentworth had left her with no children. To any titled gentleman needing an heir that made her a questionable choice.

She'd thought she had seduced Lyonsdale sufficiently that he would be willing to take the risk. She had been wrong.

Lyonsdale couldn't possibly choose an American over her. It would mean disaster for her marriage prospects. She knew Boreham valued his opinion more than any man should. If he thought Lyonsdale preferred an American over her, he never would consider her a suitable choice for his marchioness. She was running out of money. If she didn't marry soon, she didn't know what she would do. She couldn't appeal to her brother for help. The insolent nob would rather see her live in the streets than offer her assistance.

As fate would have it, at that very moment Lyonsdale appeared from the path that ran along the hedgerow and strolled into the maze with Hartwick. The very same maze Miss Vandenberg had entered a short time ago. Helena clenched her jaw to prevent herself from screaming. It couldn't possibly be true. He *couldn't* have left her for an American!

'Was that Lyonsdale who just walked into the maze? What an odd coincidence. I thought I saw Miss Vandenberg enter it earlier,' Lizzy said with a bemused expression.

It was taking all Helena's effort not to beat Lizzy with her parasol. 'I hadn't noticed.'

This was not to be her fate. She would *not* be taken to debtors' prison. She would find a way to end this association between Lyonsdale and the American for good—before it was too late.

Chapter Twenty-Two

As Katrina and Sarah strolled further into the maze the sound of rhythmic splashing grew louder. After making yet another right turn, they were rewarded with the sight of a marble fountain situated in the middle of a large gravel-covered square. The statue at the centre of the fountain was of a Greek or Roman woman, with water pouring from the urn in her hand and splashing into the pool below her. If Katrina had saved all the tears she'd cried over Julian they would have filled numerous urns.

She took off one of her white silk gloves embroidered with forget-me-nots and skimmed her fingers through the cold water in the fountain's base. 'It is lovely here.'

'I told you we would reach the centre. Now let's find a way out.' Sarah marched across the clearing towards another break in the hedgerow.

Katrina watched the water droplets slide from her fingers. 'There is no reason to leave. We are fortunate no one else is here. Can we not simply enjoy the solitude for a bit longer?'

Sarah took her time walking over to her, and sat next to Katrina on the rim of the fountain. 'You cannot hide here forever.'

'I have no intention of remaining here for the rest of
the day. Just a few more minutes. Please?'

The noise of the garden party seemed far removed from
where they were. Katrina closed her eyes and concentrated
on the sound of the water splashing and the birds chirping.
For a few minutes, at least, she could pretend she was far
away, sitting on a rock alongside the babbling brook that
meandered through her home in Tarrytown.

Only now she would be returning to a very different
home. Her great-aunt would no longer be there. Her home
would never be the same.

She took a deep, steadying breath. Miraculously, Sarah
appeared content with the silence between them as well.

Then the sound of crunching gravel ruined everything.
Their solitude would soon be interrupted. They agreed
that it was time to leave and walked towards another opening in the hedgerow. Hopefully they would get lost for
hours, trying to find their way out, and Katrina wouldn't
have to pretend her heart wasn't shattered into countless
pieces as they spoke to the other guests.

As they entered the hedgerow Katrina bumped into
the large form of Lord Boreham. Sarah caught her by the
elbow before she tumbled to the ground.

'Forgive me, Miss Vandenberg,' he mumbled, looking flustered after their accident. 'I was not aware you
ladies were in here.'

Katrina rubbed the back of her neck. 'And we were
not aware you were walking this pathway. I fear we are
all to blame.'

He appeared to be grasping for something to say. She
had no interest in prolonging an encounter with the man
and thought it best to spare him the misery.

'Well, do enjoy your time here, my lord. The fountain
is lovely.' She curtsied and edged around him, pulling
Sarah with her.

He mumbled his goodbye just after they had turned the first corner on their journey out of the maze.

Julian stepped into what he assumed was the centre of the maze and was surprised to see Lord Boreham on the opposite side of a Grecian fountain, bent over with his bottom raised to the sky.

'You present an interesting sight, Boreham,' Hart called out over the splashing water.

Lord Boreham jerked his body into a standing position, his face flushed bright red. In his hand he held something white. As they strolled around the fountain and stepped closer to him Julian could see that the slip of white was a delicate silk glove with a line of blue flowers trailing down its length. Where had he seen it before?

His heart flipped over when he realised why it looked familiar, and he snatched it out of Lord Boreham's hand. 'Where did you get this?' he demanded.

Lord Boreham went to take it back. 'Miss Vandenberg must have dropped it.'

Her name felt like a kick to the chest. 'And how would you know this is Miss Vandenberg's?' he asked, holding the glove out of Lord Boreham's reach.

'Because she was just here.' He reached for it again.

'I shall return it to her.' Julian knew Hart was watching him. He didn't care. This was all he would have left of Katrina, and he was not letting anyone take it from him.

The next night when Julian arrived home from Parliament he took off his tail coat, grabbed a bottle of brandy, and entered the portrait gallery to find some reassurance from the men who had come before him. He walked from painting to painting, studying the men staring down at him, as he drank from the bottle. They were all very good at appearing to be intimidating and grand, but they did look like a miserable lot. Had any of them been happy?

If anyone had ever understood the heavy weight of being the Duke of Lyonsdale it had been these men. They had known that life entailed sacrifice. They had known that their wants and desires did not matter. Every decision they had made had been made with the consideration of how it would impact their legacy. His father had understood this.

Julian took a long drink. The brandy burned all the way down.

He knew nothing of the women these men had married. Portraits of the duchesses hung in his various estates. He had never had any interest in looking at them before. Now he wondered about the women who had spent their lives alongside these men. Had any of them had the fire and charm of Katrina?

He pulled the flimsy white glove from his waistcoat pocket and touched the raised stitching of the forget-me-nots. He laughed to himself over the irony. He would never forget her, but he wondered if she thought about him at all—even for a fleeting moment each day. Did she feel the heavy weight of their parting? Did she long to hear his voice as much as he longed to hear hers?

The glove held faint traces of her lemon scent. Some day soon he would no longer have even that small reminder of the woman who had come to mean so much to him. He raised the glove to his nose and took a deep breath—holding her scent in for as long as he could.

'I'm surprised to find you here at such a late hour,' his grandmother called from the doorway.

Julian shoved the glove back into its hiding place. *Couldn't a man find a bit of solitude in his own home!*

'I wasn't aware there were restrictions upon when one

might visit a room in one's own home.' He took another drink.

She walked slowly towards him, adjusting her shawl and glancing at the six candelabras that lined the room. 'I don't recall ever seeing this room lit with so many candles.'

'The better to see my illustrious ancestors,' he said, waving the bottle towards the portraits. 'I didn't think they would approve of me skulking around in the dark.'

She eyed the bottle in his hand. 'I see. And what have you noticed about them at one in the morning that you hadn't noticed before?'

'The Dukes of Lyonsdale are a bloody surly lot.'

'I can't speak for all of them, however, your grandfather was known to smile on occasion.' She gestured towards the bottle. 'What are you drinking?'

'Brandy.' He handed her the bottle.

She took a small sip.

Had any of the other duchesses drank brandy from a bottle?

Looking at these men, he doubted it. He walked over to the portrait of his grandfather and tilted his head. 'What was he like?'

She followed him and looked fondly upon the man she had married. 'He was a fine, just man who cared for the people who depended on him. He enjoyed country life more than coming to Town. And he loved his family deeply.'

'Did he love you when he married you?' He motioned for the bottle and she handed it to him.

'No. We came to love each other in time.'

That was what he would do. He would fall in love with Lady Mary. Why hadn't he thought of that before?

He took a long drink and wiped his mouth with his sleeve.

'I hear you have been here for quite some time.'

He had almost forgotten his grandmother was standing next to him. She had been unusually quiet. Perhaps she was feeling poorly.

'I've been here since I returned from session.'

'Have you eaten anything at all? I've noticed you seem to have little appetite of late.'

Had he eaten? He must have, although he couldn't recall. 'I suppose I have.'

She threaded her arm through his. 'Why don't we call and have something brought up to my sitting room?'

They walked towards the doorway, past the blank wooden panel that should have housed the portrait of the Fifth Duke. Julian dragged his grandmother back to stop in front of it. He cocked his head and stared at the grains in the wood.

'He wasn't fit to hang with the others,' he mused out loud.

'That is what we have been told.'

'Why?'

'I do not know.'

He looked down at her and squinted till her image came into view. 'But haven't you ever wondered?'

He took another swig from the bottle. *This brandy was exceptional!*

'I'd wager it was something dreadful,' he said. 'Or, worse yet…scandalous! That was it, wasn't it? He did something scandalous.'

The floor dipped. He should mention that to Reynolds in the morning. They might need to fetch a carpenter.

He looked back at the empty panel. 'Poor cove. I'd wager he fell in love with an unsuitable woman and married her. Worst thing you could ever do, you know. There is no redeeming yourself from that.' He tilted his head to his grandmother and pointed the bottle at himself. 'No one will take *my* portrait and shove it in some dusty attic. *I* will not be marrying the woman I love. Some American lob will get that privilege. I will have the honour of marrying a seventeen-year-old chit who, as far as I can tell, has never had an opinion of her own.'

The floor dipped again, and Julian stamped with his booted foot to get it to stop.

His grandmother reached up and patted his cheek. 'You look very tired, my boy. Perhaps we should walk to your bedchamber.'

'That is very far. I think I'll just sleep here.' He went to sit down on the floor, but the annoying woman wouldn't let him.

'Your rooms are not that far, and on the way you can tell me about the new curricle you have purchased.'

'It's beautiful…very shiny. But I'll not drive Lady Mary around in it. She can have her own carriage.'

He trudged down the hall and went to take another swig of brandy, but the bottle was empty. They should make these bottles bigger.

'I'm marrying her, don't you know? Plan to ask Morley soon. Maybe tomorrow. Best to do it quickly. No need to wait. It's inevitable.'

Chapter Twenty-Three

Where was he?

Katrina worried at her lip as she stood in the ballroom of Finchley House, studying the guests who meandered around the elaborately decorated room in various costumes. The columns had been dressed to resemble trees and there was greenery tied with flowers that hung from the crystal chandeliers. Even though each guest wore a mask, she was certain she would be able to recognise Mr Armstrong in this imitation woodland forest. At least she hoped she would. Perhaps she should have asked which costume he would be wearing when they had spoken briefly at the Hipswitch garden party.

'May I help you find someone, my dear?'

Katrina jumped at the sound of the Dowager Duchess of Lyonsdale's voice. 'Your Grace, you startled me.' She turned to find the sweet, diminutive woman dressed like a man, with a ruffled collar, jacket, doublet and hose. For the first time in days Katrina had the urge to smile.

The Dowager turned in a circle and bowed. 'What do you say, Miss Vandenberg? Don't I cut a dashing figure?'

A soft laugh bubbled up in Katrina's throat. It sounded scratchy from lack of use. 'That you do, indeed. Are you a particular gentleman?'

'Why, Shakespeare, of course.' The Dowager stood a bit taller—or at least as tall as a woman of her height could. 'That is a beautiful costume,' she said, admiring Katrina's gold armbands.

The warmth of the Dowager's smile tugged at the scattered pieces of Katrina's heart. She missed this woman who had kindly offered her friendship and had taken her under her wing. How she wished she could reach out and hug her.

'Thank you. I must confess I wasn't certain what I wanted to be.'

'I'd say a Greek goddess was the perfect choice.'

It definitely was an improvement over the three hundred shepherdesses she had seen milling about the house since her arrival with the Forresters.

The Dowager scanned the area around them. 'You appeared to be searching for someone. May I offer some assistance?' She raised herself up on her booted toes to improve her view.

Katrina crossed her arms and fingered her armband, fighting the urge to be honest with the Dowager. 'I was just admiring the dancers.'

The Dowager lowered her heels and turned an assessing eye on Katrina. 'From over here?' She leaned closer and lowered her voice. 'You cannot fool me. Now, tell me, am I acquainted with this person?' Her eyes sparkled with anticipation.

Katrina bit her lip again. 'I'm trying to determine what Mr Armstrong is wearing this evening. Do you know the gentleman?'

The smile on the Dowager's face dropped to a frown. 'Yes. I know the man. I was not aware you were well acquainted.'

There was no sense in holding back her sigh from the

Dowager. 'We have been brought together on a number of occasions. I only wish this not to be another.'

'You are trying to avoid him.' The smile was back, brightening the Dowager's face.

'I am. However, if you share that with anyone I will deny it.'

The Dowager placed her finger to her lips. 'I am the soul of discretion.'

As Katrina scanned the room once more she finally spotted him. He was dressed as an ancient emperor with a crown of gold. It was no coincidence. How had Madame de Lieven found out what Katrina was going to wear?

'I have found him,' she said, and groaned.

The Dowager was back on her toes, scanning the crowd. Then she turned sharply and covered her smile with a gloved hand. 'Oh, heavens. He does look very pleased with himself.'

'I've yet to observe him *not* looking pleased with himself.' Katrina stepped behind the Dowager. Unfortunately the woman's height would do nothing to block Armstrong's view of her. 'He is bound to find me. I'm certain he knows what I am wearing. There aren't many women draped in gold gowns walking around this evening.'

'You are only the third I have seen as yet.'

Coming here had been a mistake. While Katrina loved spending time with the Dowager, it brought back memories of the time she had called on the woman at Lyonsdale House—the day Julian had almost kissed her in his library.

How long would the pain last? Perhaps when Sarah's dance ended she would be able to keep Katrina's mind off her broken heart.

Julian stood in the ballroom of the Finchleys' masquerade between Winter and Lord Andrew Pearce, trying to concentrate on what the brothers were talking about and not on the skull-crushing pain pounding in his head. Did the Finchleys *really* need this many candles in one ballroom? Didn't they realise that a darkened ballroom was preferable to one that appeared to be lit with the brightness of seven suns?

He looked down into his untouched glass of champagne and wished it were coffee. *Could one actually hear the sound of champagne bubbles?*

One of his friends might have just asked him a question. He wasn't certain. 'They are a valuable trading partner, and our borders in North America will be expensive and difficult to defend should another war break out. It is in our best interests to improve our relations with them.'

Could he go and lie down now?

'Thank you for clarifying that for us, Lyonsdale,' Andrew said with a smirk over the rim of his glass. 'Should I have any interest in Anglo-American relations in the future, I will be sure to inform you.'

That reply had seemed to work with everyone else this evening. Why were his friends so difficult?

'Pardon me—I thought you had asked me a question.'

'I did,' Andrew replied. 'I asked you what it was you drank this morning?'

'Last night. It was last night. From what I can recall it was brandy. I am not completely certain of that, however.'

Both men shook their heads in pity.

Winter removed the glass from Julian's hand. 'This will not help.'

'I need something to do with my hands that does not include squeezing my forehead so tightly that my brains pop out.'

His friends laughed—which was a very cruel thing to do since the sound bounced around in his head.

'Why did you even bother attending this evening?'

Andrew asked. 'You've been avoiding all forms of entertainment recently anyway. Two days ago you attended Hipswitch's garden party. That alone should have left you free to avoid any other outings for at least another two weeks.'

'I need to see Morley and arrange a time to call on him.'

There was no mistaking the look that passed between Winter and Andrew. 'And what would you have to discuss with him?' Winter asked.

He was a tall man, of intimidating size. If Julian hadn't know him so well, he might have taken his question as a demand.

'I've decided to ask for Lady Mary's hand.'

Andrew began to choke on his champagne, and Winter's sharp eyes bored into him through his black mask.

'She is a logical choice,' Winter commented evenly. He understood the personal sacrifices one must make as a duke.

Julian rolled his shoulders and glanced around the room until he spied his grandmother. Whatever had possessed her to choose the costume she had? Then his attention shifted and every muscle in his body locked at the sight of Katrina standing next to her. He needed a deep breath, but his lungs refused to cooperate.

As if some cruel force in nature had called to her she suddenly looked up, and their eyes met through their respective masks. His dying heart gave one weak effort to stir.

He couldn't look away even if he wanted to. Which he should—but he didn't.

She was breathtaking, in a sleeveless gown threaded with gold that sparkled in the candlelight. Her hair fell past her shoulders in ringlets, and bands of gold encircled her upper arms. She was Andromeda—and he was no Perseus.

Everything he had ever wanted was across the room from him. And he could not have it.

'Lady Mary will come into her own some day,' Winter said.

A sharp pain stabbed at his chest. Julian blinked and Katrina turned away. The connection was gone, as if it had never existed. Two people who had known each other once—now were strangers.

He needed to go somewhere—somewhere dark— where he could be alone and lick his wounds. The Finchleys had a library. No one would go to the library in the middle of a masquerade ball. It would be his refuge.

Julian locked the door behind him after he entered the unoccupied room and untied his mask. It was dark enough that the moonlight streaming in from the terrace doors cast a bluish white light into the room. He dropped into a plump wingback chair near the fireplace and closed his eyes. There was an advantage to dressing like a pirate. They did not wear restrictive tail coats.

The rattling of the library doorknob broke the peacefulness of the room. Thank God he had had the forethought to lock the door. Let whomever it was find another room to carry on an assignation. This room was his, and he needed to be alone.

After some time he realised he must have dozed off. He stood and stretched, but it did nothing to alleviate the tension coiled tight in his body. He couldn't put the inevitable off any longer. It was time to approach Morley.

He rubbed the ache in his chest, finding it was becoming hard to breathe. With luck the cool night air might help.

As he turned towards the French doors leading to the terrace he stumbled at the sight of Katrina's familiar silhouette in the moonlight.

He recalled standing with her on the Russian Ambassador's terrace the night his life had changed. No woman had ever affected him the way she did. And deep down he knew no one else ever would. Would there come a day when he stopped caring about her? *Caring?* It was much more than that. It was more than anything he had ever felt for anyone.

Julian gripped the back of a nearby chair. Suddenly it all made sense. He loved her—he had from the moment he'd spoken with her under the stars. That was why he had such a burning need for her. That was why no other woman could compare to her—and that was why, now they were apart, all he wanted to do was hold her in his arms and never let her go.

The terrace appeared to be deserted except for her lovely form. The need to know if she felt the same was consuming.

But before he could take another step towards the door, a man dressed in a black domino costume with a half mask and tricorn hat approached Katrina's side. Julian would wager one hundred pounds it was Armstrong. His heart sank. It was too late.

His vision clouded over with images of Armstrong dancing with her at the Whitfields' ball. It cleared just in time for him to see the man covering Katrina's nose with something white, shortly before her body fell limply into the man's arms.

Julian's brow furrowed. Katrina never swooned.

Before he was able to react, the man had hoisted her into his arms and carried her off into the darkened garden.

What the bloody hell was going on?

Julian ran for the French doors, raced down the terrace steps and through the garden. Just as he charged through the gate onto South Bruton Mews a carriage pulled away. Julian was certain Katrina was inside it. His almost dead heart now pounded furiously in his chest. He ran after it, but wasn't fast enough, and the carriage made its way over the cobblestones towards Bruton Street.

Julian slammed his fist into the garden wall, not even feeling the pain. There *had* to be a way to reach them.

Finchley House was one of only two houses on Grafton Street whose gardens backed directly onto the mews. All the other houses had stables separating the mews from their gardens. Julian scanned the long narrow lane, searching desperately for a horse. What he found was Hart's driver, sitting idly on his bench in an unmarked carriage a few doors down. Thank God his friend was always prepared for a hasty departure.

Julian whistled for Jonas just as Hart ran up beside him.

'I saw you hurry past. What has happened?'

'Someone has taken Katrina. I'm taking your carriage.' Julian climbed onto the driver's box, next to Jonas, and looked down at Hart. 'Find Miss Forrester and let her know. You both must keep this a secret. Watch for my return.'

Hart nodded, and stepped back as Julian and Jonas sped away.

The carriage rocked as it travelled over the bumpy cobblestones. There was a bend in the lane ahead. Hopefully the other carriage would be visible once they had made the turn.

'There was a carriage here just now, Jonas. Did you see it?'

'Aye, Your Grace. The one with the unmatched pair?'

'That's the one. We need to follow it.'

Jonas nodded as if chasing down another carriage was a common occurrence and then called out to the horses. 'Come on, boys, on with you.'

The carriage picked up speed.

'We won't know which way they went once they

reached Bruton Street,' he pointed out to Julian over the sound of turning wheels and clattering hoofbeats.

'I'm aware of that. Let us pray they are not that far ahead of us and we see them.'

Julian had no idea what he would do if they did not. He clenched his right hand into a fist.

Thankfully when they reached the end of the mews, they spotted the driver's green coat and the mismatched pair of horses as they turned right onto New Bond Street. Julian knew that once they were away from the street lights of Mayfair it would be harder to track them.

'Whatever you do, do not lose sight of them,' he ground out.

They followed the carriage out of Mayfair towards Cheapside. He thought of trying to overtake it, but was afraid it might cause an accident and Katrina might not survive. He would follow this carriage to the far corners of the land to get her back, and when he did he was going to beat Armstrong senseless.

If it *was* Armstrong, could it be possible that he was taking her to Gretna Green? Was he that desperate? Certainly by the way he had rendered her unconscious, this elopement was not by choice.

If they were headed there they would have to change horses in two hours. Julian needed to force himself to remain calm until then. He would do Katrina no good if he could not think clearly. In two hours he would have her back. And Armstrong would regret the day he had planned this.

When Jonas lost sight of the carriage near St. Paul's it was nearly impossible for Julian not to lash out at the coachman. They could not have disappeared. They had to be somewhere close by.

He gripped the rail in front of him until his knuckles were white. *Dear God, please let me find her.*

The streets in this part of London were not very familiar to him. Thank God Jonas appeared to know his way around. After circling the streets for what felt like hours, but had probably been less than fifteen minutes, they spotted the carriage parked on Newgate Street. He had Jonas stop far enough back that their presence would not be easily noticed.

Looking closely at his surroundings, Julian realised he knew this place. The carriage was parked in front of the Crypt of St Martin's le Grand. He, like other people in London, had ventured out here to inspect the crypt when it had been uncovered not long ago.

The implication of where they were made his palms sweat and the hair on the back of his neck stand on end. This was not a forced elopement. What was Armstrong up to?

Before Julian had a chance to determine the best way to approach the situation the cloaked figure hurried out of the crypt empty-handed, and re-entered the carriage. Julian's blood ran cold. His gut told him Katrina was in the crypt.

As the carriage pulled away Jonas spoke up. 'Shall I follow it?'

He shook his head. He knew where to find Armstrong—and he *would* find him. But first he needed to reach Katrina. He only prayed he wasn't too late.

Chapter Twenty-Four

Katrina's head felt as if it was being squeezed between two bricks. She tried opening her eyes and found her lids exceedingly heavy. Raising her chin from her chest was also proving difficult. The air had the earthy scent of a root cellar, and the smell made her nose twitch. She should leave this place. If only she wasn't too tired to move from this chair.

'Oh, you're waking up,' a female voice drawled. 'That should make this a bit more interesting. I suppose the ropes were necessary, after all.'

That velvety voice was familiar, but Katrina couldn't recall who it belonged to. With much effort she forced herself to blink, and when her vision cleared Lady Wentworth slowly came into view a few feet in front of her. She was wearing a dark cape over a jonquil gown.

Katrina had no recollection of leaving the Finchleys' with this woman. In fact she couldn't even remember leaving the ball at all.

Lady Wentworth cocked her head, and Katrina felt like a butterfly pinned in a case.

'I've tried,' the woman mused, 'but I still cannot fathom what he finds attractive about you.'

Katrina tried to place where in Finchley House they

might be. This was not any of the beautifully decorated rooms she had seen. The floor and walls were made of crumbling stone and dirt. Aside from the chair she sat on, the only other furniture was a little table near Lady Wentworth. There were items on it, but she couldn't make out what they were in the shadows. No windows were evident, and the only light came from a lantern on the floor.

Not far away was a deep stone box, large enough to house most of Katrina's gowns. She tipped her head back and squinted at the arched vaulted ceiling divided by stone pillars.

Katrina swallowed hard. It did little to relieve the scraping at the back of her throat. 'Where are we?'

'In a crypt. A very convenient choice on my part.'

A cold chill ran up her spine. Why couldn't she remember coming here? Her chest tightened as her muddled head started to clear, and she tried to suppress the panic that was taking hold. Why, of all places, were they in a crypt? Dead people belonged in crypts. She needed to leave.

Her arms felt numb. When she tried to lift them up she couldn't, and realised her hands were tied behind her back. She tugged on the rope, but it wouldn't budge. When she tried to raise her body, she saw her ankles were tied to the spindly chair.

'You have tied me up?' Katrina let out an incredulous breath. 'Why would you do that?'

'My associate did it before he left. It seemed prudent at the time.' There was an odd, satisfied glint in Lady Wentworth's eyes. 'The ropes are very secure. Struggling will not help. Your waking has forced me to adjust my plan,' she said, picking up a small bottle from the table, 'but rest assured you won't be leaving. The man I hired will make certain of that.'

She glanced pointedly at the large stone box in the centre of the room and Katrina realised it was a tomb.

Muscles and veins strained against Katrina's skin as she pushed with all her might to break the ropes that bound her. Warm rivulets trailed down her hands but she barely felt the pain.

Julian had followed the darkened steps that led down into the Crypt at St Martin's le Grand, holding the carriage lamp Jonas had handed him. The rapid pounding of his heart echoed in his ears as he navigated the underground stone passageways. Rounding the second corner, he spied the faint glow of light far up ahead and hoped it meant he had found Katrina.

Not knowing what or who he would be facing, he turned down the flame in the lantern. He crept slowly along, trying for the hundredth time to imagine why someone would take Katrina. As he made his way closer to the entrance of a chamber he could hear the sound of muffled voices and listened closely for hers. When he heard it, he almost stumbled to his knees in relief. *She was alive.*

He placed the lantern down outside the entrance, and when he looked inside was dumbstruck to see Katrina with Helena. None of this made any sense.

The domino wasn't Armstrong?

'What the bloody hell is going on?' he bellowed, advancing into the earthen chamber and avoiding the stone coffin in the centre.

Both women let out a gasp. Helena jumped and something fell from her hand, shattering on the floor. She backed away, moving closer to the wall.

Katrina was sitting in a chair about twenty feet to his left. Her eyes were closed, probably out of relief. When she opened them she glared at him.

'You have horrid taste in women!' she yelled at him. 'That's what is going on. Now untie my hands and feet so I can beat her to a pulp!'

He took a step towards Katrina, uncertain how he would handle her when she was this furious.

'Stay where you are,' Helena ordered.

She was aiming a pistol at his head and looking him directly in the eye. The sound of her rapid breathing could be heard across the chamber.

This could not be happening.

He was about to extend his hand and demand she give him the gun when he noticed the dead calm in her eyes. An unsettling shiver ran up his spine and he recalled her violent temper when he had ended their affair. He had seen how unpredictable she could be. The question was, would she use that gun?

He glanced over at Katrina, who sat frozen in place. It almost looked as if she had stopped breathing. Thank heavens she had stopped talking. Her eyes darted to his and he gave her a restrained nod. Her eyes seemed to say she was willing to stay quiet and allow him to determine how best to disarm Helena.

Now, if only he knew what the best way was...

She liked expensive things—he would start there. He looked back at the woman who had a gun pointed at his head.

'What is it you want, Helena?' he asked, hesitant even to move his hands.

She laughed and shifted on her feet—the gun didn't waver. '*Now* you ask...now that I have your life in my hands. That is rich,' she spat. 'I want the life I was destined to have. The life I deserve to have.'

'No one is saying you cannot have it.'

She shook her head. 'I cannot have it now. I might have before you arrived, but not now.'

'Why did you do this? Why did you take Miss Vandenberg?'

'You chose an American over me,' she ground out.

'An *American*!' She licked her lips nervously. 'It was bad enough when I thought you were going to listen to that harpy of a mother of yours and marry Morley's brat. But then the *ton* would have assumed you had finally given in to your mother's pestering. That chit ranks higher than me. It would not be seen as an insult to my person. But this…' she waved the pistol towards Katrina '…this is an *American*.' The final statement was said through her clenched teeth.

He needed to direct her attention away from Katrina. He took a step closer to Helena. The pistol was back, pointing at his head.

'Don't. Move.' She cocked it. 'No one of worth will want me if they think an American is above me. You don't understand. You're a *man*! You live in your lofty world, with all your money and power. You are free to choose the life you want. You. Have. *Everything!*'

At the moment it felt as if he had nothing. He raised his hands in an attempt to steady her.

'You have built a fine life for yourself since Wentworth's death.'

'I have *nothing*! I have taken to selling my possessions to pay off my debts. The money is gone and there is no way for me to get more unless I marry well.'

How could he not have realised she was in such dire straits? 'But the gambling… I have sat in card rooms with you,' he muttered out loud.

'I was there to attract men like *you*! *You* have reduced me to spreading my legs in search of the money and prestige that already should be mine. Every time I had one of you inside me I earned that title! Every time I waited for you and turned down other invitations I earned it! And every time someone asked if a proposal was imminent, and I had to smile and say nothing, I earned it!

That chatterbox Lizzy Skeffington should not be a duchess! *I* should!'

All her screaming had made her voice hoarse.

'Surely you could find a husband with a lesser title? There are many wealthy men who would beg to marry you.'

Her body began trembling with rage. 'You expect me to marry a viscount or a baron?' she shrieked.

He put his palms back up. It was like trying to settle a skittish horse. His brief moment of sympathy at her situation had clouded his knowledge of her pride and her sense of entitlement. Knowing he had once felt affection for her was making him physically ill.

'How will taking Miss Vandenberg help? I still do not understand?'

She let out a mean laugh. 'You stupid man—this isn't about taking her. It's about *killing* her. If she is dead you can't marry her, and my reputation as a desirable woman will be secure.'

Every bone in Julian's body seemed to disintegrate, and it was taking great effort for him to remain standing tall and firm. Katrina wasn't going to die tonight. Somehow he would make certain of it.

'You have it wrong about Miss Vandenberg and myself. We barely speak.'

Helena's eyes darted between the two of them and for the first time he could see her confidence waver. 'You're lying. I saw her enter the maze at the Finchleys' shortly before you did.'

This was all for nothing. Katrina wasn't even his. And if Julian hadn't witnessed her being kidnapped he would have been asking Morley for his daughter's hand about now.

He shook his head sadly. 'It was simply a coincidence. I never saw her.'

He looked over at Katrina, bound in the chair. He could tell she was frightened. So was he. But she was remaining quietly composed, allowing him to try to defuse the situation. He prayed he knew how.

'His Grace is telling the truth,' Katrina called out, keeping her eyes on Helena. 'We barely know one another.'

Helena licked her lips and shifted her feet slightly, staring at Julian. 'I've seen the way you look at her. There is something between you.'

He shook his head. 'I find her to be attractive.' *Beyond compare.* 'She is American, so her mannerisms are different.' *And charming.* 'But, as I said, we barely speak.' *But she will have my heart forever.*

Helena's eyes darted between them again. Her bravado was weakening. But if he grabbed for the pistol it could go off, and the shot might hit Katrina.

Slowly he held out his hand. 'Give me the pistol, Helena. No one needs to die tonight.'

She steadied her hand. 'I know I will swing for what I've done.'

'It does not have to come to that,' he said reassuringly. 'Now, hand it to me.'

Her knuckles whitened around the gun and her face set with determination.

He motioned for the weapon. 'As angry as you are with me, you will not shoot me. You are not that evil.'

Dear God, he hoped it was true!

Her breathing had become erratic, and in the glow of the lantern he saw tears rim her eyes.

'If I hand you my pistol, what will happen then?'

He took a step closer. 'I will untie Miss Vandenberg and the two of us will leave. That is all.'

From the corner of his eye he saw Katrina look his way. *Keep silent, Katrina. Do not say a word.*

He knew he needed to take her back to the ball. If the *ton* found out she had been kidnapped, her reputation would be beyond repair. He would find a way to deal with Helena later. Debtors' prison would be enough of a punishment. If he involved Bow Street in this, the kidnapping would be all over the newspapers by morning.

'Give me the pistol.'

She took two deep, uneven breaths and uncocked the gun.

He stepped closer and motioned again with his fingers. This time she handed him the pistol.

Relief flooded through Julian, and it was a wonder he had the strength to hold the gun in his hand.

He rushed to Katrina's side and began untying her hands. She rubbed her wrists as he worked on the bloody knot near her ankles. He needed to get her outside before Helena did something else irrational. When the knot was finally free and he had unbound her legs, he stood, ready to take her in his arms. But she lunged for Helena instead.

Julian grabbed her by the waist before she was able to get close to Helena and pulled her back. 'We need to leave. *Now.*'

She tore herself free from his grip, her eyes drilling holes into Helena. His former lover was sitting on the floor, staring sightlessly at the ground. It appeared the realisation of what had transpired had hit her.

He needed to get Katrina out of there quickly. Helena was too unstable. He would deal with her tomorrow. They needed to return to the ball.

Julian tugged Katrina's arm and together they escaped out into the passageway and to freedom.

'There is a carriage waiting for us above ground,' he said, taking her hand. 'I will return you to the masquerade. All will be well.'

* * *

In the darkness of the rocking carriage Katrina wrapped her arms around herself, attempting to alleviate the chills that had begun racking her body the moment they left the crypt. All she wanted was to crawl into bed and tuck herself into mountains of blankets. With any luck she could remain there for days, and avoid telling her father about any of this for as long as possible.

'You're shivering,' Julian said from his seat across from her. His body jerked in hesitation before he crossed the carriage. 'Forgive me—in this costume I have no coat to give you. I can only offer you my warmth.' He shifted closer to her on the bench and drew her to his side.

Her body should have melted into his. Instead it stiffened into stone. Although she would be forever grateful to him for coming for her, he was still the man who didn't want her. She was afraid that if she let herself find comfort in his embrace she wouldn't be able to let go of him when they arrived at Finchley House.

'She told me she had hired someone who would dispose of me later tonight. We were fortunate he did not return.' She rubbed her forehead. 'What do you think will happen to her?' she asked into the darkness.

Julian shrugged. 'She will not say anything about tonight. She would be sealing her fate at the gallows. I will make certain her debts are called in tomorrow. If she cannot pay them, as I suspect she can't, she will be taken to debtors' prison.'

She turned to him and met his gaze for the first time in the dim light of the carriage lantern. 'Won't her family help her?'

'I do not believe so. I do not know the particulars, but I am aware that she does not speak to her brother.' He cleared his throat. 'Are you in need of a physician? Were you harmed?'

The sound of his true concern was evident. It was breaking her heart all over again.

Katrina shook her head. 'There is no need. I have come to no harm.'

It occurred to her that the last time they had spoken it had been in a carriage such as this. As far as she knew, this might even be the same carriage they had travelled in.

She hugged herself tighter as the shards of her heart crashed around her chest. 'How did you find me?'

'I saw you taken from the terrace. I followed you out to the mews and was lucky to find Hart's driver parked nearby. We tracked you to the crypt.'

Silence stretched between them. After some time Julian cleared his throat. 'We will be arriving at the Finchleys' soon. As much as it unnerves me to leave you alone, I will enter the ball and send Miss Forrester out to bring you back in through the garden. Although it's a masquerade, and everyone is in disguise, it would be best to have her with you to ensure your reputation.' He appeared to realise his commanding nature. 'With your permission, of course.'

Katrina nodded. This night could not end soon enough for her liking.

They travelled the remainder of the way to the house in silence. It didn't take long before the carriage slowed, made a number of sharp turns, and eventually came to a stop. They were back at Finchley House.

She felt the hesitation when Julian withdrew his arm from around her shoulder. 'Thank you, Julian, for coming after me.'

He gave her a solemn nod. 'I am truly sorry,' he replied before he opened the door. Looking at her one last time, he turned and left her.

Katrina didn't have the physical or emotional energy to try to determine what he was sorry for, and she rested her head back on the squab while she waited for Sarah. It wasn't long before the door opened and Sarah jumped inside.

'Oh, thank God you are back,' Sarah said, throwing her arms around Katrina and hugging her.

Katrina knew she would have to walk through the ballroom as if nothing harrowing had happened. In order to do that, she could not allow herself to sob in Sarah's arms. It was taking all her effort to remain composed.

'I was so very worried,' Sarah continued. 'Hartwick told me you had been taken. I made an excuse to my mother about you being sick. I told her you must have eaten something disagreeable and that when your stomach was better it probably would be wise for us to leave.' She hugged her again. 'Dear God, you're shaking.'

Sarah took off her highwayman's black cape and draped it around Katrina's shoulders.

'How long have I been gone?'

'A little over two hours.' She ran her hands up and down Katrina's arms. 'Are you well? Did they harm you? Who was it that took you?'

Although Katrina was relieved to see her friend, Sarah's chattering was making her head pound. She quietly relayed all the details of what had happened as she donned the mask Sarah had handed her and they re-entered the garden to find Sarah's mother.

Hopefully, it would be easy to get her to agree to leave the ball. Katrina just wanted to be safe—in her home. She should have learned that standing alone on a terrace during a ball was never a good idea.

Katrina entered her home an hour later. The familiar smell of lemon oil in the entrance hall made her muscles soften. She was home. She was safe. If only she could sleep for days.

She was well on her way to bed when her foot landed on the fifth tread of the staircase and it creaked.

'Katrina, is that you?' Her father's voice called to her from the direction of his study.

She was about to call out her answer when he entered the hall in his dressing gown. It took all her effort not to run into his arms. 'You are up rather late,' she said.

'I could not sleep. Did you enjoy yourself at the ball?'

She had never been able to lie to him. So she simply pasted on a smile.

'Come with me to my study and you can tell me all about it while I put my papers in order.'

Reluctantly, Katrina walked down the stairs and followed him. He moved behind his massive desk, closed his inkwell, and shuffled through his papers.

'Was the music to your liking?'

She nodded.

'And the costumes? I imagine some were rather elaborate?'

Again, she nodded.

This time he looked at her over the rim of his glasses and tilted his head. When he narrowed his gaze on her, she shifted on her feet. He grabbed at her right hand from across his desk.

'What has happened? Why do your wrists look as if you have been bleeding?'

She tugged her hand out of his. 'It is nothing.'

'Nothing!' He stepped out from behind his desk to stand in front of her. 'You have been injured. Was there an accident? Why was I not informed?'

His concern was too much. She could no longer continue the pretence that she was unaffected by what had happened. She threw her arms around her stunned father and held him tight.

Thankfully, he didn't say anything when she began

to cry. He just hugged her and patted her back as he had done when she was a little girl.

He waited patiently until she had finished crying before he spoke. 'Tell me what happened.'

She took a deep breath and stepped back from him. 'I am fine. Know that. The only harm that has come to me are these bruises on my wrists.'

He nodded, but there was wariness in his eyes. He guided her to a chair and she curled up on it. She told him what had happened and he listened without interrupting.

It wasn't until she had finished that he finally spoke. 'I knew any association you had with Lyonsdale would not end well.'

'It is not his fault. You cannot blame him for what that woman did.'

Her father stood and paced the room. 'That woman would not have done what she did if it weren't for his interest in you.'

'It is not as if he intended for this to happen.'

'Why are you defending him?' he demanded.

'I'm not. However, I do find it grossly unfair to blame the man when the fault lies elsewhere.'

He stopped pacing and came to her. 'We will agree to disagree on this subject.'

Chapter Twenty-Five

'You need to move it more to the left.'

The footmen rehanging the massive painting shifted it according to Julian's direction. He leaned against the wall opposite where they were hanging the portrait of the Fifth Duke and sipped his coffee. He had been having breakfast in his bedchamber when Reynolds had arrived to inform him the portrait had been located. Eager to see his mysterious ancestor, Julian had left his untouched plate and met him in the gallery.

This painting stood out from the others. It showed a man standing tall in a country setting, with a hooded falcon perched on his gloved hand. He looked out at the viewer with the expression of a man who enjoyed life. Julian almost smiled at the notion that Katrina probably wouldn't have minded having him at her dinner table.

One of the hardest things he had ever done was leaving her in Hart's carriage last night to go and find Miss Forrester. If he could have had his way, he would have spirited her off to his home and tucked her into his bed, where he would have been able to hold her in his arms for days. But it had not escaped his notice that she had not wanted his comfort. His heart ached unbearably.

During his ride home from the ball, Helena's words played over in his head.

'You are free to choose the life you want. You have everything.'

He didn't have everything. He didn't have Katrina. And she was more important to him than anything else. One day he would close his eyes for the last time, and deep down he knew he would still be thinking about her. Was that the life he wanted? A life of sadness and regret?

It was time for him to live his own life and not an imitation of his father's. His mother was wrong. He deserved more than contentment. He deserved to be happy. It was time he wrote his own story of what made a man an honourable duke.

'Reynolds told me I would find you here,' his mother said, marching into the gallery and eyeing the footmen with a perplexed expression.

He dismissed the servants as she approached his side, dressed for an outing.

'You're venturing out early today, I see,' he remarked.

'The renovations are complete. I want to inspect my home before I have my things moved back tomorrow,' she said, adjusting her gloves. 'I assume you have heard the news about your old friend?'

Julian closed his eyes and let out a resigned breath. 'What has Hart done now?'

Her forehead creased before she caught herself and relaxed her features. 'Not him. Lady Wentworth.' The crease in her forehead was back. 'Did you not read the papers this morning?'

He shook his head. It was the first day in ages he had not. He had been too busy resurrecting the Fifth Duke. His stomach bottomed out. He had planned to speak with someone about pushing for her debts to be called in today.

'She was found in her home late last night. She poisoned herself. The papers are saying she could barely pay her bills. The servants confirmed it.'

His blood ran cold. So this was how things would end between them. 'Was there a note?'

His mother shook her head. 'The papers didn't mention one.'

Part of him knew he should feel some sympathy for her, but after having a gun pointed at his head and knowing what she had planned to do with Katrina, he felt nothing but relief.

Next to him, his mother turned and studied the portrait of the Fifth Duke, now hanging where it belonged. 'Where did that come from?'

He welcomed the change in subject. 'The attic.'

'Is that the Fifth Duke?'

'It is.'

She turned to Julian and eyed him up and down. 'There is a striking resemblance between the two of you.'

Was there? The shape and colour of the eyes were similar, as was the shade and wave of the man's hair. He had a square jaw, and his aquiline nose seemed to possess the same small bump in the middle that Julian knew his had. Now that she mentioned it, he could see the resemblance.

'Why is he here? He is not fit to hang with the others.'

Julian took a slow sip of his coffee. 'I think he is.'

The Fifth Duke had been on Julian's mind since Katrina had asked about him. He wasn't sure what the man had done, since there was no reference to him in the family history. Perhaps he had simply lived a good life in the country, taking care of his estates and the people who lived on them. A man could be a good duke without needing the world to tell him he was.

Winter was right. He was not a party of one man. Others shared his political and ethical beliefs. Together they were stronger than one man alone. If he could share his knowledge and write impassioned speeches, did it really matter who said the words to get the votes they needed? And it truly was in Britain's best interest to improve its relationship with America. There were others who believed that as well. He recalled Hart telling him that Julian's great achievement might be to aid in improving relations between the countries.

He wasn't certain if he was simply convincing himself of this to justify marrying Katrina, or because it was true. What he *did* know, without a doubt, was that he would place his need to be with her above everything else. He was a duke of England, but life was fleeting—it was time he took what he wanted!

'There is something you should know,' he said to his mother, who was staring at him with trepidation.

'Why do I believe I will not approve of what it is you have to say?'

'I will be asking for Miss Vandenberg's hand today. God willing, she will accept.'

His mother blanched. 'You can't mean that. She is an American. She has no understanding of what it means to be a duchess.'

'You told me you would defer to me on who I choose to marry.'

His normally aloof mother shook with anger. 'Yes, but that was when I was certain you would be choosing Lady Mary! You assured me that caricature was a political satire and nothing more.'

'Miss Vandenberg is an intelligent, charming woman who is the daughter of a diplomat. She would make an excellent choice for my duchess.'

'Have you gone mad? Your father would never have approved of her. He understood what was expected of your title. That was why he chose Emma for you. You are

Lyonsdale. Miss Vandenberg's family isn't even English! Your ancestors fought alongside Kings and served in the courts of many of our monarchs. *She* comes from a family of shipyard owners, and her father writes novels. What honour is there in that?'

Julian placed his cup down on the nearby window ledge and tried to steady his anger. 'She will bear my heir if *I* decide that is what I wish. I suggest, madam, that you remember I am the head of this family. I will no longer tolerate your interference with my life.'

'You will lose the respect of influential men, and people will mock you behind your back,' seethed his mother.

Not everyone would feel that way—although he knew there were men who *would* be angry with him for choosing to marry an American over their very suitable daughters. 'I can manage the *ton*.'

She placed her hand on her stomach and seemed to labour for breath. 'If you do this there will be no turning back.'

He didn't want to turn back. Behind him were the choices he had made about Katrina that he wasn't proud of. He prayed she would find it in her heart to forgive him.

Hours later, Julian stood on the steps of Katrina's home, staring at the round brass knocker and wondering for the tenth time if he would be received. He was a duke from one of the most respected families in the realm. However, he wasn't certain that would make much of a difference this morning to Katrina's father. The man had forbidden him from calling on his daughter. Common decency dictated that he respect the man's wishes. Perhaps he would blame this transgression on lack of sleep.

Before he could lift his hand to knock, the door opened smoothly and he was met with the sight of her butler. The man was English, and therefore well versed in the respect a duke should be given. However, this man also knew of the times when Julian had called on Katrina in secret, and there was something in his eyes that told Julian he would bar him entrance into the home if he could.

'Good day, Your Grace. May I help you?'

'I am here to see Miss Vandenberg. Is she at home?'

There was a hesitation before the door was opened further and Julian was ushered inside. This time when Wilkins went to present his card to Katrina, he left Julian waiting in the entrance hall. It was a silent statement that Julian did not miss. He was not welcome here.

The sound of footfalls caught his attention, and he wasn't entirely surprised when Mr Vandenberg walked into the hall. The man did not extend his hand in greeting. 'Good morning, Your Grace. Would you care to join me in my study?'

The coolness of his tone could have chilled a steaming cup of tea.

What exactly did Katrina's father know about last night?

Julian followed him into the study and took the seat by the desk that was offered.

Mr Vandenberg walked around his desk and sat down. 'What can I do for you today?' His voice was professional and not the least bit friendly.

Julian pushed his shoulders back and raised his chin. 'Actually, sir, I am here to see your daughter.'

'I thought we had agreed you would not have any contact with her. Yet here you are.' Julian opened his mouth to reply but the man held up his hand to stop him. 'Let's not speak in pretence. I am well aware of what occurred last night, and I have read the papers this morning.' He arched a knowing brow. 'While I am in your debt for bringing her home safely to me, it does not change the fact that the two of you have no reason to see one another. Twice you have almost damaged her reputation. That is reason enough. Rumour has it you are a man of high moral standards. If that is true, why are you here? What do you want?'

All last night Julian had tossed and turned, worrying about how she was faring, both physically and emotionally. He had wanted to hold her in his arms until she fell asleep and assure her all would be well. But he hadn't been able to—and it had burned in his gut. He needed to apologise and he needed to do it now.

'I am sorry for all the pain I have caused her. It was not done intentionally, I assure you. I have the highest regard for your daughter.'

'And yet you do not regard her highly enough.'

The last time Julian had walked out of this house he had been devastated by the loss he'd felt. Now he knew what his grandmother had meant about finding that spark in life. Katrina was his. She had helped him realise he did not need to carry the weight of the world on his shoulders and that he was entitled to have some happiness.

'You do not understand the depth of my feelings for her.'

'I understand that, given a choice, you chose to end your association with her instead of offering for her hand.'

'To save her reputation.'

'To save your own.'

'And my heart has suffered for it every day since! I am here to speak with your daughter because of just how highly I regard her. If you would be so kind as to inform her I am here, I would be grateful.'

Her father's forehead wrinkled. 'With wealth and privilege comes sacrifice. However, certain things should never be sacrificed.'

'And if I agreed with you, how would you feel?'

'I suppose we will know after you speak with my daughter. Katrina is out on the terrace.' He stood and rang for a servant. 'I would ask you to make your visit brief. We wouldn't want the neighbours to talk,' he said with a pointed look.

Julian pressed his lips firmly together to hold in his sigh of relief. Every nerve in his body hummed as he accompanied the Vandenbergs' butler onto the terrace while the man delivered Katrina a cup of tea. She sat with her back to them on a long wooden bench with her watercolours in her hand. She appeared intent on an oak tree that was growing just on the other side of the balustrade.

'Thank you for the tea, Wilkins,' she called out, keeping her gaze on her subject.

Julian took the Wedgwood cup from Wilkins and silently dismissed the man. He placed the tea beside Katrina. She continued to look at the tree as she reached for the cup. He cleared his throat and she looked at him.

The tea in her hand sloshed from the cup into the saucer. 'How long have you been standing there?'

'Not very long.' He nodded towards the paper on her small easel. 'I wasn't aware that you paint.'

'I find it calms me.'

She calmed him. He felt worlds better, simply being in her presence.

'May I?' he asked, gesturing to the space on the bench beside her.

She hesitated, but shifted closer to the end, making room for him. Once he was seated she returned her attention to the tree.

'The weather is fine today,' he said.

Katrina kept her eyes on the tree while she continued to outline the branches with her brush. It was easier to focus on the tree than to look at Julian. 'I doubt you're calling to discuss the state of the clouds.'

From the corner of her eye she saw him rest his elbows on his knees and look down at his clasped hands. 'This is true. It could be raining. I would hardly notice.'

It had been raining in her heart for over a week, thanks to him. She placed the brush into her glass of water and faced him. If they finished their conversation quickly, it might not hurt as much when he left.

'Is there something you've come to tell me?'

His attention dropped to the bandages around her wrists, which were peeking out from the long sleeves of her pale blue muslin dress, and his brow wrinkled. 'Last night you assured me you were well.'

The sound of his tender concern tugged at her. 'I tried to pull my hands out of the ropes. These are simply abrasions. By tomorrow the bandages will not be necessary.'

'Did you suffer other injuries? Tell me truthfully.' He looked into her eyes.

'No, just my hands.' She lowered her voice even more. 'Did you read the papers this morning?'

Relief had washed over her when she had read about Lady Wentworth. She knew it was uncharitable to feel that way, but she couldn't help it.

'I have. It is now truly over.'

Silence stretched between them and then he let out an audible breath. 'There is something I need to tell you.'

Her palms began to sweat at the seriousness of his tone. Had word of her kidnapping begun to spread?

'I'm listening.'

'It is difficult for me to know where to begin.' He appeared to choose his words carefully. 'I am sorry for everything that happened last night. Had I known Lady Wentworth was capable of doing such a thing, I would have somehow stopped her before you were ever put in danger.'

'There is nothing you could have done to stop her unless you had remained in her company every hour of every day.'

'Still, I accept full responsibility.'

She shook her head slowly. 'It is not necessary. I do not blame you for it.'

He smelled of leather and…Julian. Did every man have a unique scent? He certainly did. She hoped she would soon forget it.

'If that is all, Your Grace, you may leave. Rest assured I do not blame you for what has occurred.'

She reached over to pick up her paintbrush and her eyes widened when he took her hand. Warmth spread up her arm.

'There is something else you should know.' His voice faded in the hushed stillness of the terrace.

'Go on.'

He swallowed hard, and his green eyes searched hers. 'I've come to realise something of late. It should have occurred to me earlier, however, I have had no experience with it until now.'

The intensity in his gaze held her, making it impossible to look away.

'I love you with every fibre of my being. I have from the first moment I saw you.'

A lump settled in Katrina's throat. His words were just pretty sentiment. He didn't mean them.

She was ready to pull her hand from his when he knelt before her.

The world stopped.

'Katrina, I never want to live another day without you and I pray that in your heart you love me, even just a little.

All I want to do is cherish you and call you my wife—if you will have me.'

She blinked. 'Did you just ask me to marry you?'

'I did.'

She shifted uncomfortably under his piercing gaze. 'I know you are a man of honour, and that you think offering for my hand is the proper thing to do because of what occurred last night, but there is no need. I'll return to America and you can live the life you are destined to lead, uncomplicated by our association.'

Katrina was amazed she said all that without her voice cracking.

'Did you not hear what I said? I do not want to marry you out of a sense of obligation. I want to marry you because I love you.'

His lovely green eyes looked at her earnestly.

'I will not marry a man who will cast me aside after we are wed.'

'Do you truly believe I will?'

'You suffered derision because of a carriage ride and cut ties with me. Do you believe marrying me will be easier?'

'I had everything I thought I wanted after we parted. I regained the respect of most men in Westminster. My counsel was sought on affairs of state. I was asked to give speeches again. But none of that mattered. What mattered was what *you* thought of me. Other people's opinions and esteem do not define me. My actions define me. I am finished with living the life Society tells me I should.'

Butterflies danced in her chest. 'You truly love me?'

His kissed her hand slowly. 'With all my heart.'

'Always?'

'Always. Do you love me? Even just a little?'

The lump in her throat was back. 'I do love you, Julian, with all of my being.'

He released a deep breath and closed his eyes. 'Do you love me enough to marry me?'

'I do,' she said in a rush.

He leaned over and kissed her—deeply and passionately. When he finally pulled his head away they both were breathing hard.

Chapter Twenty-Six

Three weeks later

Wedding breakfasts could be so tedious.

Julian took a sip of champagne and wondered how long he and Katrina were obligated to stay at their own celebration. Surely they did not have to remain until the last guest departed? That could be hours from now—hours that would be better spent by him exploring the enticing curves of his new wife's body.

Fortunately for Julian, the Russian Ambassador could carry on a conversation with a potted palm. Julian nodded periodically, to keep up the pretence of interest, but his attention was fixed on Katrina, who was visible to the left of the Russian Ambassador's shoulder.

Once she had agreed to marry him, he had found himself constantly preoccupied with thoughts of bedding her. He wondered how tight she would feel when he entered her for the first time. Would she cry out her release or remain silent? Would she allow him to explore every bit of her?

His thoughts were interrupted when Hart nudged his shoulder. 'I was hoping this fixation you have with your wife would end once you were married. But I suppose you will need a few days alone with her before you are cured.'

Julian glanced around, wondering what had happened to the Ambassador. And how long had Hart been standing by his side?

'He walked off about five minutes ago,' Hart explained. 'I thought I would come to your rescue. If you'd been standing alone much longer I fear Madame de Lieven would have approached you. She has been regaling everyone with tales of how she was responsible for bringing you and your bride together. I'm certain she would enjoy sharing them with you.'

'Madam de Lieven? I had assumed my grandmother would have already made certain everyone thought it was *her* doing.'

The look of surprise on Hart's face made Julian laugh.

'In truth, the only reason you and Katrina are together is due to some careful planning by Miss Forrester and myself. If we'd left it to the two of you, you would still be sending her weeds.'

Julian glanced at his beautiful wife and recalled the first time he had called on her at her home. 'Do not discount those weeds. I think they may have helped win her love.'

'Love!' Hart spluttered into his glass of champagne.

'Yes, love. We are in love. She is all I will ever need.'

'You say that now. It is your wedding day. It would be poor form to say otherwise. But no woman can hold a man's attention forever.'

Julian studied his friend, wondering if he truly believed that. 'Some day, Hart, you will meet a woman and find that you cannot stop thinking about her. You will try, but to no avail. She will frustrate you, and excite you, and make you feel as if you are losing your mind. Then one day you will wake up and realise you never want to stop thinking about her, because if you did your life would be empty. There will never be anyone else for me.'

Hart was about to reply when Julian's grandmother

approached his side. 'Lord Hartwick,' she said, 'you surprised me this morning. I had a wager with my maid that we would need a search party to find you. Well done—you arrived before the ceremony began.'

'Had a search party been required, I can promise you, ma'am, that I would not have been found.'

She narrowed her eyes at him and Julian was grateful he was not on the receiving end of her assessing gaze.

'Why don't you see what is keeping Miss Forrester? I believe I saw her step onto the terrace some time ago.'

Hart rocked back on his heels and gave her a cocky grin. 'I'm certain Miss Forrester is clever enough to find her own way back inside.'

'Then fetch me a glass of champagne. I don't want you spoiling my fun.'

'It would be my honour.' He bowed flamboyantly and walked away.

Julian wasn't certain if he was relieved that the odd exchange had ended or wary because his grandmother felt the need to speak to him with no one else about.

'That was hardly subtle,' he said.

'That man needs a woman to take him to task.'

'Do I dare ask what fun you were referring to?'

She smiled up at him, clearly pleased about something. 'He did not tell you? Capital! I was certain he would not be able to resist exposing my secret.'

The idea that Hartwick and his grandmother shared any sort of secret was making Julian's head ache. 'Is this a secret you'd care to share with me?'

'Of course. That's why I came over here. Your wedding gift from me has been placed in the study. You may do with it as you wish.'

'Would you like me to ask what it is?'

'I would.' She tugged his arm and Julian brought his head down so she could whisper in his ear. 'Do you recall that caricature printed of you and Katrina together in your carriage? You are now in possession of the printing plate.'

Julian jerked his head back and stared at her. 'How did you acquire it?'

'When I had someone I trust inform Cruikshank about your carriage ride, I specified that I wanted the plate in return for the information.'

He could not have heard correctly. '*You* gave Cruikshank the information that fuelled that caricature? Why? Why would you do that?'

It was a struggle to keep his voice down.

'He was not aware I was the one providing him with the information. I am careful about such things.'

'You never answered me. Why did you do that? Katrina could have been ruined,' Julian said through his teeth.

'Nonsense. I needed to force your hand. You did not see that you loved her, but I did. I expected you to do the honourable thing. Instead you took a different approach, you frustrating boy.'

Julian closed his eyes and began to count to ten. Hopefully by eight he would no longer have the desire to pack his grandmother's bags and send her off to his mother's house—right now.

'How did you come by this information?'

'I live in this house with you. I notice things. While I wasn't certain you would actually go on a carriage ride with her, I suspected you were spending time with her. You were much too cheery. I was correct in my assumption, was I not? Hartwick would not confirm or deny anything to me. However, that boy does not hide his amusement well.'

Julian was back to counting. He took a deep breath. 'So you have been in possession of that plate all this time?'

'I have—and now it is yours. You may thank me by producing a number of great-grandchildren for me.'

'You might want to consider remaining far away from me until Katrina and I return from Devonshire.'

She laughed and looked past his shoulder. 'Very well. However, remember I don't have many more good years left. A house filled with children would have me dying with a smile on my lips.' She tapped her fan on his shoulder and walked away.

He scrubbed his hand across his brow and shook his head. How he wished he could leave for Devonshire now. Once more he eyed his wife. How many days of bedding her would it take until she was with child? *His* child.

Katrina was deep in conversation with Winter's wife, and her tempting lips were raised in a warm smile. His gaze skimmed down her long neck to the swell of her breasts, searching for that beauty mark he knew was barely visible over the silver edging of her gown. Would her skin taste salty when he slid his tongue along that edging? Would her nipples grow hard?

This. Was. Torture.

As if sensing his gaze, Katrina raised her head and caught his eye. Slowly she sank her teeth into her plump lower lip. His control snapped. There were advantages to being a duke. Leaving his own wedding breakfast early with his beautiful duchess was one of them.

When he finally reached his wife's side, he took her hand, and brought it to his lips. It was all he could do without raising too many eyebrows and embarrassing her. 'You ladies seem to be enjoying yourselves.'

The Duchess of Winterbourne smiled congenially. 'We were discussing a new portrait painter I've recently become acquainted with. I believe you would find his work most pleasing, Lyonsdale.'

Julian looked back at Katrina. 'Of course—we will need a portrait of you for the gallery.'

The women shared an indecipherable look and Julian's eyes narrowed as he caught the exchange.

'I will leave the choice of artist up to you, although I assumed you would use Lawrence,' he said.

'Mr Lawrence is going abroad with a commission from the Prince Regent,' Katrina said. 'Olivia has been kind enough to offer me other suggestions. Although I do not know if this one particular painter's work is suitable for the gallery.'

The Duchess of Winterbourne tried to hide her smile, but was unsuccessful. 'Please excuse me, I believe I am needed across the room.'

Once she was far enough away, Katrina leaned towards Julian. 'Perhaps you should stop looking at me as if you plan on having me for dinner,' she said into her champagne glass.

'But I *do* plan on having you—as soon as I can manage it,' he said, brushing his lips against her ear. 'Now that you are finally my wife, we can be alone for longer than a few brief moments at a time. And, Katrina, I plan on being alone with you for a very long time.'

There was a catch in her breath. 'Are you trying to frighten me?'

She tried to nudge him away, but Julian tugged her back. 'I don't believe you frighten easily.'

'Then what are you trying to do?'

'I am attempting to make you want me as much as I want you at this very moment.'

She took another sip of her champagne as she glanced at the people around them. 'I don't believe any effort on your part is necessary.'

Julian could see the rise and fall of her breasts. Knowing what they looked like under her gown had Julian imagining all the different things he wanted to do with them.

He cleared his throat, trying to summon his voice. 'One

of the advantages of being a duke is that I can escort my wife upstairs right now and no one will question me.'

His voice sounded low and hoarse, even to his own ears. Moving his head away from Katrina's, he drained the rest of his glass and tried to regain some of his composure.

'What are some of the other advantages?'

Katrina's voice had acquired a husky quality. The minx knew exactly what she was doing.

Bending his head back down towards her ear, he let out a low, warm breath. 'Another is that I can taste every inch of my beautiful duchess's body for hours.'

To his satisfaction, Katrina wobbled ever so slightly against him.

'Have you been thinking up ways to scandalise me?'

'No…not exactly…possibly…'

Chuckling against her ear, he heard her *harrumph*.

'Then you're going to have to do better than that.'

Ah, a challenge! What would she do if he told her what he had wanted to do from the moment he'd first seen her?

'At this moment all I can think about is sinking into you and filling you. Do you understand my meaning?'

This time there was a more distinct wobble. It was probably visible from across the room. Before he even had time to gloat about what his words had done to his bride she had placed her glass down on the tray of a passing footman and tugged on Julian's arm, propelling them to the doorway.

As they passed her father's questioning gaze she gave the worst performance of a woman with a headache. In less than two minutes she was dragging him up the stairs towards their suite of rooms.

When they reached the landing Katrina let go of his arm and slid her gaze boldly down his body. 'Now, what was it that you were saying about all the things a duke can do?'

He imagined taking her right there, on the floor at the

top of the stairs—or, better yet, bent over the banister. She must have realised his sense of urgency, because her sweet lips parted and she began to step backwards.

There was nowhere for her to go. The hallway led directly to the end of the house, and if she wanted to escape him her only choice was to enter one of the rooms that were connected to the hall. If she did, he would lock the door behind them and take her on or against the nearest possible surface.

It didn't matter to Julian which room it was. He was finally going to make love to Katrina. And he was going to do it now!

Stalking her slowly, like a tiger after its prey, Julian began to unbutton his jacket. The faster his clothes were off, the faster he could get her out of her gown. What would she look like in just her chemise? Was her chemise plain or did it have frills? Was it thin enough that he would be able to make out the shade of her nipples through the cloth?

Katrina made a sound resembling a squeak. 'What are you doing?'

Looking down, Julian noticed his navy tail coat was open and his fingers were already unbuttoning his waistcoat. 'Undressing.' Flashing her a devilish grin, he arched his brow. 'I suggest you do the same.'

'In the hallway?'

Yes, her voice had definitely squeaked. She was still backing away from him, although her pace had slowed considerably.

'What if someone should see us?'

'News of our early departure will have reached the servants by now. I'm sure they know enough to stay away. Take your hair down.'

She hesitated.

'Take it down,' he repeated, undoing the knot of his neckcloth.

He froze as silken strands fell to her shoulders and down her back. Just like that day in Richmond, urgency drove Julian. In two strides his body was pressed against her. His hands were in her hair and he was kissing her—claiming her—exploring her mouth. She tasted like champagne and...Katrina.

She tasted like heaven.

He might have groaned, or maybe it was Katrina.

Pins fell from her hands, scattering silently on the rug. Her fingers twisted in the linen of his cravat, which now hung around his neck like a scarf. She was pulling the cloth towards her, and Julian could not have moved his head away from her even if he'd wanted to. She kissed him back hungrily, her lips dancing with his.

Julian pushed her up against the closest door. If he didn't turn the knob soon he might very well be lifting Katrina's skirts at any moment to taste her. Soft, warm hands found their way under the collar of his shirt, and she ran her palms against the hot skin near his collarbone. He cupped her breasts. They were a little less than a handful, and they were perfect. Her smooth skin tasted salty against his tongue. She moaned, and his breeches grew even tighter.

He kissed her again, needing to sink himself into her warmth. He turned the door handle and they stumbled into the room. There was just enough common sense left in him that he remembered to kick the door shut behind them.

Almost immediately Katrina pushed off his tail coat and her fingers fumbled to unbutton his waistcoat. 'I want to be closer to you,' she murmured between kisses.

He was painfully hard. He needed to slow things down or it would be over much too quickly.

Breaking the kiss, Julian tugged his shirt over his head.

Katrina's eyes widened. Her graceful fingers skimmed across his chest. His heartbeat quickened..

Leaving their wedding breakfast early had been a brilliant idea!

They might have been in a closet for all Katrina knew. Her entire focus was on the man making her tremble all over. His rounded shoulders were broad, and his chest had a light dusting of hair. Wondering at the feel of him, Katrina trailed her fingers across his chest to the thin line that led to the band of his breeches. There was a distinct bulge in the fabric. She traced her fingers over it and discovered it was thick and very hard.

His body shivered. She met his intense gaze and Julian gave a hard swallow.

'Need to see you,' he rasped, and he motioned for her to turn around.

It felt so good to finally be able to touch him that Katrina just continued exploring the contours of that bulge.

Throwing his head back, he groaned, and then grabbed her wrist. 'Turn around.'

This time she turned her back to him. Within no time he had unbuttoned her dress and helped her step out of the delicate creation. He pulled slowly on the ribbon of her corset. The confining fabric loosened, and then it too was on the floor, followed by her petticoat.

His gaze travelled over her body and settled on her breasts. The longer he looked at them, the tighter her breasts felt. It was as if her skin was too small for her body. Julian's raised his right hand and his fingers grazed over the swell of her breast. Then he rubbed his thumb back and forth over her nipple. It strained against his finger and began to ache. It was becoming difficult to breathe, and Katrina tried to pull air into her lungs.

His fingers slipped under the silk ribbons at her shoulder. 'You look lovely.'

The idea that he liked her in such a flimsy garment made Katrina smile. Slowly he untied the ribbons at each shoulder and it slid down her body. He ran his tongue across his teeth and then dropped his head, rubbing his brow.

Her smile faltered. 'Is something wrong?'

Shaking his head, Julian met her gaze. 'I'm trying to convince myself that I should lay you down before I taste you.'

She hesitated as she tried to understand why they couldn't continue to kiss while standing up. But before she came to any conclusions he'd lifted her into his arms. The next thing she knew, she was lying naked on a bed in her stockings. Julian slid her shoes off and tossed them over his shoulder. Kneeling at her feet, he let his gaze burn a trail over her body. When their eyes met, Katrina's stomach flipped and her body tingled with restless energy.

'Do you trust me?' he asked, running his fingers along the inside of her calf.

She nodded, uncertain as to why he was asking. When he parted her legs and crawled between them she almost asked him. But before she could, Julian had lowered his head and slowly slid his tongue between her thighs.

Katrina almost jumped off the bed. He was still watching her while he tasted her again. There was no way to describe what he was doing. She had licked honey off her fingers in the same way he was licking her now. Katrina didn't want to think about what he was doing, she just knew that what he was doing felt so very good.

When he slowly slid his finger inside her she tried to scamper up the bed. With his free hand he held her down. He moved his hand faster, and her legs trembled uncontrollably.

'Don't be frightened, Kat, just relax.'

That was easy for him to say. Every nerve in *his* body wasn't being pulled into a tight mess. He lowered his lips to join his finger and she shattered into a million pieces.

When she could think clearly, she realised that Julian's lips were brushing against her neck. The weight of his warm body was comforting, and his heavy breathing was blowing warm air against her hot skin.

'What happened?' she managed to ask, confident he would be able to offer an explanation.

Julian brushed his nose against her neck. 'Your body let me know that it liked what I was doing to you very much.'

After kissing her several times, he pulled himself up and sat at the edge of the bed, taking off his shoes and stockings. Needing to watch his every movement, Katrina rolled to her side and propped her head in her hand.

When he stood, Julian turned, and appeared surprised to find her watching him. 'Would you like to do the honours?' he asked, gesturing to the buttons on the placket of his breeches.

Feeling as if she was about to unwrap a highly anticipated present, she rose to her knees and crawled towards him. Kneeling before him on the bed, she stroked the pads of her fingers over his warm chest. She didn't think she would ever grow tired of feeling his skin against hers.

He caressed her arms and kissed the sensitive area where her neck met her shoulder. Dropping her hands lower, she ran her hand over his hard length. He was breathing more deeply into her neck, and when Katrina had opened the last button on his breeches she took him into her hand.

Wanting to see all of him, she moved back a bit. Their foreheads touched. They both watched Julian cover her hand with his and show her how to give him pleasure. *Was this part of him always this hard?*

The tip of his length grew slick. Lifting her hand, she marvelled at her wet finger. She wasn't the only one growing wet from all this touching and kissing. Wondering what it tasted like, Katrina licked her thumb.

'Oh, God...' Julian groaned.

She looked up at him, worried she had done something wrong. 'Should I not have done that?'

He answered by pushing her back onto the bed and stretching his body over hers. 'Please tell me you know what occurs in the marriage bed.' His chest was rising and falling as if he had run a far distance.

She nodded. Julian closed his eyes, and Katrina held her breath. Then he thrust himself inside her.

Her body stiffened at the invasion and she clutched his shoulder. His motionless body felt like marble above her. She wished he would go back to doing what he had been doing to her earlier. It had felt much nicer.

She shifted a little, to adjust her position. Julian lifted his eyelids slightly and looked down at her. 'Please, Kat, don't move.' He let out a breath and closed his eyes again.

Was this painful for him? Having him inside her was very uncomfortable. She was certain she was going to be sore afterwards. But Katrina refused even to twitch.

'How long do we have to stay like this?'

Julian opened his eyes, a questioning look on his face.

'For there to be a child,' she explained.

He started to laugh, and it reverberated throughout her entire body. Grinning, he kissed her forehead. 'We need to do a little more than this.'

Well, *that* wasn't an answer. Would they stay like this for a few minutes? Surely he couldn't mean an hour?

He must have noticed her confusion, because he lowered his head and kissed her slowly. Then he pulled his hips back. Katrina thought they were finished—until he thrust into her again. This time she grabbed his hips to hold him in place. That had felt good—very, *very* good! Her eyes dropped to where their bodies were joined and her lips parted.

When she looked back up at him, Julian arched his brow. 'You like that, do you?'

Unable to form words, she nodded and wrapped her legs around him, trying to bring him closer. What had started off as gentle soon became urgent.

He seemed to grow even larger inside her.

Katrina's muscles tightened again.

The veins in his neck became more pronounced and he let out a loud groan.

She might have made a noise. She wasn't certain.

Suddenly his body dropped down, pressing her into the bed. They were each struggling to catch their breath and the sound was loud in her ears.

He eventually propped himself up above her on his forearms and she wrapped her arms around his waist. She felt safe and secure.

His gaze was laced with concern. 'Did I hurt you?'

Shaking her head, she traced his lips with her finger. He caught it between his teeth and drew it into his mouth. His warm, wet tongue twirled around it before he began to suck on it the way he had sucked on her nipples—pulling and drawing. There was a ripple from her finger down to where they had been joined.

'Oh, you're very good at this, aren't you?' she said.

He grinned and released her finger.

'I'm glad you convinced me to leave our wedding breakfast early,' she said, drawing circles with her nail on the small of his back. 'I find I am very content with you here.'

He lifted his head from where he was nuzzling her neck. 'Did you just say you were content with me?'

'Yes, I believe I did.'

'Content. *Content?* That seems a bit…insulting,' he said with a twitch of his lips.

'Forgive me. I did not intend to injure your pride. Perhaps I should say I'm pleased with you.'

'*Pleased?* Yesterday you said you were "pleased" with the book you were reading.'

She grinned. 'Very well. Perhaps you should tell me what you think of me. It may serve as inspiration.'

'Somehow I believe you are simply looking for pretty compliments.'

'And you are not?'

His eyes sparkled with amusement. 'Had I only known I would be facing discourse such as this across the breakfast table each morning, I might have reconsidered speaking with you on the de Lievens' terrace.'

She recalled that night, and how they had bumped into one another in the drawing room. What if her father had never been asked to come to London? And what if Julian had stood somewhere else? If it had been raining, would they even have spoken? They certainly would not have done so on the terrace.

He kissed her temple. 'I love you, Katrina.'

'And I love you, Julian.'

Life could be strange that way. Moments you thought were mundane could be the moments that change your life forever.

* * * * *

This is Laurie Benson's first historical romance.
Look out for Books Two and Three
in her wonderful trilogy
SECRET LIVES OF THE TON
coming soon!